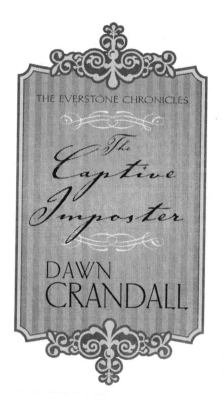

THE EVERSTONE CHRONICLES

The
Captive
Imposter

DAWN
CRANDALL

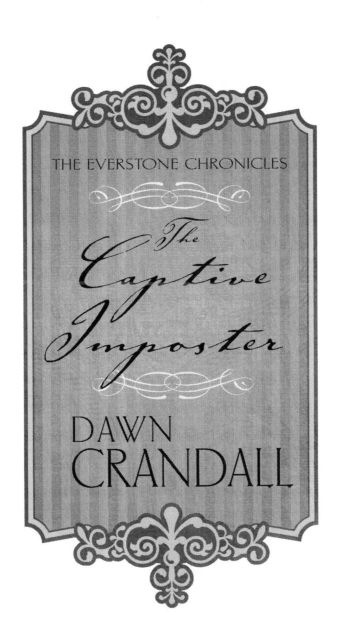

THE EVERSTONE CHRONICLES

The

Captive

Imposter

DAWN
CRANDALL

WHITAKER
HOUSE

The Captive Imposter
The Everstone Chronicles ~ Book Three

dawncrandallwritesfirst@gmail.com
www.facebook.com/dawncrandallwritesfirst
www.twitter.com/dawnwritesfirst/@dawnwritesfirst
www.pinterest.com/dawnwritesfirst

ISBN: 978-1-62911-660-0
eBook ISBN: 978-1-62911-231-2
Printed in the United States of America
© 2015 by Dawn Crandall

Whitaker House
1030 Hunt Valley Circle
New Kensington, PA 15068
www.whitakerhouse.com

ONE

Everston

"This is the forest primeval.
The murmuring pines and the hemlocks, bearded with moss,
and in garments green, indistinct in the twilight...."
—Henry Wadsworth Longfellow, *Evangeline*

Sunday, September 6, 1891 · Portland, Maine

Everston?" My voice cracked. It sounded very unladylike, which, I supposed, was allowable, considering the situation. Mrs. Macy and Mrs. Granton both turned to stare at me.

I suppose it was rather odd to them that I'd spoken. I hadn't said much in the three months they'd known me. It was generally my way, but the mention of Everston had sliced right through my otherwise resolved discreetness.

"Just think, being surrounded by all those green mountains, all that fresh air.... I think Mother will enjoy the cooler weather there. Don't you, Miss Stoneburner?" Mrs. Macy asked.

As if she valued my opinion.

She didn't, of course, so I remained silent. I was just the companion she'd hired for her elderly, recently widowed mother, Mrs. Myrtle Granton.

I was only Elle Stoneburner now.

5

What a shock it would be to Mrs. Macy if I revealed the truth. If only I could tell her that, more than being my reference, the formidable Bram Everstone was also my father, and that Everston—where she proposed sending us—one of his opulent mountain hotels.

I hadn't been to that particular hotel in thirteen years—ever since the summer before my mother had died. It wasn't that I thought anyone there might recognize me as Estella Everstone, for I'd been only eight at the time. No, the only person there who might recognize me was the last person on earth I ever wanted to see again.

Jay.

Moments later, Mrs. Macy rose from her chair and looked down at me. "Then it's settled. You'll leave tomorrow."

I took in this information as silently as I normally would have, though what I really desired to do was argue that there were plenty of other, wonderfully situated hotels in the Appalachian Mountain region of central Maine that would suffice.

Please, God—anywhere but Everston.

Mrs. Macy walked toward the door to the hall, leaving her mother and me seated upon the sofa. She turned to add, "Miss Stoneburner, you don't have much to pack. But do help Mother, will you?"

"Yes, ma'am." I never hated two words more than those! Never in my life had so much been asked of me with nothing given in return. It wore at my reserves every hour of the day. I didn't know how I would survive the remainder of the summer.

But I really didn't have a choice.

"Cheer up, young lass." Mrs. Granton smiled with a sparkle in her eye. "Don't you know what kinds of adventures await? We will likely find you a fine young husband while we're there. I'm thinking you would much prefer the position of wife over companion to someone with one foot in the grave."

"No, Mrs. Granton. You're wonderful, but I—"

"Wouldn't you like a husband?"

Jay's chocolate brown eyes came to mind, as did his warm smile. I shook my head as if to dispel the image. "A husband is the last thing I'm concerned about finding at the moment, Mrs. Granton."

Finding a way to trust my heart again…that would have to come first.

⌣

Monday, September 7, 1891 · Central Maine

"Whoa! Slow down!"

The jostling stagecoach came to a sudden halt.

Tensing, I grabbed the leather handle beside me, trying in vain not to bump against the strangers sitting on the center bench in front of me.

"Mr. Blakeley!" the coachman yelled from his seat. "Your horse is lame? You need a ride?"

Crammed next to the back westward-facing window, I could see only a dog lumbering about. He had wiry gray fur and was absolutely the largest hound I'd ever laid eyes on.

The stagecoach was already packed to capacity; I didn't know how the coachman expected this Mr. Blakeley to fit. Perhaps there was an available seat on top, but I didn't think so. The route from Severville to Laurelton must have been a popular one, for so many people to cling to the coach for the long, bumpy ride. Had I known it would be so crowded and, for lack of a better word, pungent, I would have been more than happy to wait at the train depot for the stagecoach to come back around later that night.

"There's room for you and Wulfric inside," the coachman boomed from his seat. "I'm sure of it. And we're most of the ways to Laurelton, where some of the bodies'll be gettin' off."

How wonderful that the coachman considered us mere "bodies" to be lugged across the countryside.

"And we can take it slow for your Knightley—we'll rig 'im to the back."

Mr. Blakeley walked around the stagecoach to stand next to my window, his dog with the very fitting name beside him. Although the fading light of day was giving over to twilight, I could see him quite clearly, especially as I was seated nearest the door, pushed against the glass. I could do nothing but stare.

He wasn't extremely tall, but he carried himself with an air of confidence that fairly radiated off of him. He cut a rather striking figure, dressed in a white shirt with his sleeves rolled up, a black vest, and trousers. He carried his jacket over his arm and his hat in his hand as he neared the coach door. He was only inches from me, on the other side of the glass, as he whispered something to the coachman. I studied him as he continued the intense conversation in low, indefinable tones.

His chiseled, almost statuesque, face consisted of such sharp, drastic angles. Even his sideburns added to the harshness. He looked serious with his dark brows drawn low over his eyes. Those eyes were the worst offenders of all. Dark, hazel, and brooding, they seemed to cut into everything and everyone he turned his gaze upon.

How severe he looked.

And how wonderful it would be to sketch those eyes!

I couldn't turn away, though my cheeks burned with embarrassment at such a thought. Hiding was impossible.

He caught sight of me through the window, and with the tiniest parting of his lips, he drew my attention even further with a glimpse at his straight teeth. The sight was quite unexpected. He didn't strike me as the type who smiled much.

At the appearance of the newcomer, one of the young men who'd been crowded into the stagecoach, and who clearly had not been paying attention, suddenly opened the door and climbed out. "Mr. Blakeley! Take my spot. I'll walk the rest of the way."

Mr. Blakeley didn't argue but waited for everyone else in the stagecoach to shuffle about so he could take the seat directly across from me. His giant dog occupied a significant amount of precious space on the floor at his feet.

As soon as he and his dog were situated, we were off again, only at a much slower pace than before.

A small, rather dirty boy sat on the bench in the middle of the stagecoach directly between the stranger and me, his small stature giving me another good look at the man, if I so desired to take one. The day's last light streamed in through the windows, blazing against his swarthy complexion. But I didn't wish to stare more than I already had. I didn't want him to think I desired his attention.

I gazed at the still-setting sun. Surely, he knew I'd been forced into the position—staring out the window—and that it had had nothing to do with his presence.

"I think we've found you an admirer already, Elle," Mrs. Granton breathed in my ear.

Glancing over the little boy's head, just for a moment, Mr. Blakeley, indeed, was watching me, though not smiling. I turned back to the window.

I shouldn't have been surprised to find him staring. Anyone who took a closer look at me—no matter that I wore a very plain brown travel suit—surely, would be able to tell I was from a different class than everyone else in that stagecoach. Even Mrs. Granton, who was likely the wealthiest person in the vehicle, was not from my family's class of society.

Later, when we stopped in Laurelton, almost everyone spilled out of the stagecoach, leaving only Mrs. Granton, the gentleman, his dog, and myself. Finally, I could breathe again. An awkward silence permeated the coach as we waited for any passengers who might be boarding. Sometimes, being a companion had its uses. At least I wasn't expected to make conversation. No, I was free to focus my energy on not looking at the man across from me.

Just then the coachman appeared at the door. "You takin' Knightley to the liv'ry, or we makin' him walk the long haul?"

The gentleman nearly leaped from his seat and exited through the open door, leaving his wadded coat and his hat on the bench.

"Wulf, stay," he commanded his dog with a rough, authoritative voice. The huge beast sat back on his haunches and obeyed before his master had even closed the door.

The coachman returned to his high, creaky seat upon the stage, and we waited for the gentleman to return. It was almost ten minutes later when the stranger came back and reclaimed his seat directly opposite me. The dog stood for a moment—he must have been at least four feet tall when he did so—then hunched down against the bench with his muzzle resting on his master's left knee.

Dusk had fallen, leaving only a sliver of light streaking through the purple clouds. I hoped we would travel on in silence. I wasn't sure how much farther we had to go to reach Everston—it had been so long since I'd been there—but I would have much preferred to feign sleep than to let my gaze continually stray to the enigmatic man seated across from us.

After a few minutes of travel, Mrs. Granton nodded to the gentleman and then turned to me. "Elle, I'd like to introduce you to Mr. Dexter Blakeley, the manager of Everston—"

"Is that so?" I couldn't help but be shocked.

"And one of the most sought-after bachelors in Piscataquis County, I'm to believe," Mrs. Granton said, as if I were meeting a prince. "Mr. Blakeley, this is my companion, Miss Elle Stoneburner."

"It's good to meet you, Miss Stoneburner." He nodded curtly, ignoring Mrs. Granton's comment about being so sought after. I really couldn't see why he would be; he seemed to have the demeanor of a wild boar.

"Likewise," I finally added, nodding back.

His only response to me was silence as he reached down to massage his dog's ears. Obviously, he appreciated having been dragged into the conversation as much as I did.

"It's so good to see you again," Mrs. Granton continued. "What has it been—three years? four?—since—"

"Four, I believe," he answered tersely. "Is Mr. Granton to join you soon?"

"Unfortunately, I lost my Mr. Granton earlier this year. However, I have Miss Stoneburner now—the most darling companion ever," Mrs. Granton persisted somewhat sadly. "Her last position was companion to Bram Everstone's elderly relative, Mrs. Miriam Bancroft, before she became ill early last winter."

Mr. Blakeley arched an eyebrow, as if not sure what to make of me. "I thought the youngest of the Everstone children had been companion to the aunt."

My pulse staggered. How well did this man know my family?

"Was Estella Everstone in residence while you were there?" Mrs. Granton asked.

"Yes. She lived with her great-aunt, as well...at least until her aunt became ill," I stated truthfully. "Estella was usually very busy socializing and such."

"I'd always gathered—from her brothers—that she was rather quiet, not very social, and usually wanted to stay out of sight," Mr. Blakeley put in.

I could feel his gaze on me, even in the dimming light of dusk.

"But I suppose, since Estella Everstone *is* worth four million," he continued severely, "she can very well do whatever she wants with her time."

To hear such contempt concerning my financial worth—especially from the shrewd Mr. Blakeley—was rather disconcerting. Was that how most people viewed me—as a spoiled heiress who cared for nothing but her substantial inheritance and for living out her days being pampered and waited upon?

He leaned back against the leather seat and crossed his arms over his chest. "She's actually the only member of the Everstone family I've never had the pleasure of meeting, at least as an adult. So, really, whatever I might say about her doesn't have much merit."

My stomach twisted. He'd met me as a child? When? Why did I not remember a Dexter Blakeley? Would he have been the same age as my brother Nathan? I wondered if he had been at Everston one of the summers we'd spent there. Would he recognize me when he saw me in the light?

"Estella is such a beautiful name, don't you agree?" Mrs. Granton placed a hand at my elbow. Could she tell I wasn't comfortable with this particular topic of conversation? It made me wonder how much of the truth my father had told her. She was a longtime acquaintance of his, but I was fairly certain she did not know my true identity.

"I heard her mother decided upon the name after reading Dickens' *Great Expectations*," she continued. "Though, the young lady she was named after was a cat of a girl, leading poor Pip on for all those years. I never could tell if Estella Havisham loved him and simply wouldn't allow herself to have him, or if she was just as coldhearted as the elder Miss Havisham. What did you think of the two endings Dickens wrote, Elle? Do you think Pip took her back?"

The Captive Imposter 13

I'd read the book once, and had a very firm opinion about the antagonist, which I couldn't help but share: "I think, by the end of the story, Pip finally understood Estella, even if he hadn't throughout all those pages that detailed his falling in love with her. And I do believe he took her back. What else could he have done?"

"Well, I'm sure I don't know. What do you think, Mr. Blakeley?" Mrs. Granton asked.

"I agree with Miss Stoneburner." His manners were so abrupt, so stilted—as if participating in a conversation about a novel grated his nerves. But then he added, "I believe the young lady's heart had been so manipulated over the years, it required someone like Pip, and his delusional love for her, to make her see what she'd become—to make her realize that everything she'd done with her life up to that point was utterly meaningless and self-destructive."

Although his words were touching, and a bit surprising, I could think only of my own longtime, delusional love for Jay and how it had tragically eaten up the last five years of my life. Was that how Pip had felt? Maybe Pip hadn't taken Estella Havisham back, after all.

"I had no idea you were such a lover of novels, Mr. Blakeley," Mrs. Granton remarked.

He stroked the scruff of his dog's neck. "I'm not. Dickens is a favorite of my sister's. I don't know how many times she's made us sit and listen to her read that particular book over the years. She even named her horse Pip."

It sounded to me as if my employer and this Miss Blakeley would have been a very fine match, for reading aloud was about all that Mrs. Granton required of me as her companion.

"My daughter, Mrs. Caroline Macy"—Mrs. Granton glanced my way for a moment—"planned to name her daughter Estella, but then she decided on Ursula. Miss Everstone was born earlier that same winter, you see, and Caroline didn't want to give the impression of imitating the Everstone family."

I smoothed a wrinkle from my skirt, not knowing how to respond. I had nothing to feel guilty about, yet I had the sudden urge to apologize. Mrs. Granton fell silent, and even the indomitable Mr. Blakeley took to staring at his dog. Finally, he filled the quiet with a polite inquiry: "Have you ever been to Everston before, Miss Stoneburner?"

I forced my attention from the bleakness outside my window back to him. He was now only a shadow in the darkness, a deep voice asking an innocent question.

Only the question wasn't innocent to me.

I knew I needed to twist the truth even more than I already had. For how would someone of the social standing of my persona ever have been to a hotel like Everston before, other than as an employee?

Really, I didn't know much about the past of my assumed persona—nothing beyond the fact that she had a glowing reference from Bram Everstone. I never thought I'd have to explain myself so thoroughly to a stranger.

I quickly realized that all Mrs. Granton and Mr. Blakeley—and anyone else at Everston besides Jay—would ever know of me would be lies. And if the lies were to be believable, I needed to spend time formulating a past. Time I suddenly didn't have.

"Perhaps once, but I don't remember." I looked to Mrs. Granton's form beside me in the dimness. A quiet snore rumbled between us. The dear lady had fallen asleep.

"And where are you from?" he asked. I was surprised he cared.

"Bar Harbor." I cringed as the name escaped my lips. I'd thought for a moment that it was a safe answer, but really it wasn't.

"What does your family do there?"

"They...we worked at The Grand Everstone Hotel." That was a little less of a lie, at least, and it gave me a connection to my own family, since they were my only reference.

"So, you've probably seen much of the Everstone family, aside from working for the great-aunt?"

"You could say that."

"I worked for Bram Everstone for close to eight years, managing his Bailey Hill Hotel on Nahant Island, until about a year and a half ago." No wonder this Mr. Blakeley seemed to care so much about my connection to the Everstones.

I had the feeling he was watching me, waiting for me to add something more to the conversation, so I did. "And now you're at Everston? You must be very proficient at what you do." Mr. Blakeley had to have been one of the youngest hotel managers Father had ever employed if he'd been overseeing Bailey Hill for all those years. He couldn't have been much older than thirty.

"Attaining Everston has been my goal for a very long time."

"You must love Everston as much as Bram Everstone does."

"You could say that." It didn't escape my notice that he'd used the same line I'd given him while trying not to lie. "Do you still have relatives in Bar Harbor?"

"No." None of them was actually in Bar Harbor anymore, not since Will had been killed at the beginning of June.

"May I ask what your position was at The Grand Everstone Hotel?"

"I worked at the front desk." It wasn't an outright lie. When I was a little girl, my father would take me there to visit, and I would play receptionist.

"Indeed."

"Yes...indeed."

Did he believe me? Or did he perceive the falseness of my words? Had Father telephoned to ask Mr. Blakeley to watch over me? Or would he have telephoned Jay to do that? I wished I knew. I'd sent my sister Natalia a telegram from the train station, and I was sure she would write to me as soon as possible, under the guise of being a friend. Until then, I wouldn't know anything for certain.

Mrs. Granton moaned, and a short snore escaped her lips as she wriggled next to me in an apparent effort to find a more comfortable position. I didn't like that she'd basically left me alone with Mr. Blakeley. It felt shamelessly scandalous to speak with him as I was, shrouded in the darkness of the stagecoach, hardly able to remember what he looked like, besides that he was mildly attractive.

At least when he wasn't glowering.

I focused on the bumps of the gravel road, which jostled my insides almost as much as the conversation had. The coach took a sharp turn, prompting Mr. Blakeley's dog to stand to his feet. I looked out my window and saw the stone pillars and walls that flanked the wrought-iron gates, as if they hid a secret world inside.

Once we drove past the open gate, a large, shadowy silhouette caught my gaze. A towering building protruded from the dark shadows of the mountains. That was also when I noticed the waters of Half Moon Lake glittering outside my window.

Before too long, the stage jolted to a halt at the gas lit entrance of the hotel, and Mrs. Granton made a rather embarrassing noise in her sleep. Heat rushed to my cheeks as Mr. Blakeley opened the door. Wulfric climbed out first. His master immediately followed, then turned around to offer me his assistance. He took my gloved hand and carefully helped me down.

As I stood before him, with the glow of the gaslights upon us, I had my first good look at Mr. Blakeley since I'd met him at twilight. "Mildly attractive" was hardly an adequate description. I took in his straight dark hair, which was brushed off to the side; his greenish-brown hazel eyes; his dark brows and lashes.

No, there was no "mildly" about it.

"Welcome to my hotel, Miss Stoneburner." Pride laced his every word, and I could hear the smile in his voice, even though his lips adamantly refused to comply. "Now that you're here, do you recall ever visiting Everston?"

"Perhaps, but...I don't know. Probably not." My first real, straight-to-the-core lie to him. Not that it should have mattered.

"You probably haven't if you can't remember. Everston's not a place that's easily forgotten."

I wrenched my gaze from his as he let go of my hand and turned his attention to the coach and my employer, still asleep inside. Wulfric pranced about, obviously happy to be home.

I looked to the front of the hotel and remembered with fondness the stunning door of hand-carved wood and beveled glass that led into the lobby. The bellmen came to collect our luggage, finally waking Mrs. Granton. Mr. Blakeley helped her down, then guided us up the flagstone path to the enormous front steps of the wide veranda.

In the dim light, I drank in the sight of Everston, nestled amid miles and miles of pine trees and mountains, with an expanse of stars shining brightly above. Out of nowhere, a sense of longing hit me so hard, my knees nearly buckled. How had I not realized how badly I missed this place?

I searched the night sky, the sight bringing back a flood of warm memories from my childhood. I hadn't been home in weeks. But as I walked up the path, it felt more like years.

Thirteen, in fact.

Oh, no, Mr. Blakeley. I hadn't forgotten.

TWO

Blakeley House

"Well, if I can't be happy, I can be useful, perhaps."
—Louisa May Alcott, *An Old-Fashioned Girl*

My first thought upon waking the next morning had been of a stone-encased spring I remembered visiting quite often as a child. It was somewhere along the lakeshore near the hotel, but I knew I would have a time finding it, especially as I assumed Mrs. Granton expected me to stay with her. I didn't know what her plans were, not even how long we were projected to stay.

I stretched out my arms and slipped them under my pillow, reaching my fingers to the extravagant wood frame of my double bed. Mrs. Granton had arranged for me to have my own room and a private bathroom situated next to hers. Her corner chamber was larger, of course, with two walls of northwest-facing windows. The view included the giant thousand-foot-steep slab of flint called Iron Mountain in the near distant west, and Half Moon Lake, framed by the Appalachian Mountains surrounding Everston.

I flipped the covers to the side, swung my bare feet to the carpeted floor, and stared at the wardrobe across the room. It had been months, and I still wasn't accustomed to my lack of apparel.

In preparation for my role as Elle Stoneburner, my future stepmother, Madame Evangeline Boutilier, had taken it upon herself to note the clothes my lady's maid had worn on her days off.

Then she'd bought two of the ugliest dresses I had ever seen—one brown and one gray—from her, and had had them taken in to fit my slight figure. But such clothes were expected of a companion and were therefore my only choice.

Opening the wardrobe, I found nothing but those two drab dresses—they were terribly plain compared to the bright, fashionable Paris-made Worth gowns I was used to wearing.

I should have been in mourning to honor Will's death—even fashionable mourning gowns would have been better than the dresses I'd been sent away with. My brother Vance, however, had convinced Father that my being in mourning would be too much of a clue for Jacques Gerard, in the case he should be after me, too.

Not that I thought he would be. Vance was merely oversensitive about the situation because he felt guilty for Will's death. He had been killed by mistake—the two had always looked strikingly alike.

It had all been made into such a to-do, when I really would have preferred to stay with my family so we could grieve together. Wouldn't that have been better? My sister Natalia hadn't gone into hiding, aside from being in confinement, now holed away with her baby and our father at Everwood in Back Bay. I'd never been one to depend much on relationships, but now that I had absolutely no one who truly knew me, the lack hit me quite violently.

Once I finished readying for the day, having donned the plain brown dress, and with my long dark hair pinned up in the only way I could get it, I knocked on the door that adjoined my room to Mrs. Granton's.

She opened the door and let me in without a word.

"Good morning, Mrs. Granton."

My employer silently sat upon a sofa along the wall and slowly collected a hand mirror from the powder table. Her every movement took at least four times as long as it would have taken me.

She examined the turban wrapped over her thin white hair, her face all seriousness.

Mrs. Granton's faded blue eyes finally slid to me with a coy smile.

"Would you like me to read to you this morning?" I lifted her copy of Jane Austen's *Northanger Abbey*—which Mrs. Granton and I had begun the day before in our train compartment—from the side table and opened it to the page marked by the ribbon bookmark. "Or would you like to take a walk—"

"Reading would be nice, dear…for a little while." Mrs. Granton inspected her turban again and said, still facing the mirror, "I don't want to go outside. It's enough for me to be in this room, with the view. However, I do expect you to go down without me. Aren't you interested in exploring the grounds? I'm certain Mr. Blakeley would be happy to show you around."

Perhaps when Mrs. Granton was my age, she would have thought it a grand adventure to have a late-summer romance with a handsome hotel manager in the faraway mountains of Maine. But I certainly did not.

She must have read my thoughts. "Rest assured, dearest, I don't mean that you need to fall desperately in love with him, or anything. But it wouldn't hurt to be friendly. It must be frustrating for him to have everyone cycle out of his life every few weeks. You might make the time you're here pleasant for him."

"Yes, I suppose managing a hotel could become rather tiresome." I closed the book and placed it where I'd found it. I no longer looked forward to reading, and reading, and reading some more. How tiresome my own life had become. "Do you know Mr. Blakeley well?"

"Before my Mr. Granton went home to be with the good Lord, we often visited the Bailey Hill Hotel at Nahant Island. Did Mr. Blakeley tell you he managed there for some years?"

I nodded.

"Well, my Mr. Granton always seemed to have so much to say to him while we were there. He's a man's man, you know, that Dexter Blakeley; serious and often quite callous when it comes to the young ladies always flitting about him...as if he won't allow himself to be bothered with them." Mrs. Granton rolled her eyes.

"Then why do you believe he would want to spend time with me?"

"Let's just say, I have a hunch he may have finally met his match. He seemed quite attentive in the stagecoach last night. I've never known him to say so many words to any young lady."

Mrs. Granton was mistaken, of course. She had no idea she wanted to couple Estella Everstone with the manager of one of her father's hotels. What a thought!

"I thought you were asleep for most of the ride."

"I pretended. A chaperone needs to do such things at times, you know."

"Mrs. Granton!"

"You would suit him well, you and your quiet thoughtfulness. Though he is likely 'married' to this hotel of his. Imagine how easily one could fall for such a place as Everston!"

Truly, if one was unaware that Everston was positioned upon a peninsula, he might have easily believed that the hotel was built upon an island. Poor Mr. Blakeley, indeed. Everything about his life seemed so contained. And so perfect.

⌣

Later that week, with my sketchbook and the tin of pencils I'd bought before leaving home pressed to my chest, I took the opportunity to survey the old, familiar grounds of Everston.

When I'd gone out far enough to get a good overall look, I glanced back at the towering hotel. The red and white striped awnings and two-story white pillars over the wide veranda gave it such a pleasant, cultured look, despite its being hundreds and hundreds of miles off in the mountains for society to come and find.

It was gorgeous, my Everston.

And someday—hopefully soon—it would be mine.

With Nathan in Washington, and Will gone, that left only Vance to eventually take on all of Father's business enterprises. And I wasn't sure if he was up for the task. He had just assumed Will's place over Greaghan Lumber; would he someday have control of Father's hotels, too?

I wanted only one of them.

This one.

I'd always loved Everston best of Father's hotels. There was something about its being so far removed from our homes in Boston and Bar Harbor, something so terribly freeing about being stranded in the mountain wilderness of central Maine.

As I wandered down a long drive along the west shores of the peninsula, old memories clicked into place, directing my steps. I walked for some time with Half Moon Lake to my left. It looked as it always had, with the Appalachian Mountains framing the water on all sides.

I followed the trail to the right through a hilly grove of birch and pine trees and continued down a narrow gravel path off the drive. Lined with fieldstones, it weaved through a grove scattered with pine trees, and led—much to my surprise—straight to a great stone mansion built between the high bank of Iron Mountain and the shore of Half Moon Lake. I didn't remember that!

High chimneys pointed to the sky amid gabled rooflines. Tall paned-glass windows sparkled in the late-afternoon sunshine. It was beautiful, something an English aristocrat would have used for a country house if it had stood in the land of Dickens and Austen.

But truly, the house couldn't have been more than a decade old. And who would build such a residence there? I was fairly certain the lands all around—save for the mercantile, restaurant and the row of small cottages nearby—belonged to my father, as part of the Everston estate.

I followed the path to a small hill and stopped for a moment to look out over the vast waters. I could see Everston down the rocky, tree-lined coast. Its many gaslit windows glowed in the early-evening dusk—a clue as to just how late it was getting. I didn't realize I'd been out so very long. I spun around to head back to the hotel, almost entranced by how many more shades of twilight there seemed to be at Everston than anywhere else I'd been.

Walking along near the mansion again, I came across a low patch of tiny white flowers and thought it odd to see them blooming so late into the evening. Feeling a tad wistful, I broke off one of the blossoms at the stem and tucked it behind my right ear.

As I came up to where the narrow path met the drive—which basically ended at the house—I heard the sound of hoofbeats of a horse racing over the gravel. The rider was covered in the shadows of Iron Mountain and the dark forest, his black hat and cape barely visible in the gloom of the shady twilight around us. I'd just barely made it to the patch of dense pines that ended at the well-manicured clearing when the rider yelled, "Mrs. McGuire! Anyone!"

The caped stranger slid awkwardly off his horse, carefully holding something in his arms, and he struggled not to drop whatever it was as he tied his horse. When he moved into the glow of the lamplight from the windows, I could see it was a girl lying limp in his arms. Her bright red dress emphasized the bloodless tone of her skin, and her light brown hair hung loosely over his arm. An older lady in servant's attire opened the front door for him. Light spilled onto the porch as they exchanged quiet words. Then they both disappeared into the house, closing the door behind them.

I stared at the stone house. Would offering to help be an invasion of the girl's privacy? My heart ached for her, yet I didn't want to do anything to cause her embarrassment.

Reluctantly, I directed my footsteps toward Everston, a prayer for the girl's well-being forming in my mind. In the next moment, more hoofbeats pounded toward me, scattering my thoughts to the wind.

This rider carried a lantern, and when he caught sight of me at the edge of the lawn, he pulled at his reins, and his black-as-midnight horse came to a stop.

"Miss Stoneburner?" It was Mr. Blakeley, again dressed in white shirtsleeves and a dark vest and trousers, but without his jacket or hat. "What are you doing here?" His dog—the giant gray beast from the stagecoach—bounded from behind the horse.

"I didn't realize how quickly it would— I didn't take the position of Iron Mountain into consideration when I—"

"Never mind." He cut me off, still atop his horse. He rotated away from me, ran a hand through his hair, and studied the house for a moment before returning his attention to me.

"I should get back. Mrs. Granton—"

"I will be sure to make your excuses. I need your— We could use your help."

"What do you need?" I asked. The heartfelt request was almost a shock, coming from harsh Mr. Blakeley.

He dismounted and stood before me, rather close. He searched my face for a moment and finally responded, "My sister isn't well, and my mother…she won't like this." He looked to the house again, his face reflecting the light from the windows. I could tell he wasn't comfortable with having told me even as little as he had.

"Of course. But what's wrong?"

Without an answer, Mr. Blakeley grasped my elbow and pulled me toward the front steps. He held the door for me as I entered, and I could hear someone wailing, her words garbled.

I soon found that the incomprehensible wail was coming from an older lady dressed in an exquisite, expensive-looking black mourning gown, with jewels hanging from her wrists and neck. She paced before the fieldstone fireplace in the large foyer. In the hearth, a roaring fire crackled. I hadn't realized how cool it had become until I stood there, helplessly trying to ascertain the details of the situation.

I walked past the lady, who seemed not to see me or Mr. Blakeley. She failed to acknowledge anything but the nonsense she uttered.

Mr. Blakeley pointed to his dog. "Wulfric, stay."

Then, taking my hand, he led me to the stairs.

"Blakeley, are you coming?" the cloaked stranger asked from the landing halfway up the steps. The girl still lay unconscious in his arms as he climbed the massive staircase. As he continued his ascent, he turned ever so slightly, and I realized it wasn't a stranger at all.

It was Jay.

THREE

Greenlee Cole

"What makes night within us may leave stars."
—Victor Hugo, *Ninety-Three*

Come with me." Mr. Blakeley seized my sketchbook and tin pencil case, set them aside, and thundered up the stairs, dragging me behind him.

Ignoring how inappropriate it was for me to be there, I kept my hand in his strong grip.

He stopped and stood before me on the wide landing. Behind him, the built-in lamp situated on the extravagant newel post shone, silhouetting his frame while leaving his stern features dark and indiscernible. He brought me closer and whispered, "The girl… when she awakes, she might not understand what's happened."

"What *has* happened?"

"I'll let her tell you—if she wants to." He started back up the stairs, still grasping my hand, only this time with me walking beside him.

In such a large house, there had to be more than the one servant and the sobbing lady. Had that been Mr. Blakeley's mother? And what of his sister? Why did the house seem so very empty? And, most important, how would I face Jay again?

I wasn't prepared. And with Mr. Blakeley present, as well as the servant, I wouldn't be able to explain myself.

As he led me from the top of the staircase down the hall and into the room, I stared at the floor, afraid of facing Jay so suddenly. He wouldn't like this.

"Miss Stoneburner." Mr. Blakeley stood close beside me and practically breathed the words. "Meet Dr. Jay Crawford."

Of course, Jay would be going by *that* name.

Jay—dressed to the nines in a finely cut suit, as always, no matter the situation—sat upon the edge of an ornate wood-framed double bed with his back to me, his black cape and top hat on the floor at his feet. His attention was focused solely upon the girl in the radiant red dress, who still appeared unconscious. He gently placed a palm to her forehead.

"Crawford, this is Miss Elle Stoneburner. She's acting as lady's companion to one of the guests at Everston, and she's here to help."

Jay finally acknowledged us with a quick look. But when his attention shifted to me, recognition flashed in his brown eyes. He stood, spun around, and stared at me, stunned. "You're acting as—what?"

"A companion to a Mrs. Myrtle Granton of Portland, Maine… an old acquaintance of mine," Mr. Blakeley added. "Now, what do you need for us to do?" He was all business, ready to do whatever Jay asked.

Through the open door, I still could hear the lady down in the foyer. Why wasn't she helping?

"Leave the girl here and go tell Mrs. McGuire to bring some boiled water and some clean rags, and also my bag from my saddle."

Mr. Blakeley disappeared through the doorway, and I heard his heavy footsteps as he hurried down the stairs.

Why had Jay brought this girl to Mr. Blakeley's house?

"Miss…Miss Stoneburner…would it be too much for you to undress her? Just the torn gown." He sounded as if he doubted his eyes, speaking to me as if I were truly some lady's companion brought in to help because there was no one else available. But I knew he recognized me.

The girl had started to rouse and now flailed about the bed frantically as if trying to escape some unavoidable terror. Her beautiful dress looked quite fashionable, but it was ripped in more than one place. And the side of her face, I noticed to my horror, was swollen and covered in blood.

Whatever had happened to her?

"Yes, of course." The words left me with a sudden whoosh. Nothing else mattered. I would help her in any way I could.

I perched on the edge of the bed in the place Jay had vacated. Listening to his movements behind me, I could tell that he had paused near the door, though he didn't say anything for what seemed like minutes. I'm sure he didn't understand what I was doing there at Mr. Blakeley's house, late in the evening and in the middle of nowhere, Maine. With him.

"I need to examine her injuries, but I need to also preserve her modesty," he finally said.

I turned around, and when my eyes met his, I saw the doubt transform to anger. "I will leave you." After spitting those words, he closed the door.

The girl—she couldn't have been more than twenty years old—continued to thrash about on the bed.

I reached for her shoulder, uncertain as to how to calm her. Would she fight me? She hadn't seemed to notice us; she'd simply kept on as if she were terrified of some unseen menace. I gently cupped the unbloodied side of her jaw in my hand. "Shhh. I'm here now. I'm just a girl, too."

I'd never imagined myself doing such a thing. Never in a hundred years.

The more I repeated those words over and over, the more she calmed. My hand grazed past her face and rested upon her brow.

Hopefully, Mrs. McGuire would bring the hot water and rags soon. "What's your name?"

"Where am I?" she mumbled sadly. She kept her eyes closed, as if still afraid, and twisted to face the other side of the room. For a moment, she stopped moving altogether. But then her shoulders heaved, and her breaths started coming out like sobs. After some moments, she said, "I'm out. I'm out, aren't I? Where am I? How did he do it?"

I wasn't certain if it was best to tell her exactly where, so I merely said, "Somewhere safe."

"But not at The Hawthorne?" She went from speaking the words to all-out weeping in a matter of seconds. What sort of suffering must she have endured? And what was The Hawthorne? What did that mean?

Deciding not to pry for too many details, I said, "My name is...Elle. Can you tell me yours?"

"Greenlee. Greenlee Cole," she mumbled.

"Let me help you out of your dress, Miss Cole. Dr. Crawford wants to examine your...your injuries."

"The dress isn't mine. And I don't think I can stand. It hurts too much," she muttered.

I came around the bed to get a better look at her face. "That's understandable. I'll do my best."

She stared at the wall behind me with deadness in her eyes. Their hue—light brown, almost beige—was unlike any eye color I'd ever seen. They matched her hair almost perfectly.

After I gently ripped the bodice from where it had already been torn, the gown slipped off rather easily. Once I removed the remnants, Greenlee rolled over to face the opposite direction, properly covered, with the clean white sheets and burgundy coverlet from the bed bunched around her.

"Can you tell me what happened?" I wasn't certain I wanted to know, but the thought of her having to tell Jay or Mr. Blakeley seemed even more embarrassing. Then again, perhaps Jay already knew what had happened.

"I've been—" A long-held-back sob escaped with a hiccough, and then she remained silent until she added, "I've been trapped at The Hawthorne Inn."

"For how long?"

"Maybe a year...I don't know." She wept in earnest again but went on through her tears. "All I know is, Dr. Crawford said he would find a way to save me from Ezra. And he did."

⌣

"What do you think you're doing here?" Jay hissed from behind me in the empty hall of the second story of the house. With Mr. Blakeley still downstairs, Jay obviously thought it the best place for us to have our much-needed discussion.

I'd been leaning against the railing of the stairs, waiting for Jay to conclude his examination of Greenlee. Mr. Blakeley's housekeeper, Mrs. McGuire, had just passed me in the hall. Greenlee, I assumed, now rested.

"It's not what you think."

He grabbed me by the arm and pulled me away from the top of the staircase.

"It's a coincidence," I grumbled under my breath. I tore myself from his grasp. "I'm not here because of *you*—"

"You expect me to believe that? What is your father going to think when—"

"He knows I'm here."

Jay folded his arms across his chest and stared down at me with those familiar chocolate-brown eyes, now filled with fury and indignation. "At Blakeley House? Helping me rescue a girl from a brothel in Westward?"

"Is that what The Hawthorne Inn is? A—? Really?" I couldn't even say the word. "I'm staying at Everston, like Mr. Blakeley said—"

"Does Blakeley know who you are?"

"Not that I'm aware."

"Why are you *acting* as a lady's companion?"

"Because Will was murdered. You know that. You were there." I couldn't help the tears that were gathering upon my eyelashes.

"What does your father mean by— Is he trying to get you killed as well?"

"It was Vance's idea. He wanted to hide me from Jacques Gerard—"

"So they sent you to Everston?"

"The plan wasn't for me to come here. After I spent a few months with Mrs. Granton in Portland, her daughter sent us here. It wasn't my idea." I backed against the wall, distancing myself from him. "I didn't *want* to come!"

He dropped his arms from his chest, took a step in my direction, and caught my arm in his firm grip. "And then you changed your mind and thought you might try once more to win my affections with your cunning ways?"

I didn't know why he wanted to torment me with his questions. Couldn't he tell the difference in me already? I certainly could. It was glaring.

"You're a distraction from what I know God wants me to do."

"Maybe this will help, Jay: I don't want you anymore."

"All part of your strategy, I'm sure."

"Fine, Jay. I'll just have to prove it to you, then." At last, I managed to wrench my arm from his hold. I headed to the staircase, flew down the steps, and went in search of Mr. Blakeley.

FOUR

Mr. Blakeley

"I would always rather be happy than dignified."
—Charlotte Brontë, *Jane Eyre*

I'd never stayed out so late on my own before, but I was glad I did. Even though I'd felt I had no idea what I'd been doing, and despite its having resulted in the ugly confrontation with Jay, I'd never felt as needed as when Mr. Blakeley had asked me to come inside his house and help.

Having missed dinner, I was quite famished. But it was past eight o'clock; there was no chance of having anything to eat for the rest of the night, even if I reached Everston in a timely manner.

The lady who'd been weeping before the fireplace in the hall had disappeared and the house now seemed eerily still. I lurked about, poking my head into the many well-lit rooms of the ground floor in search of Mr. Blakeley...or anyone, really.

A fire still blazed in the hearth in the spacious front parlor, but no one seemed to be there. The dining room chandelier still glowed, and the table, oddly set for what might have been an extravagant dinner party, seemed eerily out of place in these woods. And although I couldn't find a soul, I had the strangest sensation of being watched.

Finally, I peeked into what seemed to be a study at the back of the house. A single lamp burned atop a large wooden desk. I guessed it to be Mr. Blakeley's personal office, for it was a rather masculine-looking room. I stepped in, thinking he would be there waiting; but the silent stillness of the room proved me quite wrong.

Mr. Blakeley wouldn't have returned to Everston without me, would he? And why were all the lights on if no one was about?

Upstairs, I heard a startling crash. I ran from the study, through the great hall, and out the elaborate front door. Quite certain Mr. Blakeley was no longer in the house; I didn't want to confront whoever was.

As I walked along the side of the house, the lights from the lace-curtained windows flooded the side yard, guiding my way. From somewhere in the yard, I heard Mr. Blakeley's giant dog make a happy sort of sound. For some reason, hearing it made me feel strangely comforted, though I couldn't imagine why. My family had never owned a dog.

"Miss Stoneburner." The rough timbre of Mr. Blakeley's voice reached me from across the yard. As I walked to the back of the house, I saw him standing on another porch, leaning against a stone pillar, staring down at me. I could see he was still without a jacket; the white of his shirtsleeves stood out next to his waistcoat, and his tie hung loosely around his neck.

He looked tired.

Apprehensively, I took a step forward. "I need—"

"You haven't had dinner, have you?" he asked in the same instance.

"I haven't. I'd meant to return to Everston in time."

"Let me get you something, and then I'll walk you back. Wait here, on the porch." Then he turned to his dog and pointed at him. "Stay," he commanded him before disappearing inside the house.

I climbed the steps in the dark and waited. Not knowing what I was to do with a giant dog who seemed content to stare at me, I looked over at the massive clearing to the right, toward the lake. In the woods nearby, I heard the rustling of the wind through the trees and the sound of the frogs along the lakeshore forming a sweet melody. How I'd missed all of this!

And just as I remembered from childhood, it was the perfect place to observe the bright, low-hanging moon and the stars.

How had years and years gone by with my never stopping to notice those ever-constant lights forever rotating in their circles? My brothers and I had watched them turn for hours on long summer nights when I was young—sometimes at Rockwood, along the rocky coast of Mount Desert Island, and sometimes right there along the uneven shores of Half Moon Lake at Everston.

A light illuminated the window behind me, and I heard drawers and cupboards opening and closing inside. I looked in and watched Mr. Blakeley through the lace curtains as he moved about the dimly lit kitchen. He spoke to someone, so I leaned closer to the window and pressed my ear to the glass. I listened for the low rumble of his voice, yet I heard nothing but the clatter of plates. I looked in again; there didn't seem to be anyone with him.

He came out a few minutes later, leaving the kitchen lights on. He handed me a plate of exquisite Dresden china—it matched the table settings in the dining room—with a sandwich cut into quarters, a shiny red apple, and a nicely folded white linen napkin. He set a glass of water on the wide sandstone slab accentuating the top ledge of the porch wall, and then he half sat, half leaned upon it, facing me.

A little concerned about the dog's ability to reach my plate, I cocked my head in his direction and said, "That's a big dog."

"Wulfric's an Irish Wolfhound. My mother's family breeds them in Kent, England."

"Oh." I held the plate at chest level, unsure of what to do.

"He won't eat your dinner. He has better manners than I do, at times."

I carefully placed the plate next to the water glass and took a quarter of the sandwich, fully prepared to eat it standing before

Mr. Blakeley without shame. Surely, if my father would see me do such a thing—or any of the things I'd done in the last hour or so—he would telephone that instant with plans to send me home, no matter the perceived danger.

I leaned against the half wall next to Mr. Blakeley and took a bite of fresh bread, turkey, and sweet cranberry sauce.

"Do you enjoy your job with Mrs. Granton?" Mr. Blakeley asked once I'd finished the first quarter of the sandwich.

"Well, yes, I suppose. It is much better than a good many other jobs I would never want."

"There certainly are a number of less appealing jobs out there." In the dim light, I again felt as if he were inspecting me. "I think you suit her well."

I laughed at the irony that he and Mrs. Granton would both tell me practically the same thing concerning one another.

"What is it?"

"She said something similar just this morning."

"She does have a knack for discernment about such things."

He nudged the plate my way, scraping it against the rough stone between us, as if to insinuate that I needed to finish eating so we could be on our way.

I grabbed another quarter of the sandwich.

When I finished that one, he asked, "How old is Mrs. Granton, do you think?"

"I would imagine she's close to eighty."

He allowed me to finish the third quarter of the sandwich in silence and to take a few sips of water before I decided to continue the conversation—which was a rather strange prospect for me, since I'd never considered myself much of a conversationalist. But maybe that had had something to do with my being essentially invisible to everyone, hidden behind my lavish clothes and the lifestyle that went with the very public life I'd been born into.

Mr. Blakeley seemed to see me, though. I couldn't remember anyone who'd ever dared study me as candidly as he was doing just then.

"It will be sad when I—I mean, when we lose her." I'd almost forgotten to whom I was speaking. Was I really so desperate for meaningful conversation?

At a sound from the kitchen, Mr. Blakeley stood, walked to the window, and looked in. He lingered near the door as he added, "I don't think she'll be going anywhere anytime soon. She's got too much life in her yet. And now that she has you...."

For some odd reason, which went against everything I thought I knew about Mr. Dexter Blakeley, it seemed that getting to know me was all he cared to do. And, strangely enough, I hadn't run out of words for him yet.

Upon finishing the last quarter of the sandwich, I dabbed my mouth with the fine linen napkin, refolded it, and placed it upon the china plate before picking up the apple.

Mr. Blakeley took a step in my direction and stretched out his hand. "I'll take it."

Without a thought, I gave him the fruit; my fingers inadvertently grazed his hand in the shadows between us.

He cleared his throat and handed me the apple again, making sure I held it securely before he let go. "I meant the plate." His voice, always deep and rough, sounded just a tad drier than usual. "I'll take it inside."

I carefully picked up the plate and handed it to him. Before he moved away, he reached toward my right ear with his free hand, but then he stopped himself. "The Evening Primrose is still blooming, is it?"

I quickly plucked the white flower from my hair and twirled it between my thumb and forefinger. "Is that its name? It's fitting." I'd forgotten all about the flower in my hair during the events of the evening. "Do you happen to know where my sketchbook and pencils are now? You took them from me when we entered the house."

He seemed suddenly irritated; the moody gentleman from the stagecoach had returned. "Let me see if I can find them." He disappeared into the house, slamming the door behind him.

A few minutes later, the kitchen went dark, and Mr. Blakeley returned to the porch with my missing sketchbook and pencil case.

I hoped he hadn't spied my drawings, as the most recent one was a self-portrait that suddenly seemed rather vain of me.

After he handed my belongings to me, he took my free hand and placed it in the crook of his arm. "Time to get you back to Everston. You don't mind if we walk, do you? I can make your excuses to Mrs. Granton, if need be—"

"I'm fairly certain she won't be awake. Nor will she mind that I've been in your company for the duration of the evening...."

We both let my awkward statement drift into the trees and disappear as we passed through his yard to the drive, I didn't feel embarrassed, though. Walking with Mr. Blakeley in the dark seemed preferable to having him see me in the light.

After a few minutes of silence, save for the rustling of soon-to-be-falling leaves in the branches above us, I asked, "Do you enjoy working in the hotel industry?"

"Given how odd it is that it is my business...." His deep laughter rumbled over me. Was he looking down at me in the dark? "Yes, I do enjoy it, for the most part."

"If you don't mind my asking, how exactly did you come to work for Mr. Everstone? You couldn't have been very old all those years ago when he gave you the management of the Bailey Hill Hotel."

"I'd just graduated from Dartmouth and had an acquaintance with his eldest son."

"You know Nathan?" My stomach dropped a little. "Nathan Everstone?"

"He helped me secure the job at Bailey Hill, and we've remained acquaintances throughout the years. Though he hasn't been around much, of late. Just long enough to get married before heading west again."

"Did you know— Do you know the Everstones well?"

"I've met Vance Everstone a number of times. He used to come up to Bailey Hill from Boston all the time. And I met William last summer, right before he announced his engagement."

At the mention of Will, I fought back my tears.

"You probably had a chance to see something of them while you worked at the hotel in Bar Harbor…."

I took a deep breath and forced myself to say, "I knew of them, a little."

"You're probably very close in age to the youngest daughter. If I remember correctly, Estella was much younger than the rest of her siblings, though she's probably just like her older sister by now."

In an effort not to delve too deeply into what he meant by his snide remark about Natalia, I added, "But I'm not so very young, Mr. Blakeley. I'll be twenty-two next spring."

Although he had a somewhat strange view of my family, claiming them as acquaintances but also obviously harboring some sort of contempt for Natalia, at least, it felt rather nice to speak of them. As if Mr. Blakeley and I were, indeed, simply getting to know one another.

He was such a tough, serious type of man, just as Mrs. Granton had said, and I didn't feel the need to indulge him with flattery or to strive to be just as everyone always expected me to be with him. I could just be me, and he wouldn't care one way or another.

"She was quite young the only time I met her. It was here, in fact, and I remember she used to always play with my little sister, Roxy."

"Roxy?" I, too, remembered my constant companion from that summer thirteen years ago. Roxy was Mr. Blakeley's little sister?

The sister who was, at that moment, inside the house we'd just left? I could scarcely believe I'd forgotten her last name.

"I'm sorry you weren't able to meet her tonight." He laughed to himself in the darkness. "Roxy didn't stop talking about Estella Everstone for years. Like you, she was fond of sketching; she carried her sketchbook everywhere. Drawing was all the girl seemed to want to do, which is probably why I hardly remember her— that, and the fact that she was just a child at the time, and I was nearly twenty."

So, he was a little older than I'd thought. Somehow, it didn't matter. For some odd reason, I felt a strange kind of equality with Mr. Blakeley—almost as if we were kindred spirits.

It was a ridiculous notion, I knew, as much as it was absurd. Did it come from his decision to reveal so much of himself to me as we walked in the semidarkness, our path lit by the almost full moon? As guarded as he'd been the only other time I'd seen him, it was strange to hear him speaking freely with me now, without reserve.

Perhaps Mrs. Granton was right, and Mr. Blakeley and I did happen to suit each other rather well. And perhaps we would become friends.

⌒

We reached the hotel at the perfectly respectable time of a quarter to nine. Perfectly respectable for resort life, at least. Many hotel guests still occupied the main floor—the music room, parlor, and lobby. On the lower level, the hum of conversation among the jovial crowd and the crash of billiard balls could be heard from the billiards room. As we passed through the small crowds of fashionably dressed gentlemen and ladies on our way to the elevators, I felt extremely ugly in the gray dress I'd donned for the day. Next to their expensive clothes and fancy hairstyles, I really did look like a plain, unnoticeable lady's companion. And although I did somewhat enjoy the anonymity, I did not enjoy the fact I now held a station between two distinct levels of society.

It was odd that I hadn't felt those judgments upon me while in Mr. Blakeley's presence. But then again, he probably didn't spend even one moment thinking about what anyone else was wearing.

Mr. Blakeley, as well as his wolfhound, saw me to the elevator. He gave a very proper, gentlemanly bow and said, "I will see you again soon."

"But of course," I answered.

He was such a strange man, irritated and brooding one day, quietly amused because of something to do with his younger sister the next.

When I made it to my room, having to sneak past Mrs. Granton as she slept, I crashed onto my bed, sketchbook, pencil case, and all, exhausted from such an unexpectedly busy evening. I flipped over on my stomach to examine my last drawing, the primitive self-portrait.

I opened the front cover of the book and flipped through my drawings. Where the portrait should have been, a blank page stared back at me instead.

Shock propelled me to the edge of the bed. My drawing had been torn out—stolen!

How dare he! But why would someone with a reputation for sneering at the mere idea of associating with young ladies want with a drawing of me?

Of course, it hadn't been taken by Mr. Blakeley. He'd hardly remembered I'd brought the sketchbook with me until I'd mentioned it. But perhaps that had all been an act. I shook the thought from my mind. I could not fathom Mr. Blakeley's mooning over a drawing of me. Or mooning over anything, for that matter.

More likely, Roxy had taken it. Had she been watching me? Had she recognized me?

Roxy Blakeley. For as much time as I'd spent in her company as a child, I'd since become quite convinced that she'd merely been an imaginary friend, for any time I'd ever mentioned her name to any of my siblings over the years, all I ever received back was a silencing glare.

FIVE

Breakfast

"There is no exquisite beauty...without some
strangeness in the proportion."
—Edgar Allan Poe, *Ligeia*

By the end of my first week and a half at Everston, I'd made
my way through *Northanger Abbey* and *Wuthering Heights*
and partway through *North and South* for Mrs. Granton...and I
certainly didn't feel like I was on vacation. I'd been accustomed to
reading aloud to my great aunt Miriam, but that had been when
my only other option was participating in the ruckus of society
dinners and balls and the constant meeting of people whose interest in me went only as far as my four-million-dollar inheritance.

No one at Everston saw that. Well, except for Jay, but he'd
always viewed my family and my inheritance as more of a hin-
drance than an opportunity. Perhaps it was one of the reasons I'd
held out hope for us for so long. There was simply no one else in
the world who cared as little as he that I was Bram Everstone's
daughter.

I hadn't been outside since Mr. Blakeley had walked me back
to Everston in the dark the evening I'd spent at Blakeley House.
Ever since that night, I'd prayed for Greenlee and tried time and
again to imagine what it must have been like being trapped at The

Hawthorne Inn for however long she had stayed there. Not that I had the first idea.

On the morning of my third Monday at Everston, I decided I would go down for breakfast. I'd seen Mr. Blakeley almost every day during those weeks, but never with the same kind of familiarity that the darkness had afforded us the first two times we'd spoken at length.

When I reached the wide landing of the grand staircase—without Mrs. Granton, who took all her meals by room service—I immediately noticed that Mr. Blakeley, dressed in his somber black suit, stood near the formidable entrance of the hotel, speaking with a gentleman I recognized as one of the higher-up hotel employees. I'd gathered that his name was Mr. Mulduney and that he often occupied the main lobby office. He was a bit taller than Mr. Blakeley but nowhere near able to give off quite the air of gruff audacity his employer could achieve in spades when he wanted.

Mr. Blakeley directed his gaze to me as soon as I made it to the foot of the stairs, though he kept speaking to the gentleman at his side. I stayed near the stairs, not even sure why I'd come down for breakfast. It was such an awful, terrible idea. What if someone recognized me?

Eventually, Mr. Blakeley finished his conversation with Mr. Mulduney and made his way across the spacious room to me. When he reached me, he produced a small envelope from the inside pocket of his jacket. "A letter for you."

I took it, recognizing the Boston return address.

"It's from Everwood, mailed with extra postage," he noted. "Do you happen to know someone at the Everstones' Back Bay residence?"

I nodded. "An old friend of mine is a maid for the Everstone family." When my answer seemed to have satisfied his curiosity, I asked, "How did you know it was from—"

"I've been to Everwood...many times, actually," he stated matter-of-factly. "Bram Everstone has become somewhat a mentor of mine over the last year or so."

"I sent her a telegram before I came," I added awkwardly, not wanting to get too deeply into the subject of my family again. "In case she might need to reach me."

His brownish-green eyes caught mine for a second before they skittered to the opposite side of the room. Then he cleared his throat and brought his gaze back just as quickly. He opened his mouth, but when something else caught his attention across the lobby, near the doors, he clamped it shut.

An untidily dressed young man with sandy hair and dark brown eyes had come in and now spoke to the young lady with the bright golden hair who worked at the front desk.

"Excuse me, Miss Stoneburner." Mr. Blakeley swiveled away from me, in the direction of the newcomer.

The stranger took notice and walked directly toward us without a second glance at the young lady to whom he'd been speaking. "Blakeley."

"What are you doing here?" Mr. Blakeley moved to stand before me; for a moment, the backs of his broad shoulders were all I could see. And I was thankful for such a shield, that he'd felt the need to protect me from the glances of the arrogant young man.

"Who's that?" the man asked.

"None of your concern. I told you not to come here."

"She happen to be lookin' for work?"

"No." Mr. Blakeley moved to the right, and I did, as well, to stay out of the man's line of vision. Never had I felt a stronger urge to run and hide than I did from those leering gray eyes.

There was something about the scruffy man that made my skin crawl. What had he said to the young lady at the front desk? Had he made her feel a similar discomfort? She hadn't seemed too put off by him; but just the sight of him, and his words...he repulsed me.

"Yeah, well, I been lookin' for a girl I know—she has the oddest color beige eyes I ever seen. I haven't seen her for a few weeks, and I wondered if you'd seen her."

Was he looking for Greenlee? Was this the vile man who'd kept her against her will all those months?

Mr. Blakeley shuffled to the left, and I followed suit.

"And why would you think to look for her at Everston?"

"Oh, I don't know...you just seem the kind of guy who would care to help a girl out, considering what you done for Vi, and all. And you and that Dr. Crawford seem to be friendly. I know he had his eye on her; I could tell from the first time he seen her, when she was sick last spring." The stranger peeked at me from around Mr. Blakeley's shoulder and sneered wickedly. "Say, she is mighty pretty. Well, except for that dress, but we could put her in somethin' comelier....not that she needs a dress at all for—"

"Get out now, Hawthorne."

I knew it! Ezra Hawthorne, then.

Mr. Blakeley took a step toward him, which caused the man to back away and head for the door. With a quick glance toward the front desk, he said, "See ya." And then he was gone.

Mr. Blakeley turned around to face me again. "Where is Mrs. Granton this morning?"

"Taking her breakfast upstairs, as usual. Room service." I thought it odd for him to go right back to the conversation we'd begun before Mr. Hawthorne had come into the lobby.

"You two don't come down much for meals, do you?" He glanced past me into the dining room, then quickly faced me again and caught my lingering stare. The strange mix of greens and browns in his eyes was much too fascinating to ignore. "Have you eaten breakfast?"

"No, I was just thinking of going in—"

"To breakfast...alone?" He pulled out his timepiece and studied it for a moment. Then he glanced at the front doors before facing me again. "Have breakfast with me, then."

Although it had been over a week since we'd spoken, I felt familiar enough with him that, as my answer, I simply looped my arm in his.

There were a hundred impatient questions streaming through my mind after witnessing the turbulent conversation between him and Ezra Hawthorne. I wanted to know more about The Hawthorne Inn and Greenlee, why Jay had wanted to hide her at Blakeley House, and why Mr. Blakeley had allowed him to. Not that the dining room of Everston was a good place to ask.

What would happen if Greenlee was discovered to be hiding at Blakeley House? I could imagine the rumors that would spread, not to mention what Ezra Hawthorne would do to get her back. And there was no doubt that such things coming to light would affect Everston's reputation.

Did Mr. Blakeley realize all this? What would Father think?

Mr. Blakeley led me through the packed dining room to a table in a far corner of the room by a floor-to-ceiling window facing Half Moon Lake. After he had seated me and pushed my chair in, he sat down around the table from me.

From the corner of my eye, I noticed that the eyes of almost everyone in the room were on us. I could imagine what the other diners thought of me, garbed in the dull brown dress. They were thinking just what I would have thought of someone else dressed as I was.

After we were served our breakfast, he said in a low voice, "About the other day at Blakeley House...."

I lifted my teacup to my lips and took a sip, but my eyes didn't stray from his. And as I set my cup back in its saucer, I made sure to keep his attention. "Have no fear, Mr. Blakeley; my lips are sealed." I lifted the corners of my mouth in a sly grin. "I can keep a secret, believe me."

"I do believe you." Those eyes—brown one moment, green the next—shifted over my face, and he *almost* returned my smile.

This tiny glimpse of good humor from him gave me a glint of courage, enough to say, "There's a page missing from my sketchbook."

His dark eyebrows came down, and a frown marred his lips for a second. He didn't say anything, only stared at me while he slathered another biscuit with jam in a rather unforgiving manner.

I didn't like that I'd inadvertently made him frustrated with me just because I suspected that the thief had been someone from his household—even him. I hadn't intended to accuse; I wasn't even sure why I'd brought it up.

"It was torn out during the time I was at your house," I continued on, practically whispering, even though I regretted broaching the subject in the first place. I wouldn't have, if I'd known he would respond like this.

"And what was the subject of the stolen sketch?" he asked after some time, and with such frankness that I became convinced he couldn't have had anything to do with the drawing's disappearance—which I found oddly disappointing.

"Well, you see, I tried to...." Why I felt ill at ease, I could hardly tell. Someone in his household had stolen my drawing. If anyone had cause to feel embarrassment, it was he. "It was a very simplified sketch of...me."

"A self-portrait."

I could feel the heat rise in my cheeks. I didn't know what to say, so I glanced about the room intently, purposefully avoiding his gaze. Finally, rather exasperated at his responses, I asked, "Do you doubt I'm able to sketch my own likeness objectively?"

I found that his eyes hadn't strayed from mine. "That isn't what I meant...or what I said."

The clanking of silver and china throughout the large, high-ceilinged room consumed the long silence between us.

I couldn't help but stare at him as he kept his unsmiling eyes focused on my face. It was awfully brazen of him—and of me—and suddenly, a host of new, peculiar sensations raced through my veins. Along with those came a wish for some colored pencils, and the chance to draw Mr. Blakeley's gorgeous eyes before Mrs. Granton and I were to leave Everston.

"And you'd like it back?"

"You don't need to— I don't think it would be a good idea." I hardly knew whether I referred to his finding and scrutinizing the self-portrait or to the notion of his sitting before me long enough for me to stare into his eyes to get those amazing colors just right.

He gave me another almost-smile, and I didn't appreciate how the tiny lift of his lip sent my heart fluttering out of control. For a long moment, I couldn't help but stare at him. He was so complex, and the thought that I amused him, even slightly, was immensely... satisfying.

I didn't know what was wrong with me. He was one of Father's employees. What did it matter that he was incredibly good-looking, or that he seemed, at least at times, to fancy Elle Stoneburner as a person?

I wasn't Elle Stoneburner, and the thoughts streaming through my mind were utter impossibilities.

Looking down, I realized we were both basically finished with our breakfast. Apparently aware of the same thing, Mr. Blakeley stood, helped me from my seat, and led me out of the dining room. Once again, I felt every eye on us.

As we walked down the hall to the elevators, he said, "Miss Stoneburner, when you go to your rooms, would you do me a favor and ask Mrs. Granton if she would join me for tea on Friday afternoon?"

"Yes, of course." He confused me so. It was almost as if he preferred speaking to me in the dark, when we were both half hidden in shadows. How would we ever have another meaningful conversation if he insisted on acting like strangers in the light of day?

He caught my reluctant gaze and held it. "And I'd like you to come."

"I— Of course, Mr. Blakeley." I didn't know what to think. And I wondered why I even cared to think anything.

I was starved for attention. That had to be it.

When the elevator door opened, I excused myself from his company and made my way to my room, fully aware that I thought a little too much of Mr. Dexter Blakeley and his almost-smiling hazel eyes.

A little later, in an effort to momentarily forget the situation I'd found myself in at Everston, I seated myself in the stuffed armchair next to the lace-curtained windows in my room and read the latest letter from my sister Natalia.

Monday, September 7, 1891

Dearest Elle,

What a treat it must be to find yourself at Everston! Everything here is the same; we're all doing well. But I should remind you, our friend J has taken a position at Everston. Perhaps you might see him! I will write to him directly so he can watch out for you.

Also, Mr. E wanted me to pass on that there's a gentleman by the name of Mr. Dexter K. Blakeley connected with the hotel, and that if you should have any problems, and J is unable to help, you should seek out this Mr. Blakeley. He is trustworthy and has been known of the Everstone family for a long time.

Do write to me soon!

Your dearest friend,
Jane Smyth

It was a rather silly letter, but I could tell Natalia had tried her best to write it as she thought one of the young maids at Everwood might. And I knew exactly what she meant by every vague statement.

They didn't consider my being stuck in the isolated Appalachian Mountains of central Maine such a terrible situation. Natalia's newborn baby girl, Julianna, was doing well. They assumed Jay would be willing to watch over me while at Everston, and Father considered Mr. Blakeley to be someone I could depend on.

I could already tell there was something about him that fascinated me. And it wasn't just his eyes. It was so much more than how he looked, for it had begun almost exclusively while I'd been unable to see him—in the dark of the stagecoach, and again on the moonlit road from Blakeley House to Everston.

～

I spent the rest of that morning reading aloud to Mrs. Granton from *North and South*. I made a point not to look out the windows. I didn't want her to conclude—correctly—that I desperately wanted to go outside.

After Mrs. Granton insisted upon having lunch brought up, she said, "I called down to speak with Blakeley this morning. He told me he'd just accompanied you to breakfast, and I've been waiting all this time for you to mention it. Do tell me the details."

"There aren't any details." Unless the fact that Mr. Blakeley had gorgeous eyes was a detail. But I wasn't about to share that. With anyone. "I think he was angry with me for most of breakfast, but it didn't begin that way."

"Yes, I can imagine."

"And a great many people stared at us whilst we were sitting together."

"Of course they did, dear."

"Did Mr. Blakeley mention he'd like to have tea with us Friday afternoon?"

"Why, no, he didn't. Are you certain he wants me to come down?"

"He asked me specifically to invite you."

"He likely wanted only to be sure you would come. Why would he want to see me?"

"Do you not know him quite well?"

"Well, yes. But I'm a wrinkly old lady. And you're, what, about twenty?"

"One and twenty."

"Yes, I can tell you right now which one of us he'd rather spend time with."

"No, Mrs. Granton. He might have said he wanted me to come, but he was very much interested in seeing more of you again."

"Oh, very well. I suppose I can make my way down that cantankerous elevator for one measly afternoon." She grinned through her complaint. "Though I'd bet that even if I didn't, he'd be just as pleased."

SIX

Afternoon Tea

"I feel as if I were a piece in a game of chess, when my opponent
says of it: That piece cannot be moved."
—Søren Kierkegaard, *Either/Or*

Boarding Everston's massive new schooner and sailing about Half Moon Lake with a small crowd of hotel guests during my afternoon off the following Friday morning was supposed to have been a diversion. I brought my sketchbook and pencils to distract myself from thinking of Mr. Blakeley, especially his desire to have tea with Mrs. Granton and me. But with Everston ever in view as we circled about the crescent-shaped lake, Mr. Blakeley was, instead, what I found myself drawing as the wind rushed by me.

Near the end of the excursion on the crowded vessel, I thought back to my missing self-portrait. I'd come to wish I'd never mentioned it. Mr. Blakeley's reaction to my insinuations had cemented my belief that Roxy was the one who had taken it.

As I joined the procession along the path from the wharf past the boathouse to the hotel, my gaze shifted over the tall pillars of the veranda and the red and white striped canopies overhanging the multitude of windows and French doors along the façade.

How I loved Everston! I could just imagine spending every summer and autumn there, living in the private rooms of the sixth floor of the tower.

I was just about to head to my room to rescue my hair from the mess the wind had made of it when I heard the elevator ding, followed by Mrs. Granton speaking. "Oh yes, Mr. Blakeley is the finest of gentlemen. I've known him for years." She hobbled out of the clanky metal door with one hand raised. "And I'm perfectly capable of walking, Mr. Elevator Attendant."

At least with the help of her fancy brass-handled cane.

"Elle, dear!" she said when she noticed me.

"I was just coming to retrieve you."

"I don't pay you to be a retriever, dearest. I pay you to entertain me."

I met her near a sofa along the wide hall to the tea room, and she motioned for me to sit. When I did, she reached a hand to my cheek. "You're so flushed!"

"I went for a sail."

"And you took this with you?" She reached for my sketch-book, and I let her have it. I just hoped she wouldn't flip all the way through and see that I'd sketched a likeness of Mr. Blakeley.

She opened the brown leather cover and paged through the drawings without a word.

Honestly, I wasn't sure how well she could see them, since she refused to wear her spectacles. But then, to my surprise, she opened her reticule and pulled out a small case, popped it open, and took them out. She positioned the glasses on her nose and then her ears, glanced down at the sketchbook again, and beamed. "What an artist you are. You didn't tell me." She flipped through a few more pages. "Goodness, you were able to capture Blakeley quite well!"

"I guess I have a good memory," I quipped. But it didn't seem witty once the words were out. I didn't quite like how often I'd caught myself entertaining thoughts about Mr. Blakeley during the last few days.

"Well, you certainly are a natural, dear." She turned to the next page and studied a drawing of my beloved Everston. "We should tell Blakeley to have a gallery day, so his guests can show off their work. Yours would be the most lauded, I'm certain."

"Oh, no." I clasped my fingers about my tin pencil case in my lap to resist the urge to yank the sketchbook from her. I felt safe with her looking at my work, but no one else needed to see it. I didn't want Mr. Blakeley to see my sketches—especially the one of him. And I certainly didn't need to bring any sort of extra attention to myself while I was in hiding.

"I don't want anyone else to see them," I offered mildly.

"That's all right, dear. It was just an idea." Mrs. Granton pulled the spectacles from her face and put them away. Then she positioned her cane on the floor, and I helped her to rise from the sofa. "I suppose it's about time to make our way in for tea. Blakeley will be looking for us shortly."

Soon Mrs. Granton and I were situated at a small round table, and I had my sketchbook and pencils safely hidden in my lap.

"So, about your future, young lady…since you have no interest in becoming a world-famous artist, what do you think will eventually become of you?"

"Pardon me?"

"When your life is over, and you look back…." She took a sip of her blueberry tea. We'd already been served our first course of treats. Mr. Blakeley was late. "What will you have become, do you think?"

"I don't really know anymore. Until recently, I'd always imagined I would someday marry a missionary and—"

"Elle, you are a dear." Mrs. Granton laughed under her breath.

"Do you not think I could have?"

"Oh, you could, I suppose. But you must have had some particular godly gentleman in mind to have harbored such a zealous goal. You hardly speak to a soul as it is. How do you imagine you'd be any good at ministering to heathens?" Mrs. Granton's eyes twinkled. "Would you not rather go into the hotel business?" She finished her question with a wink.

I took a sip of my tea to avoid answering her just as Mr. Blakeley came to the table.

"What's this about the hotel business? Speaking about me behind my back, Mrs. Granton?" For some reason, the sound of his voice soothed my nerves. Even when it carried only the faintest hint of the gruffness I'd come to expect whenever he spoke, it was too disabling, too hypnotic. "I do believe my ears were burning."

Mrs. Granton reached over and took his proffered hand as he silently bowed to her. Then he pulled out the chair across the table from me. "Miss Stoneburner," he added courteously.

Mrs. Granton smiled rather bashfully at him. "It's about time you made an appearance at your own tea party, Blakeley." She turned to me. "Elle, would you like to know what I'm proudest of when I look back on my life?"

"Of course," I said quietly.

Mr. Blakeley's eyes connected with mine, just for a second, and heat crept up my neck as he shifted into his seat.

"It was my long, loving marriage to Mr. Lyle Granton."

A radiant smile suddenly stretched across Mr. Blakeley's face.

After witnessing only the half-hidden hints he'd allowed me to glimpse, I was stunned speechless by the sight of this display of cheerfulness. Those sad imitations—I'd taken some delight in them, but they were nothing like this full-fledged, boyish grin. A grin that unfortunately caused the foolish flutters I'd learned to control in the last days to come back with full force.

"How that man loved me…and that's what matters most, you know, Elle." This Mrs. Granton said after a rather long moment of silence.

I'd been staring at Mr. Blakeley as he continued to beam at Mrs. Granton.

"Why, was it difficult for you to love him back?" I finally asked, sensing that she expected me to respond in some way.

"Oh, no, not once I realized." Mrs. Granton took a slow bite of a tea cookie.

"Realized what?" I prodded, truly interested now.

"What deep—and often quite raging—waters can often be hidden by an otherwise remarkably calm surface." After a minute, in which Mr. Blakeley gained considerable control of his facial features, and I silently drank my tea, at a loss for something to say in response, she continued, "You know, Blakeley, I understand now." Mrs. Granton faced him again. "Now that I have the chance to see you again, I know why the two of you used to get on so well."

"We were much alike," he answered. His charming smile had mostly vanished, replaced by a rather inquisitive look. His eyes met mine briefly across the table; he'd caught me staring unabashedly.

As he quickly averted his gaze from me, I took the chance to examine him further—his muscular hands as he finally took his napkin and spread it over his lap; his fine jaw; his perfect mouth; his broad shoulders fitted flawlessly under the impeccable cut of his suit; the rich, earthy colors of his eyes….

"Seeing you again after all these years makes me miss him all the more." Looking rather somber, Mrs. Granton clicked her teacup onto its saucer. "You'll never imagine what Elle just told me. She's had her heart set on marrying a missionary."

Mr. Blakeley immediately directed his eyes to mine. The curious expression from before flitted over his face, but it was gone just as quickly, leaving his handsome, dark countenance surprisingly nondescript.

"You care so much about ministering to others with the gospel of Christ, Miss Stoneburner?" His eyes drilled through me. They were intensely green now, and suddenly difficult to read.

"All it takes is a willing heart, I've been told." That was what I'd been telling myself for years.

However, I was no longer interested in marrying Jay—not since realizing I hardly knew what I wanted. "It's merely something I've always thought...." I didn't like being forced into such a personal conversation again, especially when it seemed I always said the wrong thing.

Mrs. Granton reached for my right hand under the table, as if I needed help recovering from an affliction. Her grip was cold and clammy, like always. "It is a noteworthy endeavor, Elle. Don't let anyone tell you it's not, or that you aren't able. I know I teased you earlier about being shy, but that shouldn't keep a Christian woman from achieving her calling."

With my free hand, I gripped my sketchbook and pencils in my lap. I could tell Mr. Blakeley still watched me closely, though I wouldn't allow myself the privilege of looking at him.

"You could show Blakeley your drawings, couldn't you?" Mrs. Granton asked with a strange glimmer in her eyes, her head slightly cocked. "It's absolutely remarkable how well you were able to capture *his* likeness."

Heat flushed through my entire being. I slipped my hand from Mrs. Granton's and grasped the sketchbook and pencils with both hands. My lips wouldn't move, other than to form the shape of an *o*. Finally, I managed, "No, I don't think so."

"A drawing of me?" Mr. Blakely asked at the same moment.

To my horror, I huffed nervously, as I could hardly find my breath. Why would Mrs. Granton divulge such a thing to him? What reason could she have for wanting to mortify me completely?

"Well, I'm about finished spending time outside of my room," she said next, as if oblivious to the stir her comment had caused.

"I'm going to write letters for the rest of the day, so you needn't read to me, Elle. You can take the rest of the day off." Leaning on her cane, Mrs. Granton slowly stood from the table with the help of Mr. Blakeley. "Take a walk with Blakeley. I heard there's a lawn tennis tournament going on."

I stood, as well. "But Mrs. Granton—"

"Take your time enjoying the scenery. It is stunning, is it not?" she added with a covert glance at Mr. Blakeley. "You'll have her, won't you, Blakeley?"

"Most certainly, Mrs. Granton."

SEVEN

The Drawing

"Every heart has its secret sorrows which the world knows not, and oftentimes we call a man cold, when he is only sad."
—Henry Wadsworth Longfellow, *Hyperion*

Once Mr. Blakeley had handed Mrs. Granton off to the elevator attendant, he turned back to me. He seemed like the kind of man who would consider watching lawn tennis a waste of time. Why had he agreed?

Taking me by the arm, he continued on toward the lobby without a word. I walked beside him, my sketchbook and pencil tin clutched tightly to my chest with my left arm.

He studied me out of the corner of his eye as we strolled the length of the hall, then broke the silence. "May I see the drawing?"

I looked down at my sketchbook, then to the plain hem of my dull brown dress, wishing his attention hadn't returned so quickly to that particular subject. "I'm sure you have a dozen things you need to do other than keep me company," I said, avoiding his question. "I'd rather not watch lawn tennis."

"I'd rather not, either," he said reflectively as he led me farther down the hall and into the main lobby.

The young lady who worked weekdays at the front desk laughed sprightly at a good-natured jest one of the hotel guests had made.

Mr. Blakeley stopped suddenly. "Have you been introduced to Violet yet? I know she's wanted to meet you."

As soon as the guest had departed, Mr. Blakeley directed me across the lobby to the desk.

"Miss Stoneburner, I'd like you to meet one of my most loyal employees, Miss Violet Hawthorne. She's worked at Everston for about six months, since moving to the area." He turned to her. "Miss Hawthorne, meet Miss Elle Stoneburner."

"It's nice to meet you, Miss Stoneburner. You're here with Mrs. Granton, correct?" Her gray eyes sparked when she smiled. It was no wonder Mr. Blakeley had her working at the front desk.

"I am."

"Do please call me Violet. Or even Vi, if you prefer."

Violet Hawthorne? Ezra Hawthorne had referred to someone named Vi. Was this his sister? What could Mr. Blakeley be thinking to have someone with such a connection working the front desk at Everston?

In the hotel office, the telephone began ringing. Violet's gaze shot from me to Mr. Blakeley. "Mr. Mulduney is away at the moment, so I'll have to answer that. Excuse me."

"Of course," Mr. Blakeley replied.

Suddenly displeased with him for a multitude of reasons, I grabbed a brochure from the front desk and brushed past him on my way to the lobby doors. Shuffling past the other hotel guests, I glanced down at the brochure. When the schedule of weekly events caught my attention, I stopped mid-stride.

Mr. Blakeley was beside me again in an instant. Could he not tell I didn't want to be near him? Well, that wasn't exactly true. Part of the problem was that I liked being near him too much. But why should I? He was gruff and arrogant and made bad choices, like allowing Jay to hide Greenlee Cole at his house with his mother and sister, and permitting someone with connections to The Hawthorne Inn to staff the front desk of Everston.

It didn't matter what his smile did to my insides. What mattered was that he worked for my father, and his careless decisions endangered the reputation of Everston.

"What is it, Miss Stoneburner?"

I looked down at the brochure again, trying to pull my thoughts together, to select something appropriate to discuss. "There's to be a concert next week?" It had been ages since I'd last attended anything as culturally stimulating as an orchestra performance.

"An orchestra will perform on the veranda, yes...selections from Vivaldi." He looked at me, visibly perplexed by my behavior. "Would you...would you enjoy attending the concert...with me?"

Warring emotions coursed through me at his request. "You would like that?"

Flattered by Mr. Blakeley's marked attention to me, I knew that entertaining thoughts of reciprocating would be an exceptionally bad idea, no matter how much I wanted to.

"Of course I would."

"It wasn't exactly what I was getting at, but...." I closed the brochure and fanned my face with it, in an attempt to cool my burning cheeks. I thought suddenly of Roxy...and Greenlee...and me, together at Blakeley House.

"What I meant by asking was...will the orchestra play loudly enough to be heard across the lake from Blakeley House?"

"It ought to, yes."

"Maybe I could come, and Roxy and Greenlee...and I... could—"

"Let's take a walk." He grabbed the brochure with one hand and my arm with the other. "There's a tennis match we're missing." He shoved the brochure into his inside breast pocket.

As we crossed the lobby to the door, I noticed Violet was again at the front desk, feverishly writing something on a pad of paper, her face scrunched in concentration. She was adorable, even if she was a Hawthorne. "Is Violet Hawthorne somehow connected to the Mr. Hawthorne from the other day—and The Hawthorne Inn?"

Mr. Blakeley propelled me down the steps by the arm into the blazing heat. He scanned the veranda, where a multitude of hotel guests were lounging or milling about. It hardly offered the privacy he seemed to prefer for our conversations.

"What would give you that idea?" he asked through clenched teeth.

I could scarcely answer as he stalked across the yard with me in tow. We passed several couples taking walks along the gravel path that encircled the hotel at the edge of Half Moon Lake, and each person nodded in acknowledgment, albeit of Mr. Blakeley and not of me. I was merely an extension of him, a pretty flower tucked into the buttonhole of his jacket.

"Why does Violet work at Everston?" I asked, still being dragged along mercilessly.

He didn't answer but continued walking until we had reached the shade of some pine trees a good distance from anyone else. For a moment, I thought he might grab me by the arms, but he just stood there with an irritated frown upon his chiseled face. "You need to be more careful with what you say."

Stunned by his reprimand, I simply stood before him, my eyes locked with his. I didn't know how to respond.

"Blakeley!" Jay sprinted across the lawn toward us. He looked refreshed—much better than he'd appeared the last time I'd seen him, the night he'd carried Greenlee into Blakeley House. He walked straight to Mr. Blakeley and offered him his hand without as much as a glance my way.

"I've received a letter from my friends in Albany. They've agreed to help."

"Splendid!" Mr. Blakeley didn't seem the least bit bothered by Jay's blatant dismissal of me. He seemed to have forgotten that I stood there beside him as well. "Is it good news?"

"It's the best news."

I cleared my throat. "Dr. Crawford, have you been to check on Miss Cole? How does she fare?" I hadn't been able to ask Mr. Blakeley, for fear of embarrassment.

Jay finally looked at me, a guarded look in his brown gaze. "She's much better, thank you, Miss...what was it? Stoneburner? What a curious name." His eyes narrowed.

"It's a shame what happened to her." I dared to glance at Mr. Blakeley, and I could tell by his furrowed brow, and by his sudden inability to keep his eyes off me, that he already regretted the harsh words he'd just spoken to me.

I was aware that such subjects were deemed inappropriate for well-bred young ladies like myself to know about, let alone mention; but it didn't mean they should be ignored. Mr. Blakeley seemed to understand this, as well: that when all the useless, meaningless stuff—stuff that used to govern my world—was stripped away, the so-called inappropriate subjects were the ones that really mattered.

Even as "Elle Stoneburner," what did I have to concern myself with, other than figuring out which book I would read next to Mrs. Granton, or what awful, drab gown I would don for the day? What were those concerns compared to what Greenlee Cole had been through while at The Hawthorne Inn?

As if these new epiphanies had unlocked uncharted avenues to my mind, I realized that while I'd been living at Everwood in Back Bay, Boston, attending countless soirees, dinner parties, and concerts, helpless girls like Greenlee Cole were being forced to live as slaves at despicable places like The Hawthorne Inn in Westward, Maine...one of my father's lumber towns.

Was there nothing anyone could do to stop the vicious cycle, besides rescue one girl at a time? And was that what Jay planned to do in Aberdeen, Washington? Was that why he'd so easily rejected the idea of marrying me?

It struck me as odd that while I'd long hoped to be a missionary's wife, I'd never come to the point of realizing I was far from prepared for such a life—or that, most likely, I never would be.

I would have been a terrible wife for a missionary.

"Because the poor girl needed a way to escape."

"What?" I snapped out of my reverie at Mr. Blakeley's words. He still stood close beside me, and Jay was nowhere in sight.

He gently took my sketchbook from my hand. "Miss Hawthorne needed a way out of Westward just as much as Greenlee did." Mr. Blakeley opened the book, and a curious expression transformed his face as he watched me observing him.

"You offered her a job so she wouldn't have to work for Mr. Hawthorne? Is he her brother?"

Mr. Blakeley didn't answer; he only stared down at my sketchbook as he flipped through the pages. "These are good." He tilted the book to show me my most recent drawing of Everston.

I no longer cared what he might think of them, even the one I'd drawn of him. There were so many other things that mattered more than my silly sketches and how personal they had seemed to me just an hour before.

He turned the page and stood still, his attention completely arrested. "Is this how you see me?"

"It's fairly accurate, don't you think?" I'd drawn him as he'd been in the stagecoach, seated across from me with his hand resting on his dog's head. Although it had been dark, and my best impression of him at the time had been limited, I could see him there now, vividly. The vision of him as he'd faced me straight on for that hour drive, as he'd spoken with me so casually in the shadows—it would not leave me.

I recognized when the realization dawned on him that his likeness was the last drawing in the book. "Did you sketch this today?"

I grabbed the sketchbook from him and closed it. "Why would Violet's parents...?"

Mr. Blakeley scrutinized me for a moment, then glanced at the sketchbook and my pencil case. With the smallest of movements, he shook his head, as if to dispel some unwanted thought. "Her parents are dead. Ezra Hawthorne immediately assumed ownership of their small hotel and made it into the sinister place it is now. If she'd stayed in Westward much longer, her reputation wouldn't have survived." He pulled a hand over his face, looking beyond frustrated. "Do these things truly interest you?"

"I've lived a rather sheltered life, Mr. Blakeley. I never knew...."

"And now?" He looked at me with uncertainty. Did he doubt me? "Is it that you would do something about it?"

Could I?

I didn't know what Father would do when he found out, but I also wouldn't let myself worry about it. Hopefully, in the time I had left at Everston, I could do something. And then, perhaps, once I reclaimed my true identity, I could find a way to help, beyond making mere monetary donations through the society fund-raisers my family constantly attended.

"I'll do whatever I can while I'm able, Mr. Blakeley."

He took my arm, and we resumed our procession across the lawn. He dipped his head low and spoke with a gentleness I'd never heard from him. "Something's been bothering me since our last conversation with Mrs. Granton, and I apologize in advance if this question is too personal, but I would like an answer...for my own peace of mind."

"What is it?" I asked. Anything I could answer for him, I would. Even if he confronted me with the name Estella Everstone, I didn't think I would have been able to keep from telling him the truth.

"Is it truly your goal to marry a missionary simply for the purpose of spreading the gospel, like Mrs. Granton said? Have the rumors of Crawford's taking a mission caught your—"

"Absolutely not."

He seemed visibly surprised by my swift response, but then he went on, "Is that your answer to *both* questions?"

"No, I'm not interested in Dr. Crawford. And it was never exclusively for the cause of spreading the gospel, Mr. Blakeley. I just happened to have a fondness for the kind of men who would rather seek God's heart and will than—"

"You're speaking in the past tense. Does that mean you're no longer interested in marrying such a man?" It was a strange question, and stranger still because it came from Mr. Blakeley.

"You mean, a missionary?"

"Anyone at all. Surely, you've had your chances."

"If you must know, I was engaged once." I held my sketchbook and pencil case to my side with my free hand, as if they could comfort me. "Engaged to someone who ultimately decided he didn't want me."

Mr. Blakeley didn't respond.

"He was a missionary—at least, he'd been called to the mission field at the time, but he didn't think I was suitable—"

"What more could he want?"

My heart skipped, but I immediately determined to not dwell on those intriguing words. They weren't meant for me. They were meant for Elle Stoneburner.

"It doesn't matter now. I realized a while back that we would never suit each other, and I wouldn't have him—not for the world. Not now." What a blundering fool I was becoming. I blushed annoyingly.

"I have an odd request of you, Miss Stoneburner. It refers back to our discussion earlier about the concert." He seemed to feel just as uneasy as I had moments ago. "Would you like to meet my sister?"

The thought of seeing Roxy made me happy, despite the fact that doing so was definitely another bad idea. "I would very much like an invitation to your home, Mr. Blakeley." I couldn't help but offer him a tiny grin.

When Mr. Blakeley noticed this merry reaction from me, a smile stretched over his cheeks and into those amazing greenish-brown eyes. The sight of it made me wonder what other fascinating curiosities he kept hidden under the rigid, harsh demeanor he so often portrayed.

We made it to the lawn tennis match, just as it was concluding. As the crowd dispersed around us, a good number of the spectators seemed to take special note of our spending time together. We followed the throng of hotel guests back to Everston, and Mr. Blakeley immediately escorted me back to the elevator, where we'd last spoken with Mrs. Granton.

We'd followed her orders almost perfectly, I realized.

Upon reaching the fifth floor, I proceeded down the hall and stopped just outside our rooms, knowing Mrs. Granton wasn't likely to hear me until I walked through the door into her bedchamber.

I opened my sketchbook to the drawing of Mr. Blakeley. The idea of him, my thoughts of him—especially in the last hour—had grown to the point that I didn't think there was a single man of my acquaintance in New England who compared with his caliber of character or his irresistible magnetism.

But what did Mr. Blakeley think of me?

Nothing.

He didn't even know my name, who I was. And he likely never would.

Slamming the book shut, I took my key from my pocket and unlocked Mrs. Granton's room, completely ashamed for having indulged myself by sketching him in the first place, and even more so for spending more time than was healthy to moon over it.

EIGHT

Leightner Hollow

"She poured out the liquid music of her voice to
quench the thirst of his spirit."
—Nathaniel Hawthorne, *The Birthmark*

As my third week at Everston came to a close, Mrs. Granton insisted I take the hotel surrey to the Sunday service offered by the hotel. We'd spent the previous two Sunday mornings in the music room reading Scriptures and singing hymns, since she wasn't one for going outside much. Or at all.

After a journey up an ever-sloping hill, the hotel surreys reached their stopping point, but I didn't see a church. The drivers parked the surreys at a high meadow clearing from which we could see Everston. Just down the hill was an entrance to a forest trail.

I was surprised to have traveled so deep into the forest—but then again, much of the draw of such places as Everston was the sense of rustification.

The small crowd hiked down the wooded trail, which was covered in dried pine needles and fallen orange birch leaves. The snapping branches and rustling limbs of the tall trees were the prevalent noises as we passed under what was left of the canopy of leaves overhead. Everyone remained quiet as we walked. Had the group been instructed to treat the forest as they would a church sanctuary? Or was reverent silence simply their natural response to such a place?

Finally, we made it to a clearing with a sign that read "Leightner Hollow." There, the trees were more spread out, and huge pieces of bedrock jutted up from the ground, making high crests and hollows. I'd never ventured so far into those woods, and I was overwhelmed by the sense of otherworldliness. The biggest hollow of all was practically a wide, shallow cave that looked almost like the inside of a lady's bonnet. It was as if God had carved it out especially as an amphitheater for His people. Rows of wooden benches were arranged at perfect intervals on either side, and, front and center, a large rectangular stone protruded from the cave walls. On it stood Mr. Blakeley, next to an ancient-looking wooden chair, flipping through the pages of a Bible. He stopped for a moment when he spotted me but quickly resumed his task. I walked to the second row of wooden benches and sat down.

He didn't climb down from the rustic altar, but I could almost feel that his eyes were still on me. As I sat in my lonely seat, I covertly eyed the altar. No, he wasn't looking my way any longer; his attention was on his Bible. As it should have been.

I glanced down at my empty lap. It wasn't the first time I wished I'd remembered to pack my personal Bible when I'd gone to live with Mrs. Granton in Portland. But ever since June, when my world had been tilted on its axis—since Will's death and Jay's rejection—I hadn't really known what to do with my Bible. Yes, I usually read to Mrs. Granton from the Scriptures on Sundays, but I was too confused about what God wanted from me to think of opening the book in search of answers for myself.

I closed my eyes and covered them with my hands, almost in a posture of prayer.

I don't know what I want anymore. What do I need?

When I opened my eyes, Mr. Blakeley stood before me. Still facing me, he took a seat on the bench in front of mine, rested his elbows on his knees, and leaned forward. "Would you mind leading the hymns for us this morning, Miss Stoneburner?"

I forced myself to remain calm and steady, despite the strange, anxious sensations that his presence caused to swirl through me. "Oh, no. I sing only for my friends—"

"It's just two hymns for the benefit of the guests of my hotel." He lifted the corners of his mouth as his attention shifted to the crowd gathering around and finding their seats. This gave me a really good look at his perfectly proportioned profile.

"I sing for my friends," I repeated. "And I have no friends here."

He took his time responding to me, but he finally said, "For as long as you are with us at Everston, Miss Stoneburner, I would be honored to be counted as your friend."

I swallowed nervously. "I would be honored with that arrangement, as well, Mr. Blakeley."

"As much as I enjoy self-imposed isolation, it does become rather boring at times," he replied with a wry smile. "So you'll sing, then?"

"But I sing only—"

"For your friends. And now that we've established I am, indeed, your friend, I'm going to take that as an affirmative answer." He pinned me with his stunning eyes and gave me an approving smirk that not only prevented me from turning away but somehow made me want to do whatever he asked.

"Do you have the hymns selected?" I asked, trying to maintain a sense of composure despite my mounting nervousness. "Will I be the only one with a hymnal? What if I don't know the ones you'd like me to—"

"Fret not, Miss Stoneburner." He rose from his seat and took a quick look at his timepiece. "We have hymnals, and there will be plenty of voices joining with yours once you begin."

"Who usually leads the hymns?"

"Roxy, does at times...or used to more often than not. I'm not very good at it myself, you see. I've been in the habit lately of asking someone from the congregation, since Roxy hasn't been feeling well. But you know how it is in the hotel industry—small chance that the person I ask one week will be around the following Sunday."

"I hope to be around past next Sunday...."

"And I hope the very same thing."

I tried to ignore the thrills that shot through me at his teasing tone. "So, what shall I sing?"

"'Come Thou Fount of Every Blessing' would be appropriate. Do you know it?"

"Of course."

I soon learned, as I stood next to Mr. Blakeley upon the stone stage, why he always asked someone else to lead the hymns at the church services. Holding the hymnal between us as I sang in a high soprano, he didn't voice a single note correctly. I tried to not focus on his rough tone quality and uneven pitch, but with the way his voice echoed off the ceiling of the giant stone arch above us, it was almost as if I were compelled to listen to his every word. It occurred to me that God wouldn't care how Mr. Blakeley sounded "singing" those verses—only that Mr. Blakeley wanted to, seemingly with all his heart.

Toward the end of the hymn, I snuck a glance his way and caught him grinning to himself, as if he could tell I'd realized just why he'd asked me to sing for the sake of the congregation.

When we were finished, he gently grasped my elbow, helped me down from the stone altar, and escorted me to my seat. But instead of sitting down next to me—or anywhere else, for that matter—Mr. Blakeley strode back to the front, taking the chiseled steps two at a time until he again stood on the stage of rock.

What he did next surprised me more than anything he had done or said in the preceding weeks: He began to preach. His deep, gravelly voice echoed off those same cavern walls that had just amplified mine into something melodious and sweet.

Mr. Blakeley's voice was neither sweet nor beautiful, but it was filled with a passion that captivated my attention. I couldn't help but sit up straighter on the bench of carved log and listen with wide-eyed interest.

Was this really the same man?

His next words—"Love the Lord your God with all your heart, serve Him with your every hour, consider Him in all you do, and He will direct your paths" —struck me almost painfully with the realization of what I'd wanted most from God for the longest time: that He would answer my selfish, disillusioned prayers involving Jay and his mission to Washington. It was no wonder I'd felt lost for so long, even before June.

Why had I been so determined to have Jay?

Because, when he'd broken our short, secret engagement for the sake of God's calling, I'd convinced myself that if I could prove to him that I, too, was worthy of such a calling, he would take me back. And somewhere in all those years of pining, I'd convinced myself that marrying Jay and going with him wherever he felt called to go was my calling as well. I'd thought it was what God wanted me to do with my life. Only, I'd been wrong. And never had this truth been clearer than when he saw me immediately after I learned about Will's murder, and he turned his back on me.

It was then I'd felt my heart had finally been broken *away from* Jay instead of *by* him. Yet, for all that time, I'd been certain I knew what God wanted from me. How could I ever trust my discernment of God's will? Did He have a plan for me? And how would I know it now, when I'd thought I'd known it for years, only to be proven wrong?

"You've been freed. He wants you, your heart...and that's it. No motives, no questions, and no confusion. Just be His." Mr.

Blakeley's timely words broke into my thoughts, and my questions seemed to disappear. He'd just answered them.

I'd thought Jay was more like Mr. Blakeley deep down. The caliber of his character, his motivations...I'd believed them to be pure. I'd believed that his deepest passion was to serve the Lord as a missionary to some tiny town on the West Coast.

But his motives weren't pure. At least, not when it came to me. Even after turning me down and breaking my heart, he'd strung me along, keeping my hopes for us alive with kisses and promises that he rescinded over and over again.

What I should have done a long time ago was to make God my focus. To live for Him.

I would do that now. I had to. God was the only one who could help me find whatever it was I needed to do with my life.

Through my rambling thoughts, I heard Mr. Blakeley say, "And if we lift our eyes unto the hills, where does our help come from? It comes from the Lord everlasting."

There was something about Mr. Blakeley's preaching that made me realize things I'd never recognized before. His words, and the passion behind them, stirred something in my heart and made me want to let go of...everything.

"Miss Stoneburner, would you be kind enough to sing for us again?" Mr. Blakeley's rough voice pulled me from my thoughts. "Let us sing 'Take My Life and Let It Be.'"

"Of course." I stood, taking up the hymnal we'd shared earlier.

As he escorted me by the elbow once more to the altar of rock, I couldn't help but feel the difference his words had made in my heart. He genuinely cared about making sure that the wealthy, well-dressed hotel guests of Everston knew the truth of God's love for them. I looked down and caught a quick glimpse of Violet Hawthorne sitting in the back row. Her eyes were on Mr. Blakeley, and she sent him a wide smile.

Were the two of them good friends? Or did she want them to be?

The memory of my judgmental thoughts about Violet—and Greenlee Cole—from the week before pricked my conscience. I'd been more concerned about the danger they posed to Everston's reputation than the significance of Mr. Blakeley's determination to help them in any way he could.

Yes, I'd made a little progress, even by the end of my last lengthy conversation with him. But now that I really had a chance to examine my heart, it was clear to me that he was the better person. He didn't care only about the hotel guests, with their high-society statuses and endless money as they racked up their bills at Everston. He cared for everyone. Equally.

All of these musings sifted through my mind as I sang the verses of the closing hymn, and by the time I made it to the last line, tears threatened to spill from my eyes: "Take myself, and I will be ever, only, all for Thee."

Yes, Lord, take me—all of me. Guide me and tell me what I should do. How I should be.

NINE

The Lie

"Between men and women there is no friendship possible. There
is passion, enmity, worship, love, but no friendship."
—Oscar Wilde, *Lady Windermere's Fan*

I returned to Everston with the other hotel guests by way of the
surreys. Mrs. Granton waited for me in a far corner of the music
room, seated in an upholstered chair close to the grand piano made
of carved burl wood.

"Are you ready for lunch?" I asked her.

"That sounds lovely." She sat a little straighter. "I haven't eaten
in the dining room once, have I?"

"You haven't. Would you like to today?"

"Oh, yes." She accepted my help to stand and then shooed me
off with her cane as she slowly started toward the hall. "Would you
be a dear and find Blakeley and ask him to join us?"

"Certainly," I said, feeling a mixture of anticipation and dread.
What if he thought I was the one seeking him out, and not Mrs.
Granton? And would I even find him? He hadn't traveled back with
the guests but had instead headed down a trail in the woods. "But
do allow me to help you to the dining room. It's a rather long walk."

She stopped walking and looked me in the eye. "I'll be fine,
dear. I'll be seated and waiting by the time you find Blakeley and
bring him to me." She hobbled past me once more.

Convinced that I would never hear the end of it if I didn't at least make a good effort to find him, I went to the lobby. Surely, if he had come back, he would be in his office.

I found Mr. Mulduney standing behind the front desk.

"Good morning," I greeted him.

"And a good morning to you, Miss Stoneburner."

Had Mr. Blakeley spoken to him about me? Or had Violet, perhaps? Maybe it was simply his job to know all the guests by name. I wasn't sure. I'd never been privy to the ins and outs of running a hotel, even though Father owned dozens of them.

"What may I help you with?" asked Mr. Mulduney.

"Mrs. Granton wanted to know if Mr. Blake—"

"Miss Stoneburner, what a pleasure," Jay interrupted, coming to stand beside me. He wore a pressed brown suit. He always dressed well, his wardrobe suited to the society he'd been born into instead of the rank of a missionary.

"Dr. Crawford." I nodded civilly. "Do you happen to know where I might find Mr. Blakeley?" I questioned them both at once, though Mr. Mulduney had turned his attention to something on the desk before him.

Jay's lips formed a tentative grin.

"Mrs. Granton would like him to join us for lunch," I added. "They're old friends, you know."

Jay looked at me squarely.

"Mr. Blakeley should be here soon," Mr. Mulduney supplied. "He's preparing for a trip to Boston, heading out this very afternoon."

"Oh!" I shouldn't have felt so deflated. "Will he be gone long?"

"His trips to see Mr. Bram Everstone usually are about a week or two."

"To see—"

"Did you make it to church this morning?" Jay asked, cutting me off again. "What did you think of our Leightner Hollow?"

"It was charming. But I didn't see you there."

"I've just made it back to Everston in time to have lunch before traveling on to Westward. Do you suppose I would be a suitable substitute as a lunch guest for your Mrs. Granton?"

I stared up at Jay's familiar brown eyes. What did he mean by attempting to pry his way back into my life? The only time he'd seen me in the last few weeks, he'd acted as if I were invisible and, weeks before that, had reprimanded me for even being present. I might have been determined to have him at one time—when I was much younger and desperately eager for his affections—but not now. And never again.

"If you'd like, Dr. Crawford, I can introduce you to Mrs. Granton. If you don't mind waiting a few minutes, I should see if Mr. Blakeley is around and able to join us before he leaves." I didn't want to disappoint Mrs. Granton, and even less did I want to have to put up with Jay through lunch without the company of Mr. Blakeley.

I left Jay at the desk and went out onto the veranda. Surely, Mr. Blakeley would need to eat lunch before he left—if he hadn't already gone.

What if watching him preach that morning was the last I ever saw of him? What if Mrs. Macy decided that her mother's retreat had lasted long enough, and we traveled back to Portland before he returned to Everston?

I didn't like the feeling produced by that prospect.

Dexter Blakeley was genuine, straightforward, honest, and loyal. And I liked him. A great deal. And I wasn't ready to leave—to never see him again.

Outside, I traversed the veranda, keeping to the shade of the canopies. When I rounded the corner of the hotel, I nearly ran straight into Violet Hawthorne.

"Miss Stoneburner! I saw you at church this morning."

I smiled begrudgingly. "Yes, I noticed you from the pulpit, but I couldn't find you afterward."

"I walked back," she added nonchalantly. "We should ride together next time, and maybe sit together during the service."

"Yes, of course. Do you happen to know where Mr. Blakeley is right now?" I hurried on.

She linked her arm with mine and headed toward the hotel stables. "I saw him going this way, likely just come from Blakeley House. He's about to leave for Boston."

I walked beside her, unsure of why I kept up my search when I had a perfectly legitimate excuse for Mrs. Granton as to why Mr. Blakeley wouldn't be joining us.

"I couldn't help but notice that the owner of this fine hotel seems to have struck your fancy."

Stopping in my tracks, I stared at her. My father owned this hotel. What did she know of him? And what did she mean about his fancying me?

She looked back innocently. "And vice versa, as shocking as it is." She fluttered her remarkably long eyelashes, then winked. "I was starting to wonder what exactly he wanted—what he was looking for. I guess you're the perfect mix of culture and humility that he believes would suit him."

"Do you mean Mr. Everstone?" I asked, confused as ever.

"No, not Mr. Everstone. He no longer owns Everston. I mean Mr. Blakeley, of course."

"Mr. Blakeley owns Everston?"

"Surely, you knew that." Violet beamed with such a charming, knowing grin, I wondered if I might indeed be daft. I had to be, if what she said had any truth to it.

"He's the owner," I stated dumbly, trying to comprehend. "He's purchased Everston—from Bram Everstone?"

Violet's gray eyes flashed with apprehension as she caught sight of something in the distance. Then her gaze darted back to me. "Pardon me, Miss Stoneburner. It was a pleasure speaking with you, but I see…I should get back to the dormitory." She rushed across the crowded veranda and disappeared.

"Miss Stoneburner."

It was Mr. Blakeley…the liar. Though why he would lie about such a thing—and to me, as Elle Stoneburner—I couldn't imagine.

I skillfully measured my every breath, trying as best I could to control the urge to turn around and slam my fists into his chest. However, still a bit overwhelmed with the desire to do so, I took a few steps in the direction of the French doors leading into the reading room.

Mr. Blakeley moved to hinder my escape, a rather halting smirk upon his face. His dog blocked me from behind.

Letting out a long breath, I tried desperately to quell the disappointment that Violet's news had produced within me. I was so stunned, I found myself on the verge of tears, shaking almost visibly.

I was Estella Everstone, the master of control, the queen of composure. And I always knew what to say, what to do, even in vexing situations. Was I really so out of practice after only a few months of living with the agreeable Mrs. Granton?

"Is something wrong, Miss Stoneburner? Are you unwell?" There was a strange edge to his voice. He no longer seemed amused; perhaps he was more confused than anything else.

"I was just…." I took another deep breath. I didn't know what to do, what to think.

"Would you like me to escort you to the reading room so you can sit?"

"Yes." I sounded so pitiful. Why was I taking comfort from Mr. Blakeley—the very man who'd stolen my Everston, the man who was the source of my anguish? And to think that I'd believed him to be a friend. That I'd even admitted to myself that I liked him…more than I should have.

Mr. Blakeley commanded his dog to stay outside, and then he silently offered me his arm. I took hold of the crook of his elbow, very lightly at first, but then I found myself leaning into him because I was hardly composed enough to walk. I hated that the touch of someone I wanted to detest felt so comforting.

My stomach turned sour as I allowed him to guide me through one of the two sets of floor-to-ceiling French doors into the reading room. Once inside, I glanced around. Bookcases that lined every square inch of the walls, save for the massive mahogany fireplace bookended by the French doors.

The few times I had been in the reading room during my stay at Everston, I had viewed it through a lens of taking in something that would someday be mine, something I took pride in. Now I saw it as something stolen from me.

I let go of Mr. Blakeley and slowly approached the cozy corner of the room where the two bookcases of novels met. I absently fingered the book bindings, hardly composed enough to notice any of the titles printed on their spines.

Mr. Blakeley cleared his throat and stared at me from where he stood, next to the chair he'd expected me to sit in. I couldn't blame him for gawking; I was acting outlandishly, after all. But it wasn't fair!

I returned my attention to the shelves, searching their contents with watery eyes.

"Why don't you sit?" It was more of an order than an invitation.

"I'm better now, Mr. Blakeley." I remained silent for some moments, gathering the courage I needed to ask all I wanted. "Do you happen to know if Everston"—I stumbled over the beloved name—"if the hotel has a copy of *Great Expectations?*" Mrs. Granton had requested the title weeks before, and I hadn't been able to find it.

"I believe we do. Let's see...." He crossed the room to me and started searching the shelves for some moments, until he reached in front of me and retrieved a book from one of the top shelves. The novel was out of place—no wonder I'd failed to locate it. He silently held it out for me.

I accepted it. "Thank you." My response came out as a whisper.

"Of course. Have you finished *North and South?*"

How had he known we'd been reading that? Had he been communicating with Mrs. Granton about me? "A long time ago," I responded warily. "We've probably read half a dozen books since then."

"Is that what you spend your time doing for her? Reading aloud? You are exceptionally kind."

My traitorous heart swelled in my chest as my gaze locked with his. "How have you come to purchase such a large…such a prominent…?" I began again: "Why didn't you correct Mrs. Granton the night we met? You never told me you owned the hotel."

He stared down at me as if I had spoken in a foreign language. "Does it make such a difference to you whether I'm the manager of the hotel or the owner?"

"Yes," I uttered without a thought.

"And, obviously, the difference is not in my favor." His tone made the statement sound more like a question. "You'd rather I manage Everston, and not own it." Mr. Blakeley hadn't moved an inch, and I felt the intensity of his gaze with every fiber of my being.

"Why did you keep the name?" I whispered as I took a step back, pressing my spine against the shelf behind me. I clutched *Great Expectations* with both hands. "The name Everston…it's derived from the surname Everstone. Why did you keep it, when you have no significant connection to the family?"

He didn't respond, and I watched as confusion clouded his features. His dark, even eyebrows were drawn together. The forest-green rings around his brown irises sparkled in the sunlight that streamed through the windows, and the brilliant mix of colors stopped my breath.

I couldn't help but stare back. And I didn't ever want to stop.

"Bram Everstone insisted," he answered at last, visibly frustrated. "He wanted the transition to be a smooth as possible. He, at least, wants to see me succeed in my business endeavors."

"And why would he?" I countered. "Why does he continue to mentor you even after the sale of his hotel?"

"To tell you the truth, Miss Stoneburner, I don't know his reasons."

There was a new awkwardness between us now, perhaps because it seemed he still intended to be my friend. But I wouldn't allow it. Not ever.

"I need to get back to Mrs. Granton." The fact that I'd fulfilled her wishes in finding Mr. Blakeley had completely slipped my mind, but I wasn't about to take him to her now. It would be difficult enough to sit through lunch with Jay; I didn't need Mr. Blakeley there, too.

Mr. Blakeley's gaze darted to the entrance to the hall, then returned to me with a sudden sharpness. "Have you had lunch?"

"Mrs. Granton and I will be lunching in the dining room. She's waiting for me...and she sent me looking for you—" I hadn't intended to disclose that detail. However, I didn't have a chance to amend my statement, for he promptly took my hand, folded it into the crook of his arm, and essentially pulled me through the doorway and down the hall.

Before we reached the dining room, I dug my heels into the carpet, stalling our progress. "You didn't answer me as to why you didn't correct Mrs. Granton upon our introduction."

"Forgive me; yes, I should have clarified, only I—"

"Yes, you should have. It would have made a great difference."

I could tell I had shocked him with my candor, for his dark eyebrows rose, and his mouth gaped open for a moment before clamping shut. "If you have a problem with Mr. Everstone's decision to sell, Miss Stoneburner, I recommend you take up the matter with him. As it stands, I bought Everston fair and square last summer. It's mine now, whether or not you approve."

"I— But— But what about his family?" I couldn't help wondering how highly Father must think of Mr. Blakeley to have sold him one of his favorite hotels. The man was clearly someone Father trusted, and someone he wanted me to trust, considering the contents of Natalia's letter.

But I didn't want to trust him. And I wasn't going to.

"I think the Everstone family will survive without Everston, Miss Stoneburner. Bram and two of his sons were present when the papers were signed in Bangor last summer."

Of course, I'd been excluded. I was just a young lady, after all, with no head for business. But that didn't mean I was indifferent about what happened to my father's properties.

"Now, if you'll allow me, I'll take you in to Mrs. Granton—"

"Very well," I replied solemnly, knowing full well Mrs. Granton would likely think I'd found Mr. Blakeley for her and brought him as promised, and that he would likely—and unfortunately—join us for our meal.

TEN

Lester and Ursula Imbody

"She walks in beauty,
like the night of cloudless climes and starry skies;
And all that's best of dark and bright meet in
her aspect and her eyes...."
—Lord Byron, *"She Walks in Beauty"*

As Mr. Blakeley and I passed through the lobby, I glanced at the front desk. Thankfully, Jay no longer waited for me there. I hoped he'd completely forgone the thought of lunching with Mrs. Granton and me. Once Mr. Blakeley and I neared the dining room, we spotted Mrs. Granton standing to the left of the entrance.

But she wasn't alone. Somehow, Jay had made her acquaintance while I'd searched for Mr. Blakeley. He now stood beside her—along with a couple whom I didn't recognize.

The young lady was plain in features yet fashionably dressed; the gentleman was tall and lanky with thin blond hair and a thick beard. He watched Mr. Blakeley and me as we approached, and the closer we came, his crooked leer grew wider and more disturbing.

"Elle, look who heard we were at Everston and came up from Bangor to visit," Mrs. Granton said with a smile. "This is my granddaughter, Ursula Imbody, and her husband, Lester. Ursula, Les, meet my companion, Miss Elle Stoneburner.

Mr. Blakeley held my arm, almost possessively, as we stood before them.

Only when Mr. Imbody came forward to take my hand did Mr. Blakeley finally let go. Mr. Imbody grasped my fingers for a moment and brought my knuckles to his lips. "It's such a pleasure to meet you, Miss Stoneburner."

I pulled my hand away, my eyes flitting to Jay.

"I hope you don't mind, Elle, but I've invited Dr. Crawford, one of the two physicians Everston has in residence, to join us for lunch. Dr. Crawford, this is the lovely Miss Elle Stoneburner."

"Dr. Crawford," I said, nodding politely. Not acknowledging to Mrs. Granton that we'd already met would make things easier.

Ursula lifted her chin toward Mr. Blakeley. "And this is?" she asked rudely.

"Mr. Blakeley is the owner of Everston." Speaking the words aloud created a hollowness that started in my stomach and quickly permeated my entire being.

"I should go," Mr. Blakeley stated abruptly. "I should have left already."

"Where are you going?" Mrs. Granton asked, clearly disappointed.

"To Boston. I'll be there for the next week or so."

"That's too bad," she sighed.

I turned to Mr. Blakeley just in time to see a look of disappointment in his own brownish-green eyes as they shifted from me to Jay. "I really should go," he repeated, without moving an inch.

He bowed to me awkwardly, took my hand again, and said quietly, so I alone could hear, "I regret that my words...that my title at Everston has upset you, Miss Stoneburner. I do hope you will forgive me for any offense it may have caused. And I do hope you—and Mrs. Granton, of course—will continue on at Everston until I return."

With his warm hand holding mine, all I could do was stare, until I finally found my voice. "We hope so, as well."

I didn't know what made me offer such a response. I didn't want to forgive him, and I wouldn't. I didn't care if I never saw him again.

With one last squeeze of my fingers, Mr. Blakeley directed his attention to the others, made his good-byes, and then walked out the nearest door to the veranda, in the direction of the stables.

"Is he your beau, Miss Stoneburner?" Ursula cut a glance my way as we entered the dining room.

I felt my face flush "Indeed not."

Ursula leaned toward her husband. "Wasn't it Mr. Dexter Blakeley who led the bear hunt you went on last September, Les?"

"That he did. And I'll likely be up for the same hunt this year."

Ursula sighed. "I don't think I'll join you this time, darling. I was terribly bored."

Once we took our seats, a waiter came, introduced himself, and took our beverage orders. When he had gone, Mrs. Granton reached over to grasp her granddaughter's hand. "Dearest, perhaps Elle and I can stay until then."

"Oh, Gran-mama, I'm sure you could, but it wouldn't make a difference. I'm not so uncultured as to be easily entertained by afternoon teas, reading rooms, and walks along the lake. I need my friends around me to have any sort of fun."

"That's quite all right, Ursy; I can come on my own. Especially if your grandmother and Miss Stoneburner will be around." Les sent a covert wink my way. "A man needs a good week of hunting every year, no matter who's waiting for him in the hotel when he's finished."

I felt the back of my neck grow warm, and wondered if anyone else had understood his repugnant insinuation.

"Are you staying at Everston for long, Ursula?" Mrs. Granton asked.

"Oh, for a few days, at least. We checked in early this morning, staying in the two rooms across from yours in the fifth-floor tower." Ursula glanced my way. "I believe your Mr. Blakeley has taken the sixth floor as his residence. Isn't that right?"

"He isn't 'my' Mr. Blakeley," I muttered. "And I thought he lived in a house in the woods not a mile away."

"Does he?" Lester asked. "How interesting you should know about that. What is it, exactly, that you do around here?"

I glanced at Mrs. Granton. "We read, relax...."

"Elle spends time with Mr. Blakeley." Mrs. Granton cast me a guileful grin.

"Mr. Blakeley...who isn't your beau?" Ursula narrowed her eyes at me.

"He's not my beau," I insisted again. "We're merely friends." What was I saying? I wasn't his friend, no matter what he'd thought and said that very morning.

The waiter returned with our beverages and a salad for each of us.

"So, what kinds of things do 'mere friends' do around here?" Lester leaned over, his right elbow propped on the edge of the table beside his salad plate.

"Well, there are tennis matches, sailing, golf, bowling, billiards...." I hadn't paid much attention to what everyone else at the hotel had been doing for the last several weeks, but I knew what kinds of activities had always been offered.

"You've partaken of all those activities with your Mr. Blakeley?" Ursula asked.

I figured it was futile to correct her one more time. "Actually, we haven't done any of those things together."

"Really! Then what *have* you been doing?" Lester Imbody quizzed me in the most inappropriate way. I could tell he assumed we'd been up to no good.

"We've taken walks, breakfasted together, and Mrs. Granton and I had tea with him last Friday."

Jay had spoken not a word, other than to order more coffee. Right now, his sole focus seemed to be on clearing the salad from his plate and avoiding eye contact with me.

"Yes, he specifically invited us to have tea with him," Mrs. Granton elaborated. "Not that he's thought about *me* one whit. Not with Elle around."

"Mrs. Granton, really," I muttered. "It's not like that at all."

"I wouldn't be so sure," Jay added drolly.

I stifled a huff. That Jay would now be jealous of Mr. Blakeley! Would he ever know what he truly wanted?

Ursula stared over her salad at me, then looked at Jay. "Do you two know one another?"

"Why, no," I lied. "Not beyond just meeting in the last month. Where is it you've just come from, Dr. Crawford?"

"Bangor," he answered blandly.

"Oh?" Ursula interjected. "We're from Bangor. Lester's family owns a number of sawmills in the area. If you don't mind telling, what was your business there?"

"I had some things to discuss with Mr. Vance Everstone. He recently took charge of Greaghan Lumber, one of his father's enterprises."

Having Jay around was beneficial at least in regard to keeping me informed about my family.

"We'd heard the Everstones were considering selling out to Bartlett last summer," Ursula commented, "but I guess that's no longer the case."

"I guess not." Jay lifted his napkin from his lap and set it beside his empty salad plate. "I should be going."

"Why, we've only just begun, Dr. Crawford!" said Mrs. Granton. "Your hunger can't have been satisfied with only a plate of vegetables. Do join us for the rest of the meal."

"I assure you, I can survive on what I've eaten. It was very good to meet you." He stood. "However, as for this week, I'm afraid I shall be traveling again. I'm leaving this afternoon, in fact." Still averting his gaze from me, Jay turned and strode confidently across the room to the doors.

⌒

After a long and tiresome day spent being put down and scoffed at by Ursula Imbody and ogled by her husband, I fell into bed that night utterly exhausted. And I slept soundly—until I heard a jostling of the knob on the door connecting my bedchamber to the hall. I propped myself up on my elbows and grabbed for the only thing within reach—my sketchbook—to hurl across the room, if need be.

Paralyzed with fear, I heard a key turn in the lock, followed by the door creaking open. The silhouette of a tall man appeared against the gaslit hallway. I could smell the stench of alcohol from across the room. The door closed, and I heard the bolt slide back into place.

Without another thought, I heaved the book at the intruder, then ran for the door to my employer's room. "Mrs. Granton, wake up! Oh, please, wake up!"

"Ah, my darling," Lester Imbody slurred as he shuffled across the room and grabbed me from behind. I held fast to the doorknob, shaking it urgently, pounding and screaming as loud as I could. Why was it locked? Mrs. Granton always insisted it remain open.

"Mrs. Granton, help me!"

Lester's arms locked greedily around my waist, the heat of his searing through my thin nightgown. I was still clutching the knob as he rotated me around and pressed me against the door. I ducked my chin in an effort to dodge his lips, then shoved an elbow into his face and gave him a high kick between the legs with my knee.

The door gave out behind me, and I fell backward onto the floor, Lester landing beside me with a groan. I scrambled to my feet, although it seemed Lester had passed out upon hitting the floor.

"Elle, what's happened?" Mrs. Granton blinked repeatedly, looking from Lester to me and back again.

"He came into my room—he tried to get me." I crossed her bedchamber to the windows, striving to get as far from Lester Imbody as I could.

"But how? Why would he do such a thing?"

She nudged him with her toe, eliciting a low moan. It was then that I noticed she was standing without her cane. In the months I'd known her, I'd never seen her without it.

"I don't know," I cried. She didn't seem as concerned as I thought she should be. Did she not understand what he might have done if she hadn't opened her door?

"I'd better find Ursula." Mrs. Granton gazed absently in the direction of the hall.

"Oh, please don't! And what about him?"

"No need to fret, my dear. He seems to be asleep; I don't think he's going anywhere."

She didn't seem to understand the situation. Was she fully awake?

I followed Mrs. Granton out of the room and stood beside her as she knocked lightly upon Ursula's door.

Almost a minute later, Ursula opened the door with a scowl leveled at me. She was dressed in a frilly yellow wrapper, her mouse-brown hair tightly braided down her back. I took a step back to stand behind Mrs. Granton. Ursula's facial expression quickly reverted to sweetness when she addressed her grandmother. "Gran-mama, whatever is the matter?"

"Your husband is in my room, asleep on the floor," Mrs. Granton said simply.

"Whatever is he doing there?"

"He fell." Mrs. Granton spoke mechanically, her habitually affectionate tone oddly gone.

"Gran-mama, are you sleepwalking again?" Ursula's eyes shifted to me. "She's not truly awake. Now, tell me, what happened? Is my husband indeed asleep on her floor?"

"Yes."

"Yes, dear," Mrs. Granton affirmed. "He fell. Remember? I just told you that."

"How did he get there?"

"From Elle's room."

"Elle's bedchamber?" Ursula shot me a glare, then rushed past me across the hall to Mrs. Granton's room. She stopped in the doorway and looked in at her husband, lying sprawled across the threshold between our rooms. "And just what, may I ask, was Lester doing inside your bedchamber?"

"I don't know," I assured her, stepping into the room after her. Mrs. Granton shuffled in behind me. "But you must believe me, it wasn't by invitation. He must have been confused."

Ursula closed the door to the hall, then faced me again. "Do you always sleep with your door unlocked?"

"It was locked. It always is. We use your grandmother's door to access the hallway."

"So, you're saying you let him in?"

I was growing frustrated. Would she not accept the truth of what had happened? "No, I was shocked—"

"Indeed."

"Mrs. Granton heard me screaming, didn't you, Mrs. Granton? You opened the door—"

"Indeed, I did, Ursula. I opened the door and found them...." Mrs. Granton looked more confused than ever. She lowered herself to her sofa as if in a trance, and then, after a long moment, she looked around and asked, "What's happened?"

Ursula took hold of her grandmother's hand. "Gran-mama, I'm afraid that the companion Mother hired for you is a wanton seductress."

I faced Ursula, tears in my eyes. "I'm not a— How dare you! You don't know anything about me."

"I know enough from the way my husband gawked at you the moment you walked into the dining room this afternoon, inviting him with your hypnotic Jezebel eyes to join you in your bedchamber, even while you obviously had Mr. Blakeley wrapped around your finger." Ursula nudged her husband with her foot. "Lester, do get up. I think we need to leave Everston. Now." Her husband groaned again, clutching his thighs to his stomach. "I knew it was a mistake to come, but Lester insisted as soon as he heard Gran-mama was here," she muttered under her breath. Then she bent over, gripped her husband by the arms, and pulled him across the floor in a way that suggested she had been through this routine before.

"That wench!" Lester wailed.

"Gran-mama, we're leaving tonight. There's the late stage headed down to Severville—we'll catch that and be off. We're taking you home with us. I'm sure Mother won't mind."

"Oh, dear. And I was just getting settled," Mrs. Granton pouted. "I won't be able to say good-bye to Blakeley. He and Elle were just—"

"Who cares about Mr. Blakeley and Elle?" Ursula grunted as she yanked her husband across the threshold and into the hall. "We're leaving within the hour."

After our trunks had been packed and taken down to the lobby, I stood in the doorway of my room, overcome with regret. I didn't want to leave, and now Everston was being ripped from my grasp in more ways than I'd imagined possible.

While the others took the elevator down the four flights, I chose to descend the gorgeous staircase, knowing it was likely for the very last time *ever*. I didn't know if I'd ever muster the courage to come back to Everston, the way my latest visit had culminated.

Once our belongings had been loaded onto the stagecoach, I exited through the main door and took the front steps down to the drive. Mrs. Granton and Lester were already seated inside the coach. Ursula stood near the foot of the stairs, waiting for me. When I reached her, she caught me by the arm and hauled me into the deep shadows of the surrounding trees, away from view. "You're not coming with us."

My throat turned suddenly dry. "But my trunk—"

"You'll just have to do without it."

Fear burned in my chest at the prospect of being stranded with absolutely nothing to my name. I'd packed every last one of my possessions in my small trunk, not wanting to be bothered with carrying a reticule in the coach.

"Why?"

"Because I said so," Ursula hissed in my ear. "And because you deserve it. I noticed the way both Dr. Crawford and Mr. Blakeley looked at you. How easily they must have fallen for your charms. No doubt you've been leaving out ample bait for them, and for anyone else who might take notice."

"Y-you're mistaken," I sputtered, "and if you take my trunk, I won't have *anything*. All that I own is—"

"That's just too bad." She poked a finger into the worn material of my lightweight brown traveling coat. "And I promise, if you get on that stage, I'll tell everyone on board—and, later, everyone you come into contact with in Bangor—how you tried to seduce my husband, only to be caught in the act by my grandmother." Ursula poked me one last time, backing me into the bushes along the veranda. "Understand?"

Somehow, I found my voice. "Yes, I understand." There was nothing else I could do.

I stayed hidden in the shadows as Ursula went to the stage-coach. "Elle wants to stay at Everston," I heard her say. "She said something about wanting to work at catching Mr. Blakeley's attention."

"Why, Ursula, dear, she doesn't need to work at that. She accomplished—"

"I'm sure she did."

"Well, can I at least bid her good-bye?" Mrs. Granton pleaded.

"She's already gone back inside, Gran-mama," Ursula answered before slamming the door shut.

The coachman whipped his horses into motion, and the stage-coach gained speed as it traveled down the drive. Within a minute, it had disappeared into the darkness.

I remained huddled beneath the copse of trees, gazing hopelessly at the hotel. There was no use going back. I had no money for a room.

I couldn't believe how easily I'd accepted defeat. But I'd had absolutely nothing to fight back with. I certainly couldn't have stopped Ursula's divisive plans with the truth of my identity. Unveiling my true identity would have only made the situation worse, for then she would have threatened to spread rumors of her husband's being seduced by Estella Everstone, not just some unknown girl named Elle Stoneburner.

I looked around, feeling more alone than ever before. The moon, full and bright, shone on the gravel road; and suddenly, I knew just what I would do—where I would go. There was only one place I could go.

ELEVEN

The Rescue

"[She was] kept there in the sort of embrace a man gives to the
dearest creature the world holds for him."
—Louisa May Alcott, *Eight Cousins*

Despite my fear of what I might meet in the dark on the
mile-long road from Everston to Blakeley House, I
walked on through the shadows and shifting moonlight. I couldn't
help but think of what I would do if Mr. Blakeley's mother refused
to let me in.

Bombarded by questions and doubts, I trudged down the
semi-familiar gravel road.

I'd walked through the dark, gloomy woods between Everston
and Blakeley House once before—with Mr. Blakeley—but I didn't
recall the awful sound of wolves howling in the distant mountains.
To keep my mind off the threat of wild animals, with every terrible
step, I contemplated what I would do when—or if—I was admitted at Blakeley House. I didn't like the idea of telephoning Father
and crawling back home, having failed utterly at something that
should have been simple.

Thinking back to my stolen trunk, I shuddered at the idea that
any of my belongings would betray my identity once Ursula went
through them. I didn't doubt for one second that she would, or that
she would consider them plunder from a battle well fought and

won. The only thing I could think that might make her wonder were my French-made undergarments, which I'd refused to give up.

I stopped on the trail and palmed the rough material of the ugly traveling coat I wore—the only article of clothing I had to my name, besides the thin nightgown and the ugly brown dress I'd thrown on over it. The tears I'd fought off finally broke through when I realized Ursula had taken my pencils and my sketchbook... including my drawings of Mr. Blakeley.

How I longed to see a familiar face—especially Mr. Blakeley's, with his gorgeous eyes staring down at me as if I were some puzzle to be solved.

If only he hadn't left!

Although I'd been raging mad at him and had treated him rather callously upon his departure earlier that day, he'd been the epitome of graciousness, and I found that I liked him all the more for it.

I looked through my tears at the clearing that the road carved through the trees, then up at the stars. "God, please help me," I pleaded. "Show me what I should do now."

There was nothing else I could find to say. I just needed Him to find me, to save me, to rescue me—somehow. This I knew after years and years of attempting to make things go my own way. It seemed the surrender I'd made that very morning had been no coincidence.

When I heard a low panting noise, my heart stopped beating, and my feet froze in place. Then there was a loud rustling, and I could tell that whatever animal I'd come upon was running straight for me.

The beast ran right past me, its fur brushing my hand. "Stay away from me!" I screamed. My tears flowed in earnest, and I repeated those words, though more as a whimper. It was too difficult to scream when I could hardly breathe.

The next sound I heard was of hoofbeats on the road. Despite my fear of being devoured by wolves, I jumped off the path and into the grass, dodging behind a tree. Even more than ferocious animals, I feared a stranger—someone like Lester Imbody, perhaps—coming after me in the darkness.

"Wulf!"

I recognized the deep, gruff voice, and in the shifting moonlight, I could just make out the sight of Mr. Blakeley seated upon his black horse.

He pulled at the reins. "Whoa! Who's there?"

"Mr. Blakeley!" I ran out from behind the tree with tears streaming down my cheeks.

"Elle?" He quickly dismounted and pulled me into his arms with more tenderness than I would have expected.

"What's happened? Where's Mrs. Granton?"

"She's been taken away," I cried against his chest, resting my cheek against the smooth fabric of his waistcoat.

Mr. Blakeley kept his arms around me, soothing me with quiet reassurances. It had been such a long time since anyone had shown me any empathy, and I needed it so much. I burrowed my face into his shoulder and felt comforted in an instant. He seemed genuinely concerned, even after I'd been so spiteful and hateful toward him. Why didn't he despise me?

"Who took her away?"

"Ursula Imbody—Mrs. Granton's granddaughter. She also took my—" A sob cut short my words. I wasn't able to go on.

His dog circled us, yipping softly. Suddenly self-conscious about crying on him so shamelessly, I backed away a few inches. He let go of me slowly, as if he regretted doing so.

"What are you still doing here?" I asked, wringing my hands in front of me. "Weren't you on your way to Boston?"

"Bram wired at the last minute to cancel, but I was too...I wasn't thinking clearly this afternoon, or I would have checked.

Mulduney wired down to the station at Severville in time to stop me, and thus, here I am again." I'd never heard Mr. Blakeley speak so tentatively, as if choosing his words with extra care. "He's coming this way soon, and thought he would—"

"Mr. Everstone is coming here? When?" A different kind of fear seized me—the fear of being seen as a helpless failure by the rest of my family.

"In a week or two. Why? Nervous about seeing your former employer?"

I was filled with fear of my two separate worlds colliding. "Why, yes, something like that."

Mr. Blakeley cocked his head slightly; I could almost see the gleam in his eyes. "You were heading to my house, weren't you?"

"I...I didn't know what else to do...where else to go. I don't have a thing, and your house...I didn't think you'd be there; I just hoped your mother would...."

From what I could see of Mr. Blakeley's rugged face in the moonlight, he didn't fancy the prospect of my depending on his mother. Unless his frown had something to do with me personally. Perhaps he was more annoyed than concerned about finding me there on his road in the dark.

"What happened tonight, exactly?"

"I lost my job...I lost Mrs. Granton...Ursula's husband broke into my room—"

"He what?" Mr. Blakeley took hold of my arms and drew me nearer.

"He didn't do anything; he was too drunk, but he somehow entered my room. Mrs. Granton awoke just in time, and he passed out on her floor. But Ursula didn't— She wouldn't believe me. She thought I—"

"I have a job for you." He swallowed, almost as if he were nervous. "That is, if you'd like to stay at Everston." His voice sounded rather hoarse now.

Mr. Blakeley might not have been completely agreeable all the time, or even very charming, but at least he was kind.

Captivatingly so.

"A job at Everston?" I imagined myself dressed in the black-and-white uniform Violet always wore, and cleaning bathrooms or washing dishes.

"Not the hotel. At Blakeley House...looking after Roxy and Greenlee."

"Does Roxy need looking after?"

"She needs a friend." He let go of me but didn't back away as far as he had before.

"Would I live at Blakeley House...as a servant?"

"As an equal. You'd be a companion, just as you were for Mrs. Granton. And I'd pay you double whatever you were—"

"It appears Dr. Crawford isn't the only one with a mission to save poor, unlucky girls from unfortunate circumstances."

He grunted. "My mission is to live justly, as God would have me to do, Miss Stoneburner. I wouldn't be able to abide myself if I offered you anything less than everything I am able to."

"Well then, Mr. Blakeley." I extended my hand to him. "I gladly accept the position."

He took it in his warm, firm grip. "Thank you." I could hear the smile in his voice.

"You're thanking me for taking a job you practically invented for my sake?"

"It wasn't invented. But, yes, I suppose I should be thanking God instead, shouldn't I, for bringing you here?" He hadn't let go of my hand yet, but I couldn't complain. Just then, he caught hold of my free hand and brought it between us. "You're freezing."

"I didn't think to wear gloves tonight; everything happened in such a hurry." I relished the warmth of his large, strong hands holding mine. "Have you wanted to hire a companion for your sister for very long?"

"I had considered offering the position to Miss Hawthorne. It would have been easier to fill the front desk with another hotel employee than…than to bring a complete stranger into my house."

"You haven't already mentioned the position to Violet?"

"No." As concerned as Mr. Blakeley seemed about my cold hands, and as late as it was getting, he didn't seem to be in a hurry to return home. "Honestly, the possibility of such an arrangement came to me the night you first visited Blakeley House. I think you're…you would be a good addition." He guided me to his horse. "You're not afraid of horses, are you?"

"Of course not." I wouldn't tell him that riding them was far from my favorite thing to do.

"Miss Stoneburner, meet Knightley. Knightley, Miss Elle Stoneburner." He grinned. "Roxy named him after her favorite Jane Austen hero."

After releasing my hand, he threaded his fingers together and invited me to step up, then hoisted me into the saddle, a hand on my back to help steady me, until I was balanced upon Knightley's back, one knee about the saddle horn.

Mr. Blakeley took the reins and began leading Knightley forward. "I suppose you'll want to write or telephone someone of your change of situation."

"I'll write to my friend at Everwood, if you would be kind enough to mail the note for me. You can take the postage from my—"

"I'll cover it. And what of your family? Would they not want to know?"

"I have no one else to write to besides…besides Jane Smyth."

We were silent for the rest of the journey to Blakeley House. It really wasn't far, but I was extremely thankful Mr. Blakeley had come to my rescue before I'd had to knock upon that large wooden door. What would I have said to Mrs. Blakeley to explain my presence?

When we reached the residence, Mr. Blakeley tied Knightley to a post near the front of the house, then reached up, encircled my waist with one arm, and gently pulled me down. He held my arm as he guided me up the front steps.

"I'm so glad you found me," I whispered.

"Me, too," he whispered back.

With a shuffle of keys, he unlocked the door, then held it open as I stepped inside. It was completely dark, save for the shafts of moonlight angling through the windows. He closed the door behind him. "Wait here." He sounded nervous.

I heard him climb the staircase, his footsteps quiet upon the carpet. A few minutes later, he came back down. "Hannah—I mean, Mrs. McGuire is preparing a room for you. She'll be down for you shortly."

I couldn't see his face clearly, but somehow I could tell he was watching me closely—what he could see of me in the dim light.

"Thank you for your help, Mr. Blakeley," I whispered into the blackness. "I don't know what I would have done without you."

"You're more than welcome, Miss Stoneburner," he answered quietly as he made for the front door, probably headed back out to stable Knightley. "Now, get some sleep. You've had a long night."

"Yes, sir." I smiled to myself.

Mrs. McGuire came downstairs a few minutes later and led me to a bedchamber near the top of the staircase. A small brass lamp on the bedside table cast its flickering light on the wainscoting and the wallpaper, a floral pattern of olive green and cream. There was a large fieldstone fireplace, not unlike the one in the foyer, at the center of a wall of built-in shelves. A tall double bed with a headboard of carved wood was positioned in between the two windows, beside which sat a small upholstered chair. And the door on the interior wall, which led to a private bathroom, was flanked by a wardrobe and a vanity table.

Once Mrs. McGuire had left me, I crossed the room to one of the windows and pulled back the white lace curtain to take in the view of the barn behind the house. I searched the moonlit yard as much as I was able, but there was no sign of Mr. Blakeley. He did live at Blakeley House, didn't he? Or had Ursula been correct in saying he occupied the sixth floor of Everston? For some reason, I didn't like the thought of his living down the road at the hotel instead of at Blakeley House.

My search was hindered by the trees surrounding the residence. Blakeley House seemed to be completely hidden away... which was perfect.

Despite everything that had happened in the last day, God was taking care of me. Strangely enough, by way of Mr. Dexter Blakeley.

TWELVE

The Blakeley Family

"The best thing one can do when it is raining is let it rain."
—Henry Wadsworth Longfellow, *Tales of a Wayside Inn*

The next morning, I awoke to the sound of something scratching against the door to my bedchamber. I sat up in bed and threw off the covers. What a dream!

But then, with groggy, sleep-filled eyes, I stared at the unfamiliar, massive stone fireplace across the room from me.

Where was I?

Leaning over, I peered out the window next to the bed and saw a barn. Then I remembered where I was.

Blakeley House.

Details from the night before returned to me with shocking intensity, startling me with an urge to run from the room, out of the house, and down the road to Everston...and back into Mr. Blakeley's arms. Surely, that part of what I remembered from the night before must have been a dream.

Sitting upright on the edge of the bed, I was confronted with a troubling recollection of a number of things: Jay Crawford's utter lack of concern for me after my brother's murder, and his hateful words to me right there in the upstairs hall of Blakeley House; all that had conspired between Mr. Blakeley and me over the past several weeks, especially the previous day and evening, when his embrace as we'd met on the road had somehow met my deepest need. My heart hardly recognized the jumble of emotions those two men aroused within me: confusion, regret, bitterness; relief, security, and gratitude.

I didn't know why I felt such deep appreciation toward Mr. Blakeley. Yes, he'd saved me from having to face his mother alone in the dead of night, or perhaps my spending the night on the front porch. That was all.

And he would have done the same for anyone else in need of help. He would have cared as much for anyone else. It wasn't me; it was only the situation in which I happened to find myself.

The scratching sound on my door that had awakened me resumed, followed by a tiny purr. Still wearing only my nightgown, I opened the door just a crack. A kitten with gray and black stripes butted its head against the door, pushing it open enough to slip inside. Once my furry guest had been admitted, I closed the door quickly, hoping no one had seen or heard me do so.

The kitten jumped up on the bed and curled into a ball amid my messy covers. It appeared Mrs. McGuire had given me the room belonging to this cat.

With a sigh, I opened the wardrobe and took out the only dress I had to my name. I didn't know what I would do about obtaining more clothes. I didn't imagine Mr. Blakeley's sister would want to share her wardrobe with Greenlee *and* me.

I dressed, then turned my attention to my hair. Whatever was I to do with it? In the chaos of the previous night, I'd lost most of my hairpins.

At the recollection, I pictured myself in Mr. Blakeley's arms, in the dark, with my hair down. What had I been thinking to let him hold me?

I shook the thought away, only to feel a sudden jolt as I wondered if Mr. Blakeley would be at breakfast—even though I knew he took most of his meals at Everston. Might he be downstairs, waiting to see me? He would likely want to introduce me to his sister and his mother, and perhaps to reintroduce me to Greenlee.

A light knock on my door made me practically jump out of my skin. I crossed the room and reached for the doorknob, but I hesitated before opening the door. This bedchamber was the only safe place I had left. Was I ready to start a new scene in the unpredictable play my life had become?

After about thirty seconds, I dared to open the door. There stood a grown version of my childhood friend Roxy, her arms full of colorful gowns. A cream-colored cat at her feet darted over the threshold and into the room.

Roxy walked right in without an invitation and unloaded the dresses onto my bed. Then she twirled around and hugged me. "I'm Roxanna Blakeley. I was so impatient to meet you, and I thought you might need these." She motioned to the pile of bright lace-edged gowns, which, from the look of her, would probably fit me rather well. "Dexter told me you would need some clothes."

Dexter. His name always struck me as harsh and sharp—much as he seemed, at times.

Had he asked her to part with those dresses? I couldn't deny how thankful I felt toward him, even as I wondered what had prompted him to realize I had no clothes besides what I'd been wearing the night before.

"I'm Elle Stoneburner," I said, "and thank you."

"I know who you are. You can call me Roxy."

Roxy's greenish-hazel eyes and wavy brown hair looked just as they had when she was a child; her hair flowed down her back, immediately reminding me that my hair was far from presentable.

"I know you met Greenlee the last time you were here. She also borrows my dresses…when she feels like getting dressed, that is."

"Yes, we've met. So, she doesn't come out of her room much?"

"Practically never."

I knew that I would have to be very careful in my associations with Roxy Blakeley, even though thirteen years had passed since last we'd seen each other.

"Is it time for breakfast?" I asked with a smile. "I'll confess I'm famished."

"Are you ready to go down?"

"Almost. My clothes...and my hair...I have to do something with it."

"No, you don't. Not for us. And your clothes are fine, for now." Roxy took me by the arm and pulled me into the hall and down the stairs. "I'm certain Dexter will think you're the prettiest thing ever to meet him for breakfast at Blakeley House."

So, he would be there.

When we reached the dining room, Mr. Blakeley stood from his seat at the far end of the table. He grinned but quickly sobered as he shot a look at his mother, who stood across the table from me, gawking at her son. She had yet to acknowledge me.

Her eyes matched her son's, and as they cut to me, she frowned.

Mr. Blakeley came around the table toward me. "Mother, this is Miss Elle Stoneburner. She'll be staying at Blakeley House for a while."

His mother nodded at me. "Miss Stoneburner," she said harshly. She wore the same black mourning gown I'd seen her in before, and now that I had a better look at her, she seemed rather young to have a son in his thirties. Her hair was still very brown, with hardly any gray mixed in; and she was slight of build—nearly the same size as twenty-year-old Roxy.

"You may call me Beatrix." After the words were out, she looked as if she wanted to take them back; she hardly seemed happy to meet me.

"It's very nice to meet you...Beatrix."

Roxy took me by the elbow and guided me to the side of the dining table, where Mr. Blakeley pulled out a chair for me.

"Thank you, Mr. Blakeley."

As soon as I was seated, the other three took their places around the table, and Mr. Blakeley blessed the food. Then Mrs. McGuire appeared in the doorway with a platter of sausage, a bowl of scrambled eggs, and a carafe of coffee.

"Hannah, you've met Miss Stoneburner," Mr. Blakeley added as the woman arranged the plates at the center of the table.

"Yes, it's nice to see you again, dearie." She nodded sweetly as she filled our coffee mugs, then returned to the kitchen.

Roxy took a few links of sausage from the platter before passing it to me. I helped myself to a small portion, noting how closely Beatrix watched me with narrowed eyes. As if my goal for being there was to steal her precious son from her clutches.

"I'm glad you brought Elle to us, Dexter," Roxy said, as if I weren't seated directly across the table from her. "How long have you known her?"

"I met Miss Stoneburner when she came to Everston, about a month ago." He lifted his gaze from his coffee and caught me observing him.

Out of the corner of my eye, I saw that Beatrix still watched me cautiously.

"Aren't you glad to be staying?" Roxy asked me. "It's so romantic, don't you think?"

"Yes, I am glad," I said simply before taking a quick bite of sausage and a long sip of coffee.

"Roxy." The way Beatrix spoke her daughter's name, it was almost a threat.

"But don't you think it's romantic?" Roxy implored.

I choked on my coffee and set my cup down, unable to keep from coughing.

"Roxy." This time, it was Mr. Blakeley's turn to use a threatening tone.

"I must apologize, Miss Stoneburner," he said to me. "Roxy doesn't get out much." He sent her a severe look. "She compares everything to the plots of her favorite romance novels and has no real idea about what she's talking about."

Roxy huffed loudly. "Love is real, Dexter. Even romantic love."

I wasn't sure what to say in response. It seemed as if they were picking up a conversation they'd had time and again, judging by the provocative looks they gave each other.

"Have you ever been in love, Elle?" Roxy asked wistfully.

Mr. Blakeley placed his mug of coffee on the table with a thud. "Roxy, Miss Stoneburner has had enough questions this morning."

"But wouldn't you like to know if—"

"Let's give Miss Stoneburner a day to get acclimated before you start bombarding her with any more invasive inquiries."

Roxy sat straighter in her chair and remained silent for the remainder of breakfast.

Mr. Blakeley didn't seem like the same man who'd found me on the dark road the night before—and I was glad. I didn't know what I would do if he continued to behave so heroically.

I laughed inwardly at myself for thinking such a thing. Mr. Blakeley, my hero? He may have come to my rescue the night before, when I was vexed and distraught. In such a state, I would have clung to just about anyone.

Well, with the exception of Lester Imbody, of course.

I knew Mr. Blakeley could very well have let me stay the night at Blakeley House and then shipped me off on the next stagecoach to Severville to catch a train to somewhere else that very morning.

But, for some reason, he hadn't.

I would be his employee, which was the extent of what he'd offered me—a job, plus room and board. That wasn't heroic. It was business.

After breakfast, Mr. Blakeley left for Everston, and both Roxy and Beatrix went to their rooms without a word. Greenlee had spent the morning in her room; I guessed that was the way of things at Blakeley House.

For the first time, I wondered why Mr. Blakeley didn't just encourage Roxy and Greenlee to spend time together instead of hiring me as a companion for them. But perhaps he'd already tried, to no avail.

Companion or not, I shut myself in my room, as well. It seemed like a better idea than wandering about the giant, lonely house, constantly afraid I might come across Beatrix. It also felt good to finally have an entire day to myself.

It had been months.

At noon, when Mrs. McGuire delivered a tray of lunch to my room, I told her that I would take my dinner there, as well—unless Mr. Blakeley planned to rejoin us for the meal, although I didn't think he would.

Mrs. McGuire confirmed that he had no such plans—he usually took his meals at Everston. But I'd already known that. I wasn't sure why I'd asked the question, and with such hopeful expectation. Did I think he would spend more time at his home just because I was staying there?

Through late afternoon, gray-blue rainclouds dominated the dreary sky, giving me no incentive to explore the grounds. I remained secluded in my dim bedchamber and wrote a letter to Natalia, explaining that my employment with Mrs. Granton had concluded, and that Mr. Dexter Blakeley had generously offered me a position as companion to his sister. I also penned a letter to Nathan and Amaryllis, for Natalia to send when she next wrote to them.

My written correspondence completed, I took dinner in my room, then finally ventured out in order to return my tray to the kitchen. The sky had brightened somewhat, and so, rather than going immediately back into seclusion, I crept out the front door. The stillness of the woods at dusk was one of the things I'd missed most about Everston and the surrounding area.

Though the rain had stopped, it was still muggy as I strolled around the perimeter of the grand, English-looking stone house and past the manicured garden. Off to the left, I found a trail into the woods, and I headed down it in hopes of finding the spring I remembered so fondly.

But before I could go far enough for the trees to block my view of Blakeley House, cold raindrops began to fall, slowed only slightly by the branches of the birch trees and huge pines overhead. I hurried across the yard toward the house, my boots plodding through the mud of the lawn. I climbed the steps to the porch, opened the screen door, and pulled on the handle of the front door. It didn't budge.

I pulled again, with no luck.

Peeking through the lace curtains covering the nearby bay window, I saw only darkness inside. Had Mrs. McGuire locked up, thinking I was still in my room?

I banged at the door with my fists, but there was no answer. I rushed around the side of the house through the now-pouring rain to try the door to the dining room. I just managed to turn the knob and push when the door was shoved back and slammed in my face.

"You're not welcome here!" Beatrix yelled from inside.

I knocked on the window next to the door. "Please let me in! It's raining again and getting cold."

"Go back where you came from! It's bad enough having that harlot of Dr. Crawford's upstairs. We don't need you, too!"

I stepped back to the railing of the porch and looked to the windows of the room above the kitchen, which I knew to be Mrs. McGuire's quarters. "Mrs. McGuire? Mrs. McGuire! Can you hear me?"

No response. I swiveled around to face the drenched grove of birches and pines. What was I to do?

I walked to the end of the side porch and took a seat upon a long cushioned rattan settee. There was nothing to do but sit and wait…and possibly sleep, if I could manage to drift off. Fortunately, I wasn't too wet from the rain, so I curled my knees to my chest and looked out through the trees to the darkening sky above the clear blue lake.

It wasn't long before I was sobbing into my hands, my resolve utterly spent from everything I'd been through in the last day. Why did it so often seem as though I was purposefully placed in such painful situations? Had I not just offered my everything to God the day before? Why was He doing nothing to help me?

I lowered my feet to the planked floor and stood, determined to stop my tears. I would telephone Father. I would go home, and he would fix everything. If only it weren't raining, and Everston weren't a mile down the road.

I returned to the settee and lay on my side with my knees bent, my back pressed against the cushions. As I waited for sleep to come, I thought of Mr. Blakeley the night before…how compassionate and kindhearted he'd been. As if it had truly meant something to him to help and comfort me in my predicament.

But that was just how he was. He'd done the same thing for both Greenlee and Violet, in a way. He just couldn't help but act the hero whenever he saw the need.

THIRTEEN

Unlocked

"I arise from dreams of thee
In the first sweet sleep of night,
When the winds are breathing low,
And the stars are shining bright...."
—Percy Bysshe Shelley, "Lines to an Indian Air"

Sometime in the night, I awoke from a dream that had seemed to repeat over and over, each time with more vibrancy, more force.

Yes, I had been sleeping outside, and I wondered who would come and find me. Rescue me.

I already knew, of course.

But, if I had the choice, whom would I choose? Would I choose him?

Or would I choose Jay, who'd stolen my heart and held it captive all those years?

I'd always hoped that the next time he saw me, he would kiss me, he would want me, and everything would go back to the way it had been for those few months of our secret engagement.

But it never had, and now it never would. I knew that now. And it didn't matter, because I didn't want him, anyway.

And then, there was Dexter Blakeley.

Dexter Blakeley, who cared about strangers he'd just met—enough to give them anything he could. For Greenlee and for Violet.

And even for me.

But then, Violet had said I'd caught his fancy. And she'd winked, as if it had pleased her. And then she'd told me the truth about who owned Everston.

My Everston, lost to me forever! Oh, how I hated him!

But I couldn't hate him. I liked him entirely too much—exceedingly too much.

I tossed and turned on the settee. I was still dreaming; I had to be dreaming. These feelings weren't real. Nothing at Everston was real because I wasn't real.

There was no Elle Stoneburner, only Estella Everstone...and this wasn't my life.

Mr. Blakeley's image filled my mind again. The sketches I'd drawn of him—the ones in my stolen sketchbook—how I wished to have those drawings! How I wished to see his intense eyes staring at me, wanting me.

Always.

⌒

"Miss Stoneburner." A deep, quiet voice startled me awake.

I opened my eyes, propped myself up on my elbows, and looked around, a little lost.

Morning had dawned, and Mr. Blakeley knelt before me in the shadows of the side porch. Staring at me. His hands braced the bottom edge of the settee. Wulfric, sat obediently beside him, panting happily.

I sat up straight, startled at how very glad I was to see him.

He let go of the settee as my feet met the porch floor.

I shook my head and lifted a hand to my hair. "What time is it?"

"Why are you sleeping on the porch?" Mr. Blakeley asked in the same moment. He still knelt before me, looking me in the face, his forearms resting on his knees. "It's somewhere between four and five o'clock. Now, tell me what happened."

"I went for an evening walk—it's so beautiful around here at dusk, don't you think?—and, well...your mother locked me out."

I couldn't see his eyes in the dim light, but I could tell by the slow breath he let out that he probably knew just how it had transpired.

"There's no excuse for how you've been treated the past two days, first as a guest at my hotel, and now under my own roof. Miss Stoneburner, I beg your forgiveness—"

"There's nothing to forgive you of, Mr. Blakeley. You're the only one who seems to care for me anymore." I rubbed my cheeks, not caring how unladylike it was to do so. I'd never awakened in front of a gentleman before, and it felt exceptionally unseemly to continue speaking with him while I struggled to collect my thoughts. But I didn't want to stop, or to leave his presence. I didn't know when I'd see him next. "It's really so early in the morning? You come home at such odd times."

"I've had a difficult time sleeping lately." He wasn't smiling now, and I had a feeling he'd revealed more to me than he'd wanted to.

"I'm sorry. You must be very busy. You spend a great deal of your time at Everston, don't you?"

"I'll try to come around more, now that you're here."

"Do you think I should stay? Your mother—"

"Yes," he whispered emphatically. "You should. I'll deal with my mother. If you do want to stay, that is."

"I would prefer it." My only other option was far too humiliating. As resolved as I'd been to telephone Father only hours before, now that I sat in Mr. Blakeley's presence again, I realized what a mistake it would have been. I didn't want to leave.

Mr. Blakeley didn't say anything for a long while but remained on his knees before me. Finally, he said, "Not many of the young ladies I've known…are as kindhearted as you are."

His gentle words took my heart by surprise, and I had a difficult time keeping my appreciation from bursting forth in the form of hot tears.

I straightened my back. "Do you know many young ladies, Mr. Blakeley? It seems to me most of the people you meet eventually leave."

Mr. Blakeley finally stood and leaned against one of the stone pillars supporting the porch. "Yes, they do…but most of them are also the kinds of young ladies I despise. I've known enough of the sort to realize that true kindness is a rarity."

"I'm not really kind," I insisted, more disturbed by his comment than flattered. He'd been referring to young ladies like the real me, the wealthy socialites who flocked to his hotel for the enjoyment of doing absolutely nothing for days and weeks on end. "But you are kind, Mr. Blakeley. You insist on helping others out of their unfortunate situations. Just think of all you've done for Violet, for Greenlee…for me."

Mr. Blakeley studied me with a quizzical expression. He must have been in love once, to have such a cynical view of it. And of course he had been. He was as appealing a man as one was likely to meet.

"Has someone broken your heart irreparably, Mr. Blakeley?"

He gave me a hard look that made me wish I hadn't asked the question. "The answer is no…but it's also yes. Not directly, but damaged just the same. It was my brother's heart. But it was much more…it was his will to live."

"I'm sorry." Though I wasn't quite sure what he meant.

"I wish there were more young ladies like Roxy…and you." He rubbed his eyes, as if he, too, were just waking. "I want to thank you for taking the position. Roxy seems to like you tremendously."

I raised my eyebrows. "Tremendously?"

"She came down to breakfast with you yesterday." He paused, as if searching for his next sentence. "I was surprised, is all. She's never had many friends, much like me. It's our lot in life, I guess. And, to tell you the truth, I'm quite all right with it. But I don't think she is."

It was a bizarre twist of fate that Mr. Blakeley seemed to be the only friend I had anymore. No matter how I looked at it, I felt as if he was the only person who truly knew me, no matter what name I went by.

I stood from the settee. "I can understand a little as to why Greenlee would want to spend most of her time in her room, but why does Roxy?"

He frowned. "Has she been avoiding you? I didn't expect that after this morning, but perhaps I was a little too severe with her. She needs to learn that love isn't something produced from bouquets of flowers and good intentions, but something that can hurt quite deeply."

Again, without his knowing how precisely his words had pierced me, he had spoken the truth so openly. Something terrible, indeed, must have happened to the brother.

"I should have made a point to be around more today," he went on. "Then this wouldn't have happened. You must wonder why I hired you."

"You're not going to send me packing now that you know how ineffective—"

"I would never send you packing, Miss Stoneburner. I plan to keep you around here for as long as possible."

My stomach flipped at his words, though I knew very well he hadn't meant them the way my ears had heard them. "But do you think I'll be needed—"

"Yes, I do."

As the sun rose and the sky grew brighter, I could see Mr. Blakeley more clearly with every passing minute. He still leaned against the stone porch pillar, his arms folded across his chest, looking much more relaxed than usual. Wulfric still sat at his feet with his tongue hanging out.

"And Roxy has something called Ménière's disease. That's why she hides. It causes her to have severe dizzy spells and headaches, as well as extreme fatigue."

"Does Dr. Crawford know? Has he seen her?"

"Dr. Jennings—the other physician at Everston—sees to her. We've tried different treatments, but so far, nothing has helped." He pulled a ring of keys out of the pocket of his trousers. Before heading to the door, he took my hand and helped me to stand. "Is there anything I can do to make up for last night? Anything at all, perhaps something Mrs. McGuire might not have already seen to?"

"For me? Oh, no, I don't need anything."

"There must be something…and I bet I know just what it is."

I let go of his hand and picked at the atrociously plain cuff of my right sleeve. "My drawing pencils and sketchbook *were* stolen," I finally admitted.

"Just like your self-portrait from your first night here. I'm still fairly sure Roxy has it, though I don't know what would have induced her to—"

"It's all right. I don't need it. She can have it. Honestly, I'm more upset about Ursula Imbody's stealing my entire sketchbook." I started down the porch toward the door to the dining room.

He followed close behind. "Don't let yourself think of her, Miss Stoneburner. She can do you no more harm."

"I know. I just don't know how to rid myself of the feeling I've been trampled upon."

He gently took my arm and looked down at me with regret in his eyes. "I'm sorry I wasn't there." His voice cracked, and he cleared his throat. "I'll do my best to get you anything and everything you'd like as long as you're staying under the protection of my roof."

"Thank you, Mr. Blakeley."

He seemed to have something more to say, but he remained silent.

I'd been thinking about him too much for weeks—first while still under the impression that he was merely the manager of Everston, working for my father, and now, when I knew the truth: that Father was mentoring him as the new owner of Everston.

With sudden clarity, I realized how backward my thinking had been since meeting him. Hadn't I been ready to leave everything behind in order to follow Jay out west? What was the difference between my falling for a missionary and my falling for anyone else? What was there now to keep me from falling for Mr. Blakeley?

There had always been something about him, above and beyond the fact that I always enjoyed his company.

As he moved toward the door, a vision of the nearby spring—the one I had yet to rediscover—and its burble of waters escaping into the lake came to mind, and I imagined how wonderful it would feel to let go of the tight rein I'd been keeping on my emotions and somehow allow myself to enjoy getting to know Mr. Blakeley better.

But then, as I stood there on the porch with him, I realized that the woman he saw wasn't me.

Mr. Blakeley didn't know who I was. And from his mentions of me—the real me—I had a strong suspicion he wouldn't particularly welcome the knowledge of my true identity.

"What will your mother do when she finds out I'm staying?" I asked him, desperately struggling to keep character.

When I looked up, I caught him studying me. "You don't have to worry about Mother locking you out again. I promise. And I'll give you a key, in case." He unlocked the door and held it open for me.

Inside the house, Mr. Blakeley went straight to this office, and only then did I take the time to examine the extent of my rumpled clothes. Combing my fingers through my loosened, falling-all-over hair, I almost regretted spending all that time out there with Mr. Blakeley looking at me, studying me, really seeing me, when I looked such a fright!

I raced to my room, intent on rectifying myself before facing him again at breakfast.

Over the years, hardly anyone had ever seen the true me. Not even my own family seemed to care whether I erected a façade or presented my true feelings on a given subject. I'd been invisible for so long. How odd that it was here, in the middle of the mountainous woods of Maine, and while I pretended to be someone else altogether, that a man had finally cared to look.

Although I'd known Dexter Blakeley for only a few weeks, I felt I could be myself with him.

Despite his blunt manner and the no-nonsense attitude he sometimes presented, he was real, true to himself, and he didn't seem to care what anyone thought of him.

And that made me like him all the more.

FOURTEEN

Roxy's Favorite Things

"There is no charm equal to tenderness of heart."
—Jane Austen, *Emma*

Although he did join us for breakfast the next several mornings, Mr. Blakeley spent most of his time at Everston. I guess he was perfectly content to leave his mother, Roxy, Greenlee, and me under the care of Mrs. McGuire and her husband, Virgil, who took care of the grounds and the animals.

Beatrix had started ignoring me once she realized Mr. Blakeley wouldn't stand for her theatrics. And he'd given me a key to the kitchen door, just in case.

In the rare glimpses I caught of Roxy during my first few days at Blakeley House, she seemed as friendly as she'd been when we were children. Her sickness kept her mostly to her room, and I left her alone, hoping she'd eventually let me in.

No matter that the Blakeleys were a strange family, I was happy to be hidden away in the woods at their residence. I almost liked it better than Everston. Surely, my family would see the situation as mutually beneficial. I just wondered when I would begin "working." So far, I'd seen Greenlee only once, when she poked her head out from behind her bedroom door—only to slam it shut once she saw me. And I hadn't seen Roxy much at all, catching only brief glimpses when she would sneak downstairs in the evening to speak with her mother in the parlor.

For this reason, I wasn't prepared for the exuberance I met with when I answered a knock at my bedchamber door on Thursday evening.

Roxy stood there, dressed in a pretty green and white gown, her long, wavy brown hair braided over her right shoulder. In her arms, she held her cream-colored kitten, Creamy. "Will you come with me to my room?" she asked, grinning broadly.

"What is it?"

"Oh, nothing...." She motioned down the hall with a curtsy and a nod. "Only that you are cordially invited to spend the evening with Creamy and me, doing all of my favorite things."

"And what exactly does that entail?" I had no idea what Roxy liked best besides being in her room alone for long periods of time. The quiet conversations with her mother usually seemed to wear her out to the point of exhaustion. Seeing her so bright and cheery and desirous of my company made me happy.

"You'll see." She took me by the hand and guided me down the hall.

"Is Greenlee coming?"

"I asked her to, but she probably won't. She never does."

My stomach dipped at the thought of being formally introduced to Greenlee Cole. We had met under rather unusual circumstances, and Mr. Blakeley probably thought my taking care of her that first night had been introduction enough.

Roxy escorted me into her bedchamber. I could hear the water running in the connected bathroom, and the heavy scent of lavender assaulted my senses. She set her kitten upon her bed, where it curled into a ball.

Roxy's room had been quaintly decorated, much like mine. From the wainscoting to the ceiling, paper patterned with green swirls covered the walls. A dark double bed of ornately carved wood was the focal point of the large room, and it faced a massive fireplace flanked by two tall windows. Next to a gray chaise-longue nestled in the corner was a pile of newspapers and magazines. Across the room stood a wardrobe, as well as a desk, on which was an open scrapbook in the process of being decorated. And next to the scrapbook was a framed photograph of Mr. Blakeley, wearing the rare smile I wished to see more often upon his lips.

Just as I pulled my lingering gaze from the image, Mrs. McGuire came into the room carrying a tea tray with service for two in the Dresden china I recognized from the first night I'd set foot in the house.

I moved out of Mrs. McGuire's way and leaned against the foot of the wood bedframe as Roxy showed the maid into the bathroom. Were we going to have tea in there? Why was the bath water running? My curiosity got the better of me, and I followed the two women into the small room.

Mrs. McGuire set the tea tray on the wide porcelain pedestal sink, then left the room.

I looked up to see Roxy grinning at me. "This is what I do every Thursday evening."

"Have tea in your bathroom?"

"It isn't just tea in the lavatory. I make every Thursday night special by soaking my feet in the lavender bath salts Dexter buys for me when he goes to Boston."

"Does he go to Boston often?" I peeked into the bathtub and noticed that the steaming water was already a couple of inches deep.

"A few times a year. He meets with Mr. Bram Everstone—Dexter's a favorite of his."

"Yes, I've heard something about that."

"He was supposed to go to see him this week, but the trip was cancelled, fortunately. Mr. Everstone has been mentoring him ever since he sold him the hotel last summer, but Dexter always has to go to Boston to see him. Mr. Everstone never comes here."

"Oh, but Mr. Blake—your brother told me Mr. Everstone was coming to see him soon."

"Did he?" She looked at me curiously. "I wonder why he would decide to come now."

I stared at her without an answer.

"I don't blame him for not coming before," Roxy went on. "With the way Mother speaks of his family, he must know—from Dexter, likely—that she hates the Everstones for some reason. Mother hated that Dexter used to work for him at Bailey Hill, and that he had to associate with him further in purchasing Everston. She hates it even more now that Mr. Everstone insists on mentoring him."

"She hates all of them—the entire family?" I swallowed hard. As if the woman didn't despise me enough already. I dreaded to think what she might do if she knew I was Bram Everstone's daughter.

"I don't know why. It seems we were friends once. Family friends. Although I was too young to understand much at the time, I thought that the one summer our families found each other here, it wasn't a newly acquired friendship." Roxy leaned over the edge of the tub and dangled her fingers in the scented water, then stood up again. "Dexter told me you attended church at the hollow last Sunday. Did you enjoy it?"

"Very much." I purposefully refrained from elaborating on how her brother's words had made such a difference to my bruised and battered heart. Had that only been days ago? It felt more like months, with all that had happened.

"I felt well enough to go the week before last, when Dr. Crawford spoke."

"Dr. Crawford spoke at the hollow?" I lifted my eyes to meet hers. "I—I'm sorry we missed it. Most weeks, Mrs. Granton and

I stayed at Everston and held our own service in the Music Room. She didn't like to venture outside."

"I'm sorry your time with her ended badly." Roxy motioned for me to follow her back into the bedchamber. "But I can't say I'm sorry you're here now. Maybe Dexter will start coming around more often. I do miss him. I saw him a lot more when we lived with him on the top floor of the tower at Everston...out of everyone's way." She plopped onto the bed.

I sat down beside her. "I used to—" I stopped abruptly, just short of mentioning that I had fond memories of staying in those very rooms. Having Roxy beside me made me forget myself. "I stayed in the tower with Mrs. Granton, on the fifth floor."

"I miss the hotel, but Mother doesn't. I don't think she's been there once since we moved out. But Dexter practically lives there anymore. Sometimes I suspect that a young lady there has caught his interest, but then I always remember his stance on falling in love. According to him, it is the most terrible thing anyone could ever do in all the world."

My stomach threatened to climb into my throat.

"Did he seem interested in anyone while you saw him at Everston?" she asked.

"Your brother doesn't tell me anything," I stated simply. "We hardly know each other." The latter statement was far from how I really felt, of course.

"He must feel he knows you, or he wouldn't have brought you here." She leaned in and placed her hand on mine for a moment. "And while it's true that he doesn't like to talk much in general, when he does speak, he actually says quite a lot—just with fewer words than most people use."

I smiled politely. "Did your family used to come here often... for the summers?" I already knew the answer, but Elle Stoneburner wouldn't have.

"More when I was much younger. We would take the train up from Portland…that's where we used to live. It was the summer I was eight that the Everstones came. That summer, their youngest daughter was my closest friend. During the months following our departure from Everston…well, to put it bluntly, we lost both my father and my oldest brother the following spring, and then, a few months after that, I heard that she'd lost her mother in a shipwreck."

It was true that my mother had died the following summer.

Roxy lifted her lazy kitten from the bed and cradled it in her arms. "Father and Cullen were killed while they, along with Mother, were in the process of relocating our family to California. I went to stay with some relatives at my aunt Eugenia's in Portland."

"They were killed? What happened?" Part of me dreaded finding out, but I felt I needed to know. Whatever had happened was intricately linked to the man Mr. Blakeley had become, and something in me needed to know as much as possible about his family and their past.

"Honestly, I don't know what happened, only that Father and Cullen died…and Mother's never been the same since."

"What about your brother? Was he changed because of what happened?"

"Dexter is the same as always, doing what needs to be done, no matter what. Like working all those years for Mr. Everstone at the Bailey Hill Hotel, saving everything he possibly could. I've gathered that Father lost a great deal of money in California before he died; Dexter had to work a long time to finally purchase his Everston."

I frowned at the sound of "his" Everston before I could stop myself, but Roxy must have read the look as one of concern, for she said, "It's all right, Elle. I didn't know Father or Cullen that well. I feel bad mostly for Mother and Dexter. Cullen was more than just a brother to Dexter; he was his best friend."

"That must have been awful, I can't imagine." Although I, too, had lost a brother, the previous summer, Will and I had never been close. Not like Nathan and I had always been. Mr. Blakeley's relationship with his sister reminded me very much of how Nathan related to me, always looking out for my best interests.

"A few years later, Dexter graduated from Dartmouth and took the job at Bailey Hill. He and Mother moved into the manager's quarters at the hotel, but there wasn't room for me. That's why I lived in Portland. But then, when Dexter had the opportunity to buy Everston last year, he brought me here, where he built Blakeley House for me and Mother. Everston has always been my favorite place in the world, and he knew it."

Dexter Blakeley was quite the hero, from his sister's standpoint.

Just then, Roxy cringed as she blurted out, "I'm sorry, but I need to confess something. I just lied to you. Please forgive me, Elle, but I want to tell you—I never lived with Aunt Eugenia in Portland. She was always very close to Mother, and the reason she moved from England when Cullen and Dexter were small is because Father was always away on his ship. But when Mother, Father, and Cullen traveled to California, she thought it best that I stay at the sanatorium, hoping that I would be healed of my headaches and dizziness."

I'd heard the news of her condition from her brother only days before, but hearing the words from her, and learning that she'd been separated from her family, grieved me deeply. I was equally touched by the way she'd quickly corrected herself. As if she simply couldn't stand not telling me the truth.

And there I was, lying to her...to everyone.

"Will you forgive me?" she asked.

"Of course!" I smiled reassuringly. "You don't have to tell me anything you aren't comfortable sharing. It's not a crime to keep such things private."

"I know; I just didn't want to keep it from you. I also want you to know that my self-imposed seclusion is something I do because I'm not feeling well, not because I don't enjoy spending time with you."

"Thank you, Roxy. And I understand. I, too, like being alone."

"I'm glad we understand each other completely." Roxy put her cat down, slid off the bed, and started toward the bathroom. "I bet the tub is full enough now."

I rose from the mattress and followed her.

I entered the bathroom just as she reached for the spigot and turned off the water. "Go ahead and put your feet in first, and I'll serve you your tea," she offered. "I'm used to having to do it for myself when it's just me."

As I sat upon the closed commode and began unlacing my boots, I envisioned Roxy as the little girl with whom I'd played at the spring and run about Everston while our families spent time together. We'd felt more like sisters than mere friends back then; in fact, we'd often talked about how wonderful it would be to truly be sisters.

After I stripped off my stocking and very ungracefully rolled up my French cotton drawers—striving to hide their fineness from Roxy—I gathered my skirts and stepped into the tub, placing my bare feet in the silky hot water. I bunched the extra material from my skirts to pad the hard edge of the claw-foot tub.

Never had I sat with my drawers pulled high and my bare legs completely exposed. Fortunately, the water was so deep, it reached my knees.

Once I was situated, Roxy asked me how I wanted my tea. From the aroma, I could tell that it was blueberry, and I made my requests. She served it to me before preparing her own, which she set on the edge of the tray, just within reach after she had placed her feet in the steaming lavender-scented water. She assumed much the same position as mine, with her skirts wadded behind her, and we didn't say anything for a little while as we sipped our tea.

In all honesty, sitting there with my calves soaking in that silky water while I sipped my hot tea was the closest thing to perfection I'd experienced in months.

After I'd drained my cup, I placed it on the tray and decided to break the silence. "Do you think Greenlee will ever talk to me? I feel as if I hardly earn my keep, spending most of my time doing as I wish without you or Greenlee. It hardly feels like I'm working."

Roxy shrugged. "Perhaps that's what Dexter had in mind all along." She set her teacup back on the tray next to mine. Then her lips formed a wry smirk. "Maybe he doesn't want you to have a *position....*"

I knew what she was getting at. But hadn't she said that her brother was set against falling in love? That it was the last thing in the world he wanted to do?

"Your brother likes to help damsels in distress," I insisted. "I'm not the only one." As much as I wished to be....

"You can call him Dexter if you'd like, Elle. At least with me. You could probably address him by his Christian name, too, if you wanted. I think he would welcome it."

"Oh, I wouldn't want—"

"I think when you first came to Blakeley House, he was half frightened of you...and too afraid to ask you to call him Dexter, if he hasn't already."

The thought of Mr. Blakeley being afraid of anything—especially concerning me—was ridiculous.

"You could call him Dexter, and he could call you Elle."

I remembered how I'd felt the single time I'd heard him say "Elle," on the road to Blakeley House in the middle of the night. It was if a blanket of safety had been wrapped about me...before his strong arms had imparted the same feeling.

Although Elle wasn't my true name, it was a nickname most of my family used quite often. And hearing him utter it...I knew that it wasn't smart for me to dwell on the feelings it had aroused.

"Miss Roxy, do you need anything else?" Mrs. McGuire inquired from the doorway of Roxy's bedchamber.

"No, Hannah, we have everything we need; but thank you," Roxy answered. Once we heard Mrs. McGuire pad down the stairs, she added, "You know, there's a trunk in the attic that Dexter brought over from Everston when we moved into the house last fall. It has Estella Everstone's name engraved on the nameplate."

"My—" I shook my head and scrambled to correct my blunder. "My goodness!"

"I go through it often, fondly recalling that summer, but Dexter doesn't know."

"Has your brother...Dexter...told Mr. Everstone about it?"

"Yes, but he didn't seem too interested. The contents are thirteen years old, not to mention they belonged to an eight-year-old. Estella probably never missed them. Well, except for possibly the sketchbook and colored pencils—"

I stifled a gasp. "Her sketchbook! And colored pencils?"

"I bet Dexter would let me give them to you, since yours were stolen. Do you want to go see the trunk?"

"Right now?"

"Why not? There's a light in the attic."

"Well, yes, I suppose."

Roxy lifted one sopping-wet foot out of the water, then the other, splattering the tile floor. When she stood, she did so with far more grace than I would have expected. Of course, she'd had some practice, since this was apparently a weekly ritual. "I'll have to go get the key. It's in Dexter's study downstairs."

Before I knew it, she'd left the room. I could hear the patter of her bare feet as she crossed the hall and started down the stairs.

I sat there for a moment on the edge of the tub, my legs soaking in the now-lukewarm water, the fronts of my skirts and undergarments clutched in my fists. I had to mentally prepare myself before I dared to set eyes on that trunk again, on that sketchbook...especially in front of Roxy. I could barely remember what I'd drawn that summer, but I did know that most of the sketches were of my family...and that some would have been of my mother.

I heard footsteps on the stairs, so I stood, still grasping the bunched folds of my skirts in an effort to keep them dry. As I maneuvered my way out of the tub, I realized that Roxy really had made it look far easier than it was. I soon became rather stuck, with my left leg hanging over the edge of the basin; and then, as my right foot lost traction, I had to grab the edge of the tub with both hands to avoid landing wholly in the water.

"Hey, Rox! You in here? Oh, it's Thursday, isn't it?"

To my horror, Mr. Blakeley's frame casually filled the doorway, looking frustratingly handsome as his hazel eyes widened with the realization of who he'd walked in on with her skirts lifted past her knees.

Mortified, I didn't know what to do. Should I try to step completely out of the tub without displaying to him any more of my bare legs? Or should I plunge fully clothed into the water to hide from him?

I chose the third option—doing nothing. I could do nothing, frozen in place.

Mr. Blakeley averted his gaze, looking at everything but me. His eyes were on the far wall as he sputtered, "I thought you— I thought Roxy—"

The sound of his voice snapped me into action. I flung my skirts over my exposed knees, no longer caring if my garments got wet. That still left my wet bare foot dangling immodestly between us. Still gripping the edge of the tub with both hands, I lowered my left foot to the floor, carefully, lifted my right foot out of the water, and stumbled gracelessly backward onto my feet, facing the far wall. I hoped with everything in me that Mr. Blakeley had already left the scene, for then I could pretend what had just happened... hadn't.

I took one step, slipped on the wet tile, and landed with a thud on my side in a pile of skirts and petticoats, exposing even more of my bare feet and ankles to Mr. Blakeley, who still—quite unbelievably—stood in the doorway. I twisted away from him, desperate to conceal as much as possible, and trying to ignore the throbbing pain in my hip.

"Forgive me, Miss Stoneburner." He entered the room, crouched down, and lifted me beneath the arms to the commode, where I sat miserably, not looking at him. He knelt on one knee before me, almost as he had done the other morning in front the settee. "I'm sorry, but I simply couldn't leave you on the floor like that."

He picked up my boots, which I'd stuffed with my stockings, and handed them to me. "Are you all right? Nothing hurts, does it?"

I grunted. "Only my pride."

"I have a feeling it'll make a speedy recovery, if your general resilience at life's hardships is any indication." He stood and awkwardly patted me on the head. "I should go."

Still burning with mortification, I hurried to my bedchamber, boots and stockings in tow, ignoring the drips of water that ran down my calves. Roxy would be back soon, ready to go to the attic to explore my long-lost trunk.

As eager as I was to reunite with my belongings, I didn't want to think about the past. I had plenty to think about regarding my present state of affairs...and Dexter Blakeley...and how the stunned look on his face when he'd walked through that bathroom doorway had done something peculiar to my heart. Something I had a feeling wouldn't be so easily undone.

FIFTEEN

The Trunk

"More things are wrought by prayer than this world dreams of."
—Alfred, Lord Tennyson, *Morte d'Artur*

For the next two nights, Dexter dined at Blakeley House and even stayed afterward to spend time in the parlor with his mother. But even this didn't bring Roxy out of her room.

Perhaps it was better that she hadn't come down. It was bad enough that Beatrix was witness to his strangely high-spirited behavior around me. I knew that his mother didn't like it, and I didn't need Roxy to notice and then forever taunt me by insisting that she'd known her brother had feelings for me.

It sounded a bit scandalous, but I knew that one look at a bare leg wasn't enough to capture someone's attention; Dexter's reluctant awareness of me had been there for weeks. I'd simply tried to ignore it, which was becoming more and more difficult to do.

With a sick feeling in my stomach, I constantly reminded myself that he harbored this obvious attraction to a woman who didn't really exist. Were he to find out my true identity as the spoiled socialite daughter of his business mentor, his interest would surely wane.

Despite these concerns, I couldn't help but continue to cultivate our friendship. For, just as I'd learned over the previous month at Everston, the more I got to know Dexter Blakeley, the more I enjoyed being near him. Just sitting in the same room together—albeit under the watchful eye of his mother—did something to me I'd never experienced. I gained untold courage of heart just watching those strong shoulders move under his well-fitted jacket as his sharp eyes took in every detail of whatever was set before him.

Oftentimes, I found, it was me he studied so closely...and those were the moments at Blakeley House, I lived for.

⌒

Roxy finally came out of her room on Sunday. She met me in the hall near the top of the stairs as I was heading down for breakfast.

"If you were planning to attend church this morning, I'm afraid you're too late," Roxy said. "You would have had to catch the early stagecoach into Laurelton." She ran her hand casually along the banister.

"Why? Has something happened?"

"We received a message from Dexter this morning that he and Dr. Crawford were needed in Westward last night. He wasn't sure when they would be back." Roxy hadn't spoken to me since Thursday night. I knew she didn't understand why I hadn't opened the door to my bedchamber when she'd come for me with the key to the trunk. I'd been beyond mortified after her brother had walked in on me with my skirts to my knees, but how was I supposed to explain that to her?

"What shall we do—"

"Elle...listen." Roxy grabbed my hand. "I'm sorry I've ignored you the past few days. I was hurt; but I think I've figured out the reason behind your reluctance to see the trunk."

I let her hold my hand, but I didn't answer. What could I say without giving too much away?

"You were scared because I'd brought up Estella Everstone, weren't you? And I came too close to the truth, because, well, you see…I can tell. I've always been able to read you. Then and now."

"Then?" I asked, my panic mounting, as she pulled me from the hallway into my room.

She let go of my hand to close the door, then stood with her back against it for a moment. "You're Estella Everstone," she whispered. "It all makes sense now. The drawing from your sketchbook—yes, I stole it that first night! I'd watched you, and I wondered, and I just had to have it. I'm sorry I'm a thief! And then, there's also…the way you are."

"The way I am?" I swallowed and turned away from her, utterly shocked and unprepared for all she was saying. "I don't know—"

"You haven't been seen in Boston or Bar Harbor for months. After what happened to Will, some people are saying you followed your brother Nathan and his new wife west. But you didn't. And Dexter told me that your references were from Mr. Bram Everstone…your father."

I clamped my lips together and struggled to keep myself from bursting into tears. It actually felt good to have Roxy recognize me. But what if she blew my cover?

I didn't like the idea of Dexter finding out. Surely, he would stop treating me with such sincerity, such kindness. If he learned my identity, everything about our relationship would change. For some reason, most people treated me as if I lived in a glass box. Now that I'd had a taste of what it was like to be outside that box, I didn't look forward to going back.

"I'm right, aren't I?" Roxy asked.

"Yes." I nearly sobbed the word.

"I hope you don't think I'll tell Mother. I think it is better that she not know, considering the way she feels about your family."

I felt a measure of relief. "Thank you. I believe that's wise."

"But what about Dexter? Don't you think we should tell him? I'm certain he fancies you. And you like him too, don't you?"

"Oh, I'm really not certain he'll want to know." I faced her again, purposefully ignoring her final comment. As attracted as I was to her brother, I wasn't sure of my feelings for him; they were clouded with confusion.

"I still think you should tell him."

"My father will be here soon to see...Dexter." I forced myself to say his name. "He'll probably want to take me home, so I suppose everyone is bound to find out, at some point."

"Precisely the reason you might as well tell him now." Roxy almost smiled—just like her brother was apt to do—but then a shade of worry darkened her features as she sat on the edge of my bed. "I've missed you, Estella, and I am truly sorry I stole your self-portrait from your sketchbook. Do you want it back?"

"No, you can have it." I sat down next to her.

"Have you been to the spring since coming back?"

I jumped back on my feet, excited she'd remembered. "I wasn't certain where to find it." A boom of thunder suddenly shook the house, followed by the sound of heavy raindrops pounding the windows.

"It's not too far, but today obviously won't be a good day to go." She leaned back and lifted the lace curtains to reveal the stormy sky. "But I have something else we can do that will be equally enjoyable." She sat up and fingered the string about her neck. Hanging from it was a key. "It goes to your trunk."

I could only smile.

"Do you want to go right now? I can't wait for you to see it, Estella." Roxy grinned as she stood. "It's good to call you that."

"You shouldn't. What if someone hears you? Your mother might be right outside my door, listening. Or Mrs. McGuire."

"They would probably think I'm losing my wits, is all." She led me from my room a door I hadn't noticed before. "Aren't you excited to see your old sketchbook and drawings again?"

"And the colored pencils...." Maybe I *would* have the chance to draw Dexter's eyes. I followed her through the door, closing it behind me before climbing the stairs to the attic. "How is it that Dexter has a key? Was the trunk not locked?"

"Curiosity got the better of me when Dexter first found the trunk and brought it to Blakeley House," Roxy said as she switched on a lamp at the top of the stairs. "I snuck up soon after and pried the lock open. I wanted to be reminded of that summer. But, for some reason, Dexter had a new lock put on. Hence the key."

Roxy crossed the large, open space to my old black leather trunk and knelt before it on the wood floor. I followed suit, taking in the sight of the long-lost relic. It was much smaller than I remembered, but I'd been much smaller myself the last time I'd set eyes on it.

Roxy inserted the key in the lock and turned it with a click. "Your being here is an answer to my prayers, you know."

"I'm glad I could come." And that was the absolute truth.

The trunk popped open as if it had been stuffed full. I was anxious to see all the contents—not just the sketchbook and pencils but also my clothes and any childish knickknacks I might have kept from that summer.

Roxy rifled through a layer of ruffles and lace, then lifted out a familiar wooden lap desk. I could picture my sketchbook and pencils inside, tucked away right where I'd left them. My heart pounded as I opened the lid.

It was empty. They were missing.

Roxy gasped.

I tried not to seem too distraught as I asked, "How long has it been since you last looked at them?"

"I don't know," Roxy said. "A few weeks, perhaps."

Peering inside the trunk again, I reaching through the layers of old gowns to the very bottom. My fingertips grazed something fuzzy, and I pulled out the small stuffed white bear my mother had made for me.

Roxy reached over and fingered the soft fur. "Polaris."

My jaw dropped. "You remembered his name?"

"I remember everything about that summer." Roxy reached out to caress the back of the bear's head. "I wish things had worked out differently...that our families hadn't been touched by the trauma of death so soon after. We might have stayed in contact."

"When Mother died, they just seemed to want to move on with their lives."

"Mine, too."

"Maybe they didn't realize what good friends we'd become."

"I don't think they did. Or they didn't care." She paused. "Your mother was a wonderful person. I could tell you were her favorite. I wish I'd been Mother's favorite, instead of Cullen."

I wasn't certain my mother had favored me, but I did know I felt completely bereft when she was taken from me. "Ever since she passed away, I've been virtually invisible to almost everyone, even those who are supposed to be close to me."

"Well, you're not invisible to me," Roxy assured me. "And I don't think you're invisible to Dexter, either."

"Roxanna?" Beatrix's voice bombarded the quiet of the attic from the foot of the steps. "Are you up there? What are you doing?"

"Nothing, Mother." Roxy closed the trunk lid softly and whispered, "You keep Polaris. I'll take Mother all the way downstairs to distract her while you go down to your room. I have a feeling she won't like that you've been up here with me." Then she turned toward the staircase and bellowed, "I'll be right down!"

She quickly looped the padlock through the latch, fastened it securely, and stood. "I'm sorry your sketchbook and pencils weren't in there. I can't imagine what might have happened to them."

"Roxanna?"

"Coming, Mother!" Roxy scurried over to the stairwell and disappeared, leaving me in the attic with only Polaris, a favorite toy from a lifetime ago.

I waited until it was safe to leave the attic. Then I tiptoed down the stairs with Polaris tucked inside the pocket of my dress, and started to my room.

I knew just who had taken the sketchbook and pencils. And I also knew why.

Dexter had mentioned it once before...that he knew just what I wanted.

SIXTEEN

The Spring

"To me, love isn't all. I must look up, not down, trust and honor with my whole heart, and find strength and integrity to lean on."
—Louisa May Alcott, *Rose in Bloom*

know just who you came downstairs for—and why!"

Beatrix spat the words before I even saw her. I tried to make it from the foot of the stairs to the front door before she could apprehend me, but as I passed the entryway to the front parlor, she flew out of the room and caught me by the elbow, pinching me with surprising force through the thick sleeve of my blue hand-me-down coat from Roxy.

"I don't know what you mean!" I insisted.

"I know you want him. Why wouldn't you? You heard him ride up!"

I tried to pull my arm free from her grip. "I didn't know he—"

"Don't lie to me. You're after my Dexter! He just rode up, and here you are."

I'd known it was a bad idea to venture downstairs before breakfast—earlier than usual. But, to be honest, the last time I'd searched the side yard from my window—yes, I had been looking for him, hoping he would arrive soon—I hadn't actually seen him ride up the drive.

Beatrix finally released my arm, sending me stumbling across the front hall toward the door. I caught myself and somehow avoided landing completely sprawled out on the floor.

Hurrying out the door, I was met with the sight of Mr. McGuire leading Knightley into the barn, and, of course, Wulfric prancing about.

Stuffing my cold bare hands into my coat pockets, I started for the spring, which had been the main reason I'd risen so early. Roxy and I had been there a few times, and I looked forward to seeing it at dawn, with the daylight seeping over the mountains as the sun slowly rose over the lake.

I hastened past the barn, lest Dexter see me—and his mother spy us together. Not that there was anything to hide from her. He was simply my employer. Never mind that I had to remind myself of this truth many times each day.

I followed the wooded trail, keeping my eyes glued to the path, and felt increasingly anxious to see it yet again—my spring!

But as I rounded the final bend in the path around a ridge of pine trees, it wasn't the stone structure and flowing water that captured my attention.

It was Dexter.

He sat along the edge of the spring in a posture of prayer, his broad shoulders pressed against the tall stone wall built into the hill. As always, he wore his fitted black suit; his coat was buttoned only halfway to reveal a gray waistcoat, and he'd set his hat on the low stone wall beside him.

I stood there paralyzed, absolutely beguiled by the sight of him.

He obviously hadn't heard me, but I didn't know what to do. What if he opened his eyes to see me walking away? For I knew I needed to leave. It wouldn't be wise to see him; or for him to see me.

Especially alone.

I'd been holding my breath for several moments when he sat up—perhaps having concluded his prayer or period of meditation—and opened his eyes.

He caught me staring.

"You're back," I offered awkwardly.

Dexter stood slowly and tucked his hands in the pockets of his trousers. "How long have you been standing there?" he asked with a quizzical smile.

"I don't know. A few minutes, maybe. I didn't want to disrupt— Were you praying?"

"Something like that." He started toward me. "Do you come here often?"

"Roxy and I have been a few times over the past week. I wanted to see the sunrise this morning, so I just...decided to come."

"I'm glad you did."

"You are?"

"It's good to get out from under the watchful eyes of Blakeley House once in a while. Don't you agree?" Dexter removed his hands from his pockets and walked back toward the spring, examining the large tree near the basin. "And, in case you weren't aware of it, you're an immense pleasure to be around, Elle Stoneburner."

I swallowed the lump in my throat. "Um...thank you. It's...or I should say.... I like spending time with you, too."

"Roxy must have really taken to you to have brought you to her favorite place." Dexter walked toward the thicket of bushes and pine trees at the end of the trail by the edge of the lake.

"I was actually looking for the spring the night you found me on the road—the first time. The night Dr. Crawford brought Greenlee to Blakeley House."

"Really?" He faced me, clearly surprised. "You knew about it back then?"

"I must have heard someone at Everston mention it." I hated myself for layering lies upon lies. How long until he learned the depth of my deception? Likely soon, when Father came. When he insisted on taking me home.

I didn't want to go.

"I wasn't aware that anyone at Everston knew about it. Roxy used to come here often with a childhood friend of hers. Or sometimes I would join her."

He turned away from the trees and again came closer to where I stood next to a large boulder. "It's why I chose to build Blakeley House where I did—so she could come here whenever she wanted, when she felt well enough. That's the reason— That's one of the reasons I asked you to stay…to see if you could get her to come out more. And Greenlee, of course. She needs company, too."

"I'm trying my best."

"I'm sure you're doing a wonderful job. Roxy asked you to join her for her Thursday evening ritual…." He sent me a wry smile.

"Yes, that was lovely of her."

"I just hope you know that you're a welcome addition to Blakeley House, no matter what my mother may say or feel."

I didn't know how to answer, except to tell the truth—my name—which was suddenly resounding in my ears.

I hated lying to him. But if I told him the truth, would it put an end whatever was developing between us? I vividly remembered what he'd said, and the tone he'd used, in reference to me when Mrs. Granton had mentioned the Everstone family during that ride in the stagecoach. He believed Estella Everstone to be a spoiled brat. Whatever it was that had formed between us in the last weeks, in spite of my initial reluctance, wasn't something I wanted to let slip away quite yet.

His smile returned. "I came upon Roxy soon after finding you that night, running around the house with wet feet. Do you know what she was up to? She wouldn't tell me."

"She went downstairs to get something." I yearned to tell him the truth—all of the truth, every single time he asked it of me. Yet something in me wouldn't let it out.

I thought back to the first night I'd met him, when he'd been such a dark mystery sitting across from me in the stagecoach. Reaching Everston, and seeing it for the first time in years, I'd felt that I was finally home. But perhaps those feelings had stemmed from another source.

Whenever I found myself near to Dexter Blakeley, I felt more at home than anywhere else I'd ever been; and I wanted to keep that feeling intact for as long as I possibly could, even if its destruction was inevitable.

And it was. As soon as he knew the truth, everything would change. And I dreaded that.

My gaze was arrested by the sight of the roof and stone chimneys of Blakeley House above the tops of the distant pine trees. "Blakeley House is rather new, isn't it? Even though its style resembles an English manor house?"

He nodded. "I had it built as soon as I bought Everston, primarily for Roxy and Mother, and modeled it after my mother's family estate in Kent." He combed his fingers through his hair, making a mess of the dark, thick strands, as he turned in the direction of the house. "Roxy lived in a sanatorium while Mother and I were residing at Bailey Hill on Nahant Island."

"She told me that."

He swiveled abruptly to face me again, his eyes wide. "Really? She told you about the sanatorium?"

I knew it was my perfect opportunity to tell him just why Roxy had felt comfortable telling me such a thing—that I was her old friend Estella, and that she'd figured it out the first night I came to Blakeley House and she'd stolen my self-portrait.

"Because, because...." I made a point to look at him, willing myself to say the words. His shock seemed to be abating, replaced by a mixture of passion and fascination in his eyes—a mixture I definitely didn't want to see disappear.

Feeling restless over of the web of lies I kept piling up, I dashed over to the spring and stepped onto the stone reservoir, circled around the ledge, and took a small leap over the part that slanted down toward the lake. Hardly any water burbled from the spring; it was little more than a trickle.

"Roxy used to do that same thing."

I stumbled at his words.

"Don't fall." He reached for my hand and pressed his warm palm to mine. And he wouldn't let go.

If I told him the truth, the satisfied look on his face would morph into the frown of disdain I remembered from our first conversation, when my name had been mentioned—and a few other times since.

"I can't imagine balancing on those uneven stones in those heeled boots."

"If it weren't so cold, I would take them off." I had done so many times as a child.

Dexter released my hand and bent to pick up a fallen birch branch from the ground. I thought he would offer it to me as a walking stick, but he instead used it to catch the hem of my dress, pinning it to my leg just above my boot. "Would you now? Don't you think I've already seen enough of your—"

"Yes, well, I'm truly sorry you had to witness that horrifyingly embarrassing scene."

"It's quite all right." He cleared his throat, as if he wanted to say something more; but he remained silent as he lifted the branch higher, grazing the material of my skirt at my knees. He looked as if he was trying not to grin, but he failed quite miserably. "I just might forgive you."

I couldn't help but delight in this playful side of him. Wanting to reciprocate, I reached down to grab the stick, yanking it out of his grasp. "Thank you. This is just what I needed." I used it as a cane for balance as I continued making my way around the stone circle.

"I don't think that's all you need." He watched me closely as he said this, and I wasn't sure what he meant; but I was pretty sure it had absolutely nothing to do with the birch branch.

I started to make a second round along the edge of the well, but he sat down, blocking my path. I stood there beside him, his shoulders level with my thighs.

He tugged gently on the lavender material of my skirt. "Come, sit with me."

"No, that's alright...I'll stand. I'm not...I don't want to soil Roxy's dress." I pivoted on my heel and walked away from him, hardly able to breathe at the tantalizing thoughts racing through my mind. They had nothing to do with telling the truth, and everything to do with maintaining the persona of Elle Stoneburner forever, especially if it might mean someday feeling Dexter Blakeley's arms around me again.

Reaching the stone wall that was built against the hill, I closed my eyes, pressed my palms to the stones, and let out a deep sigh. I wasn't sure how safe it would be to sit next to Dexter on the ledge. What might he do?

And what if it was everything I so selfishly wanted him to do?

Oh, my heavens! Why was I even thinking of kissing Dexter Blakeley?

After staring at the wall for a while—basically ignoring him—I slowly turned around. Dexter sat with his back to me, and I took the opportunity to try to discern what it was, exactly, that drew me to him.

Was it his preaching? His heartfelt offer of friendship?

No, there had been something before that—before I'd learned he owned Everston. In those weeks between meeting him and coming to stay at Blakeley House, I'd become enamored of him and his blunt, straightforward ways. He presented his true self to everyone; and although I hadn't been under the impression he liked me all that much back then, perhaps that was because he hadn't wanted to.

He hadn't been exactly forthcoming about his relationship to the hotel; but, in that regard, his actions were the opposite of what one would have expected. Why hadn't he corrected Mrs. Granton? Because he was humble. Sometimes brusque yet always unpretentious, he didn't care what anyone thought of him. He wasn't concerned with impressing anybody. He was just Dexter Blakeley.

I noticed that he had taken up another thin branch he was using to trace lines in the path with. Then he turned around and caught me staring. "Are you enjoying yourself?"

"Would you like to join me up here?" I wanted to take back the words as soon as they were out. They were too encouraging. Too forward.

"All right, if that's how things are going to be...."

He stood, stepped up on the ledge, and came to stand before me, captivating me with his every move. Had we really known each other only six weeks? I felt as if I'd always known Dexter Blakeley—or at least, that I'd always been missing him.

"Well, here I am."

My mouth went dry, and my heart thudded in my ears. "Yes." I dropped the birch branch quite unintentionally.

He propped his right hand against the stone wall beside us. "You know, I've never done this before."

I sucked in a breath. "It is rather silly, isn't it?"

"No, that's...not it."

"Perhaps, then...you think it's too dangerous?"

"Something more along those lines, yes." Dexter took a step closer, his eyes entrancing me. "You *are* dangerous. Actually, you terrify me."

He was all seriousness, and for the first time, I allowed myself to imagine that we could, somehow, be together—even once he learned my identity.

The dream I'd had on the porch my second night at Blakeley House returned to me unexpectedly, and with vivid detail. It had confused me at the time, why I had chosen Dexter Blakeley. But now, it made perfect sense.

More sense than anything else had in a long time.

But what, exactly, did he want from me? Based on everything I'd heard from Mrs. Granton and Roxy, he wasn't the kind of man who went around casually capturing the hearts of young ladies, as he seemed to be doing with mine.

I took a step back but kept my eyes locked with his. Just then the heel of my right boot missed the ledge, and I lost my balance, teetering violently. He wrapped his left arm around my waist to steady me.

"Miss Stoneburner," he whispered. It was almost a question.

Was there an answer to what he'd just said, beyond the fact that he terrified me, too? That being near him felt both safe and incredibly dangerous at the same time?

It was dangerous, what I'd allowed to develop between us—this pretense that I wanted to keep. But I didn't want to stop it. Even so, I knew, deep down, that if it was to continue in the way it was now headed, I would need to tell him the truth...and soon.

I reminded myself that he did know me—the real me. As character and personality went, I'd been real with him all along; in fact, being with him felt, in many ways, more like living the truth than a lie.

The only thing he didn't know was my name.

Dexter leaned in just a bit, and I could tell his intent from the palpable passion in his gorgeous eyes. I knew he would kiss me if I let him.

And I suspected that was what he'd been referring to when he'd said he'd never done this before. The thought thrilled me, entranced me—that he'd lived his whole life without kissing anyone, and now he wanted to kiss me.

But I couldn't let him. Not without first telling him the truth. He might not want to kiss Estella Everstone. In fact, he almost certainly wouldn't. And so I stepped aside.

As politely as any gentleman, Dexter released my waist and let me go.

"How long does Greenlee plan to stay at Blakeley House?" I asked quietly, hoping that my avoidance of his unspoken question and the near kiss was one step in the direction of telling him the truth.

Dexter cleared his throat and swallowed hard. He seemed a little agitated that I'd changed the subject, but I could tell he didn't necessarily fault me for doing so. "Crawford is headed on to Boston from Westward this week to meet with the board from the Boston Inland Mission Society. He plans to marry Greenlee and take her west by the end of the month."

He might as well have ripped out my heart with such unexpected news, though he never could have guessed that it would wound me so. I jumped down from the spring and started for the gravel path leading to the house, not wanting Dexter to see the tears brimming in my eyes.

They were odd, the feelings that raced through me. I didn't love Jay, I didn't want to go west with him, and I certainly didn't want to marry him! But it hurt that he would let me go, then so easily pick some girl out of a brothel to fall in love with.

Though it seemed I was running away from Dexter, I didn't care. I just wanted to retreat to my bedchamber, where I could effectively sort through the conflicting emotions, thoughts, and heartaches that flooded through me—especially the question of why it was that Jay still had such power to hurt me.

Before I made it far, Dexter was beside me. He grasped my arm at the elbow and rotated me to face him. He stood so close, I could see the intermingled hues of browns and greens in his eyes as they reflected the light from the sun rising across the lake.

His eyes—they always seemed to say so much. Sometimes too much. At that moment, they revealed intense longing, mixed with apprehension—and a hint of jealousy that caused my heart to jolt against my chest.

"I thought you said Crawford had nothing to do with—"

"Believe me, Mr. Blakeley, he doesn't," I answered calmly. After blinking away my tears, I lifted my face to his. "I promise."

"I want to believe you, but I also want you to tell me what's wrong." He still held me by the arm. Not that I minded.

I wanted to bury my face in his chest and confess to him everything that was wrong in my life, just as he'd asked me to. But I couldn't do that—not without telling him who I was.

"I can't tell you everything. I don't understand it all, myself." There was at least some truth to that, albeit not enough to give me peace of mind. "It's just…it's just that Greenlee will have the future that I…a similar future to the one I always thought, or at least I used to think, I'd have."

Dexter's lips parted for the briefest of moments before he pressed them together in a frown. "You mean, how you wanted to marry that missionary who wouldn't have you?"

"Yes."

"Anyone can be mission-minded, Elle. One need not travel to far-off lands to reach the lost. Plenty of lost souls come to Everston every summer, and I do my best to share with them the Word of God and the message of salvation, along with the rest and relaxation they are seeking. The types of people who frequent the hotel—spoiled young ladies, dissipated young gentlemen—are in particular need of hearing the truth, and my hope is that it will make a difference in the way they live their lives." He looked down at me, straight into my eyes.

If only I wasn't from the class of people he had just described.

"And then, there's what Crawford and I do in Westward. Greenlee's just one of the girls he's been able to rescue."

"That's what it's all about, isn't it?" I blurted out. "He chose Greenlee on purpose, didn't he? But why would he?" I hoped Dexter hadn't noticed my voice cracking, for I didn't want him realizing that it mattered to me. It wouldn't make any sense to him.

Dexter shook his head. "During Crawford's visits last spring, when Greenlee was ill, he ministered to her, and she was able to put her trust in Christ again—"

"Even while being kept by Ezra Hawthorne?" What strength of character she must have to trust God in the midst of one of the worst situations I could imagine.

"She has an evident heart for the Lord now, Elle, despite what she's been through. Ezra is the one who beat her when he found out she was with child."

My hand flew to my mouth. "Is she still—"

"No."

I couldn't get over how that single piece of information completely transformed my view of Greenlee.

"Hearing of the beating she'd taken—that was the last straw for Crawford. He'd been praying for months for a way to rescue her—"

"He's really in love with her, isn't he?"

"It does seem to be something that grows out of the most peculiar places." The look in his eyes held me captive, and suddenly there wasn't a single thought in my head that didn't have to do with Dexter Blakeley…and for the future I hoped for with him.

"They do seem well-suited for each other," I admitted slowly, studying the gnarly tree roots protruding from the ground between our feet. "And you're right in saying that one can do mission work anywhere. Take yourself, for example—the owner of a high-class mountain resort, and you're more mission-minded than almost anyone else I've met. I've never known anyone who displayed as many Christlike characteristics as you. You're so...."

Quickly realizing I'd already disclosed too many of my feelings, I stalked away through the trees toward the house.

Dexter silently took my hand in his, intertwining our fingers.

I inhaled a deep breath, relishing his familiar touch.

He led me toward the house, keeping beneath the canopy of trees, likely so that his mother wouldn't be able to see us. "Is that what's bothering you, Elle? Something to do with your...growing regard for me?"

I sighed. "You're too— You don't know me, who I really am. I can't...."

"You don't think I *really* know you?" He stepped closer, drawing me against his chest, and wrapped his arms around my shoulders. "You're wrong. I do know you." He breathed the words into my hair. "Elle, you're kind and sensitive...and beautiful, inside and out. And I have an idea you feel you're all alone in the world. But you don't need to be. You don't have to feel like that anymore."

I relaxed against him, pressing my cheek to his chest. I wished I could stay there forever. His arms, strong and comfortable around me, felt just as I remembered them.

He cared so much for others. And he cared especially for me; I knew that now.

With his left hand, he playfully fingered the fine hairs at the nape of my neck, until the tingles rushing down my spine made me tremble.

Hesitantly, I wrapped my arms around his waist, giving into him. "Dexter...."

"Dexter?" At precisely the same moment, we heard his mother's summons; it sounded as if she were standing on the balcony that faced the lake—or perhaps on the porch, in which case she was apt to come around the corner of the house and spy us together. "Dexter, are you out here? Are you with that girl? Do come in!"

I wrenched free from his embrace and started across the lawn, lest she see us.

SEVENTEEN

The Engagement

"My heart is set,
as firmly as ever heart of man was set on woman."
—Charles Dickens, *Oliver Twist*

Dexter took both breakfast and dinner at home every day of the following week, and in the evenings, he stayed to visit with his mother, his sister, and me until it was time to retire. I did my best to appear unmoved by his attention; but, as I coveted it, that proved rather difficult. It wasn't that he sat close beside me and gazed into my eyes all evening. I wouldn't have been able to handle that. I was barely able to handle his ardent glances at small intervals from across the room.

On the seventh day, he didn't come for breakfast.

Late that afternoon, missing him more than I would have thought possible, I sat in the parlor with Roxy, embroidering a pillow with ribbons—something she'd insisted I attempt, since she enjoyed it so much. Around four o'clock, we heard Mr. McGuire yell a happy welcome down the gravel drive.

Jay was back from Boston.

No sooner had I heard the shout of his name than I heard footsteps race down the main staircase. Dressed in one of Roxy's gowns, Greenlee made a beeline for the window beside the front door. She held back the curtains with one hand and her long light brown braid with the other, drinking in the sight of Jay as he approached.

Roxy and I joined her at the window, but I stayed back a bit. I didn't need Jay thinking I'd been watching for his return. Because I most certainly hadn't been.

Over Greenlee's shoulder, I could see that Jay still sat upon his horse, looking as handsome as ever. When he noticed Greenlee in the window, his face lit up.

He dismounted and spoke to Mr. McGuire for a minute before they both headed for the house. It was nearly dinnertime, and I wondered if Dexter would finally come home for the meal. At dinner the previous evening, he'd said nothing about Jay's imminent return. I wished I'd had some advanced warning, though I wasn't sure how a foreknowledge of his coming would have mitigated the inevitable awkwardness of the next several minutes.

Jay stepped into the front parlor, where Mrs. McGuire took his hat and coat.

"You remember Miss Stoneburner, I guess?" the servant asked.

Jay frowned as his dark eyes caught mine. It was clear he didn't approve of my presence at Blakeley House. The last he knew, I was staying at Everston as Mrs. Granton's companion.

Jay took my hand just long enough for a proper welcome. "Yes, I recall meeting."

"Dexter hired Elle as our companion shortly after you left," Roxy added.

He didn't respond to this comment but beamed at Greenlee as he took her hand in his, wrapped it around his arm, and led her into the parlor.

I followed them, suddenly feeling out of place when Roxy went to join Mrs. McGuire in the kitchen. But I sat down in my favorite chair in the corner facing the window that offered a spectacular view of Half Moon Lake, and returned to my embroidering.

I kept my eyes averted to either my stitching or on the window to allow the lovers some measure of privacy. How I longed to sketch the arresting view outside. I'd grown accustomed to always having my sketchbook with me, and since it had been stolen, I'd felt the lack of it quite profoundly. Lately, whenever I felt this lack, I also thought of my old sketchbook and pencils missing from the trunk in the attic. I wished I'd found them before Mr. Blakeley had collected them—even if he'd done so with the intention of giving them to me, as I presumed.

What other reason could he have had for taking them? And why the delay in giving them to me?

Was it because he'd sought to kiss me, and I hadn't let him?

Turning my gaze from the window, I peeked at Jay. He looked positively enamored by Greenlee's stunning, rare beige eyes. He was being extremely pleasant with her—much more pleasant than he'd been with me in the past few years—and Greenlee absolutely glowed in his presence. Doing my best to focus on the embroidery project in my lap, I still found I couldn't stop watching them, no matter that it produced an odd sort of turmoil inside.

I stuffed the pillow down into the cushions beside me. How could he just sit there and pretend I didn't exist? Or had he been doing that for so many years that he no longer needed to pretend?

I had an urge to leave the house and take a long walk...to go find Dexter.

But I couldn't leave. It was my duty, as companion to Greenlee, to chaperone her time spent with Jay. What if he kissed her?

He'd kissed me so many times and told me he loved me, only to take it all back. I found myself wondering if he'd kissed me so often simply because I'd let him.

Taking up the pillow again, I resumed my embroidery but soon stopped at the sound of hoofbeats out front. I lifted my eyes from the ribbons in my hand, but as my gaze traveled toward the window, it was arrested at the sight of a small white envelope in Jay's hand. He whispered something in Greenlee's ear as he pointed to it.

In the next moment, Mrs. McGuire opened the front door and took Dexter's hat as she greeted him. Seconds later, he entered the parlor with long, purposeful strides. Stopping in the middle of the room, he raked his fingers through his hair and sent me a spirited glance before turning to Jay and Greenlee on the sofa. "Crawford, I heard you were back…and just in time for dinner, if you can stay awhile."

Jay accepted the invitation as Dexter took a seat in the chair next to mine and lounged back with an easy smile.

Sensing his closeness, I let out the breath I'd been holding without realizing it. I stole a peek at him and felt my shoulders relax. But they tensed just as quickly as I recalled the last time I'd been in his arms. The air in my lungs felt trapped. And all this from merely having the man sit near me.

I was about to go back to my stitching when Jay cleared his throat. "Now that you're here, Blakeley, I have an announcement I'd like to make." He scooted a little closer to Greenlee and took her hand in his, causing her cheeks to flame bright pink. "I corresponded with Miss Cole while I was away, as you know, and she's agreed to marry me."

My hands faltered, resulting in a painful prick of the embroidery needle. The news was not unexpected, so why did I feel such an overwhelming sense of shock?

Dexter didn't seem fazed at all. He stood and offered Jay a brief handshake. "Let me be the first to offer you both my hearty congratulations. We must celebrate this happy news."

A moment later, Roxy entered the room. "What's all the excitement about?" Her smile told me she already knew.

Jay wrapped his arm about Greenlee's shoulders. "We are engaged to be married."

"Oh, how romantic!" She took Greenlee's hands in hers. "I'm so happy for you. Hannah has been cooking up quite a storm for our celebration dinner."

"Yes, there are a few Norwegian dishes my family always prepares in honor of an engagement, and I wanted to be sure to observe the tradition, even though my family is gone."

Roxy brought her hand to her chest. "It's such a lovely thing to do!"

Fortunately, Roxy and her overzealous felicitations gave me a chance to collect myself. I also hoped they would compensate for my utter failure to congratulate the happy couple.

"When are you to be wed?" I asked.

"As soon as Reverend Whitespire can make it, I suppose," Jay replied. "What do you think, Greenlee?"

"Yes, as soon as possible," she agreed.

"And I guess you'll be off to Washington soon after?" Dexter asked.

"Right away," Jay affirmed.

"Excuse me, but I'd like to check on the meal preparations," Greenlee said as she stood.

"I've been watching Hannah closely, and I think you'll be pleased," Roxy assured her, following her out of the room and down the hall that led to the kitchen.

After raising his eyebrows at Jay and me, Dexter went after them, apparently curious to know what kinds of Norwegian dishes would be on the dinner menu.

Jay stood and faced me. "What happened to your employment with Mrs. Granton?"

"The plan changed. I'm employed by Mr. Blakeley now, and—"

"Estella, you need to go home, where you belong."

He pivoted on his heel and headed for the kitchen, leaving me with his awful pronouncement ringing in my ears.

But then, I pictured Dexter striding into the parlor, smiling at me as he nervously raked his fingers though his hair.

Who was Jay to tell me where I belonged? He hardly knew me anymore.

But Dexter Blakeley knew me, and far better than Jay ever had—even if by the wrong name.

EIGHTEEN

The Sketchbook

"I may have lost my heart, but not my self-control."
—Jane Austen, *Emma*

Needing to escape the house and everyone in it, I walked out the front door and circled around to the side yard. It was nearly suppertime, I knew; but Mrs. McGuire would ring the dinner bell in plenty of time for me to make my way back. For October, the day was unseasonably warm, and it felt good to be outside. By the barn, Mr. McGuire was still busy brushing down Knightley. He waved to me, and I returned the gesture.

As I took a seat upon a grassy knoll, Dexter Blakeley came to mind. The memory of my chance meeting with him at the spring taunted me. How relaxed he'd been, and how playful, too. I could scarcely believe he'd almost kissed me.

If he tried again, would I allow it?

The answer was a resounding *yes*.

I sighed at the muddle I'd made of my life.

I should have come right out with the truth the last time he'd mentioned Jay. I should have told him then and there that he had no reason to be jealous—that I wouldn't have Jayson Crawford Castleman, even if he got down on his knees and begged for my heart.

That thought had me envisioning Dexter in that very position. Were that to become a reality, I was quite sure I wouldn't have the strength to resist.

I stretched out on my back and placed my hands behind my head as a pillow, choosing not to worry what such a position would do to my hair. I closed my eyes and focused on the feel of the refreshing autumn breeze as it traveled over my face, as it wisped my hair about. I listened for the noises of nature—the wind in the trees, the crows cawing in the distance.

After a while, a group of geese flew overhead, honking loudly and when I opened my eyes to see what the fuss was about I found Dexter Blakeley sitting mere inches beside me; his arms rested upon his knees, his gaze on the sky.

I sat up quickly as he turned his attention to me, though I had a feeling he'd averted his gaze only seconds ago, so I wouldn't know he'd been watching me as I lay there.

"May I call you Elle?" he asked abruptly. Somehow, the way he would blurt out such things had become rather endearing, especially when he had that little-boy smirk on his face and that strange resolve lighting his eyes.

"What are you doing out here?" I asked, brushing twigs and grass from the skirt of my dusty rose dress. Roxy's dress, rather.

"Sitting with you."

Dexter *was* sitting with me. On the grass, wearing his fine-tailored trousers from Boston. He'd taken off his jacket and wore only shirtsleeves and a waistcoat on his top half.

"Where's Wulfric?"

"In the barn. I told him to stay there when I arrived."

"He's a very obedient dog."

After a long, awkward silence, he blurted out, "Elle…? You never answered my question—may I call you that?"

I couldn't help but smile at his abruptness. "Of course. I suppose you can call me whatever you'd like to."

"I'd like that. To call you by your name, that is. If you don't mind. I feel as if we've moved past the need to observe the formalities of strangers or mere acquaintances. What do you think... Elle?"

No matter how I relished the sound of the name on his lips, deep down, I knew hearing him say "Estella" would be infinitely better. If only I could be guaranteed that he would speak that name with equal fervor.

"I agree." I didn't know what else to say. My heart pounded and I wanted to wrap my arms around his neck, pull him to the ground, and whisper his name a thousand times into his ear. To redirect my wayward thoughts, I asked, "How are the special dinner preparations coming along?"

Dexter ducked his head almost bashfully. "Dinner's taking a little longer than planned. It's my understanding that Roxy attempted to help...." His eyes met mine again, and he grinned. "But we'll eventually have the celebration Jay and Greenlee deserve."

"You're a true friend, Mr. Blakeley."

"Will you call me Dexter?"

"I will, I promise."

We sat there in silence for a moment, until he reached behind his back and produced a package wrapped in brown paper and string. He scooted it across the dried grass between us. "I brought you something."

I lifted my gaze from the package to him.

"Because I know what you'd rather be doing out here." Now he was beaming.

I knew what was inside, and the ceremonious presentation he'd chosen sent a strange tremor through me. My hands shook as I untied the string and unwrapped the paper.

Sure enough, it contained my old sketchbook—the one I hadn't seen in thirteen years. And my child-sized case of colored pencils. I almost cried at the sight of them.

"The sketchbook is used, but more than half the pages are blank. And the pencils are old but their quality undiminished. They belonged to Bram Everstone's youngest daughter, left at Everston over a decade ago. They were left at Everston, forgotten."

I opened the sketchbook to the first page, eager to recall what I'd sketched that summer.

The first drawing was of Everston, viewed from the front lawn. How my style had improved in the years since then! And thankfully so, or Dexter might have realized that the artist was the same. This sketch looked nothing like the one I'd done of Everston only weeks before.

"Quaint, isn't it? I'm sure she eventually developed her craft to match even yours, though I must concede she was quite talented for her age." He reached over and turned the page. "Take this one, for instance. This sketch of her older sister is remarkably close to how I remember Natalia Everstone looking."

I'd always wished I looked more like twins Natalia and Nathan, with their blonde hair and green eyes. Instead, I resembled Will and Vance with my thick chestnut hair and dark eyes.

"Did you find her attractive?" I asked.

"Everyone who knew Natalia Everstone thought she was beautiful. She seemed like a very genuine person, at the time."

"Did you know her as well as you knew her brothers?"

He averted his gaze, looking at the grass, the trees, the lake—at everything but the portrait. "Yes." His tone was suddenly harsh.

I flipped to the next page, frightened by the questions skipping around in my head. Had Dexter felt something for Natalia that summer?

The next drawing was a portrait I'd drawn of eight-year-old Roxy...and Dexter.

How could I have forgotten a near-twenty, strikingly handsome Dexter Blakeley posing for me with his little sister?

"Roxy was always so exuberant as a child," Dexter said wistfully. "You can see it in that drawing, the fire in her eyes. It's gone now, for the most part; though your presence seems to have rekindled it somewhat."

I decided not to comment on his observation, or to question why he said nothing of his own presence in the picture.

I went on to the next drawing, which was of Mr. Collins, the young man Natalia had spent time with that summer. I was surprised I even remembered his name, as I'd hardly associated with him.

As I studied the picture, I remembered being quite positive that Natalia had fallen in love with Mr. Collins and would marry him. But something happened, and we never saw or heard of him again after that summer. And then Natalia had married someone else a year later, soon after Mother's death.

Which seemed odd, even now. Who got married while still mourning her mother?

"Why don't you draw something?" Dexter nudged my shoulder with his, then picked up the box of pencils and handed it to me.

"What should I draw? You?" I'd meant it to sound like a tease, but too much of my heart had come out in my voice.

"You can if you want. You drew me once already...remarkably well, I might add, for not having me there to sit for you." He observed me quite openly, and I couldn't look away. "I certainly don't know why you chose to, though."

I could feel a blush stain my cheeks. "I wanted to draw you ever since meeting you. You have such a striking face, such extraordinary eyes."

Dexter lowered his head, his bewitching hazel gaze now focused on the ground before him. Had I embarrassed him? Pleased him?

I popped the lid off the pencil case and selected the graphite pencil, which I'd always preferred for making initial sketches.

Dexter reached over and picked out the green pencil, then playfully held it over the bridge of his nose. "Is it a perfect match?"

"Yes," I sighed as my eyes locked with his. Not that I needed to check their color. I knew it very well.

And that he was the perfect match for me.

I couldn't think of anything I would enjoy more than having him sit for me, so I would have an excuse to stare at him for hours on end.

Well, almost anything. I still had the raging desire to wrap my arms around him and kiss him—a desire I continually fought against.

He tapped me on the nose with the blunt end of the pencil before letting it land in the grass between us. "You're very charming, Elle Stoneburner. Do you know that?"

My cheeks blazing now, I dropped my gaze to the sketchbook in my lap and took up the graphite pencil, intent on beginning my sketch of him.

At the same time, he leaned over, supported by his left hand on the ground near my back, and lifted his right hand to my left temple. He plucked a twig out of my hair, then grazed my jaw with his fingertips, moving toward my ear to caress the strands tucked behind it.

I held my breath, too mesmerized to do anything but lift my eyes again and study him...as he studied me.

I couldn't speak or move. It felt as if he'd wound a cord about my heart, somehow linking us permanently. I knew this because with every breath I breathed in his presence, the cord shortened. Every time he looked at me, it grew taut. And every time he spoke in that deep baritone, it sent a tangible reverberation through me. He loved like no one I'd ever met.

And I desperately wanted him to love me.

"Elle." He combed his fingers through my hair, and I closed my eyes and leaned in. He was everything safe and courageous and true.

And he was interested in me. At least, me as Elle Stoneburner.

But, again, I hadn't acted outside the bounds of my character or behaved in any way that was not true to myself. In fact, I'd never known myself to the depths that I'd discovered while at Everston and then Blakeley House. And it was due partly to Dexter—his uncanny ability to perceive my heart with only a few well-placed questions and astute observations. He seemed to have known me—everything I should be, could be—before I knew it myself.

Dexter's fingers inched down to the edging of my ribbed white collar and came to rest at the base of my neck. But he didn't kiss me.

"Mr. Blakeley," I sighed.

"It's Dexter, remember?"

I opened my eyes and sucked in my breath. "Oh, yes...."

And I remembered then who I was. Estella—not Elle—falling completely in love with Dexter Blakeley.

How could that be? How would that ever work? It wouldn't. Dexter wasn't falling for me; he was falling for poor Elle Stoneburner, who had no family, nor a penny to her name.

And when he knew the truth, the affection in his eyes would fade. He wouldn't dare touch me as he was now doing. He might not even speak to me at all.

"You will remember to use it next time? You promised."

"Yes, I did promise. I will." I swallowed past the lump in my throat as his right hand glided from my neck to my collarbone.

"I've never met anyone like you."

"Surely, you have."

His hand lingered at my shoulder a moment before sliding down my arm. "I don't think so," he whispered. "Because no one else has ever—"

The dinner bell clanged from the side porch, and I blinked. What was I doing?

As the clanging continued, I returned the pencils to their case, clicked it shut, and closed the sketchbook, regretting that I hadn't made as much as one stroke of his gorgeous likeness.

"Dinner's ready!" yelled Mrs. McGuire, giving the bell a break.

I stood at the same moment Dexter did, disregarding the hand he offered. "Thank you for the sketchbook and pencils. You have no idea how much it means to me that—that they're mine."

The clanging of the bell resumed, and I hastened through the trees, down the hill, and across the yard, clutching my long-lost sketchbook and pencils to my chest. With my free hand, I smoothed my hair—what a mess I must have looked!

Once I reached the porch steps, I swiveled around to wait for Dexter, ready to apologize for running as I had.

But Dexter wasn't there. All I could see was the dim, gray haze overtaking the yard as the sun made its descent behind Iron Mountain.

I climbed the porch steps, fighting the urge to call his name, to search for him, to propel myself into his arms. To ask him to keep me there—in his arms and at Everston—forever.

His, forever. But as Estella Everstone.

The question of our future together could be decided only after he knew who I was. I couldn't spend the rest of my life as Elle Stoneburner.

I somehow needed to make him realize that, whatever name I went by, the "me" he knew was the real me. Not the frivolous ninny I'd been for years.

For as long as I could remember, I'd always had more than I could have asked for. More gowns, more jewelry, and more money than I knew what to do with. And now, stripped of all those things, what was left? A woman dressed in borrowed clothing, with nothing to call her own but an old sketchbook and a case of pencils.

At Blakeley House, I had nothing. And I had never felt more content.

NINETEEN

Iron Mountain

"I hope that real love and truth are stronger in the end than any
evil or misfortune in the world."
—Charles Dickens, *David Copperfield*

After dinner that evening, Dexter didn't return to the
house for a few days. And when he did finally come back,
he quickly shut himself into his study with his mother and Mr. and
Mrs. McGuire for their weekly household meeting. I was almost
positive that this week's discussion had something to do with me.

Greenlee had never needed me, and she certainly wouldn't
require my services once she married Jay. They were scheduled to
be wed as soon as the pastor of the small church in Laurelton could
make it to Everston, likely sometime in the next week.

Until then, ironically, she needed me as her chaperone. In the
afternoons, when Jay would visit, I sat with my sketchbook in my
favorite corner of the parlor, Wulfric lying at my feet.

Honestly, I couldn't wait for the moment when they would
no longer require my company. The sooner they were married, the
sooner I could stop pretending not to notice their smiles and whis-
pers from across the room.

Now that my old sketchbook and colored pencils had been
returned to me, they were my constant companions. I wondered

if they would ever tire of the subject matter I seemed stuck on: Dexter's likeness.

"Elle, what would you think about taking a ride to Iron Mountain with us?" Greenlee asked me one afternoon. "Jay says there's an incredible view of the lake, but I can't go with him unless accompanied by someone else."

"Oh, I don't know," I stalled. "I'm not terribly fond of riding. Perhaps, once his meeting is through, Mr. Blakeley could...?"

The pocket doors across the hall opened, and I saw Mr. McGuire exit the study.

Wulfric left me, clearly eager to reunite with his master.

Dexter squeezed through the doorway between Mrs. McGuire and his mother, as if he couldn't get away fast enough. He looked mentally spent. "Not now, Mother. We can speak on that subject another time."

"And just when will that be?" Beatrix followed him into the hall, her arms crossed over her narrow chest. "You're never here, except to see—"

"That isn't true."

I saw his eyes flit briefly to me, and I quickly dropped my gaze to my sketch.

"It needs to be addressed. You know what you've allowed to happen is foolishness. You would do well to remember your brother. Your father."

"Yes, Mother, I know."

Forcing myself not to watch him leave, I listened to his steps as he moved down the hall toward the front door.

"Now, if you'll excuse me, Mother, I need to—"

"Oh, Mr. Blakeley—please, wait!" To my horror, Greenlee vaulted off the sofa and scurried to the hall.

"Miss Cole?" Dexter stepped into the doorway from the hall to the parlor.

Jay went to stand beside his fiancée, while I slouched lower in my chair. I suddenly had a fairly good idea what she was about to ask of him.

"Would you accompany Elle, Jay, and myself on a ride to the top of Iron Mountain? Elle doesn't feel capable of making the journey without you."

That was most certainly not what I'd said or implied, but I couldn't help wondering what his answer would be—even as I remained slouched in my chair, my back pressed against the cushions.

"It would be my pleasure, if that is indeed what Miss Stoneburner desires."

"It is," Greenlee answered for me.

I could almost feel Dexter's gaze, though his view of me was obstructed somewhat by the chair.

After a moment, he asked, "Is it, Elle?"

I swallowed past my discomfort, leaned over the arm of the chair, and quietly uttered, "Yes."

"Virgil?" Dexter called down the hall to Mr. McGuire. "Would you go ready Knightley and Pip, please?"

Riding was far from my favorite thing to do, especially on steep bridle trails. But I would have agreed to just about anything if it would mean spending time with Dexter.

And time spent with Dexter would be a chance to tell him my real name.

I stood, leaving my sketchbook and pencils on the side table.

Dexter hardly looked at me as we followed Jay and Greenlee out the front door and to the barn, where Mr. McGuire was fastening a sidesaddle to the second of the two horses.

Once Greenlee and I were situated in the saddles, we started the journey, Jay and Dexter leading our mounts by the reins. Wulfric pranced happily alongside us. The trail started off level, but as we moved deeper into the woods, we reached the intersection of the steep bridle trail and the steeper still "Indian" foot trail at the base of the mountain. I studied Jay from behind as he led Pip along the trail, about twenty feet ahead of us. His kindness toward Greenlee was still so odd for me to behold.

When had he ever treated me so tenderly? For all those years I'd believed I was in love with him, I couldn't think of a single instance in which he'd put my feelings before his own.

"Elle?" Dexter's voice broke through my mental meanderings. "You seem preoccupied."

He would eventually learn everything—who I was, why I was there. I needed to tell him the truth. Now.

"I need to tell you something that might surprise you. A few things, actually."

After a few heart-thudding moments of silence, he finally said, "Go on."

"Dr. Crawford…I imagine you know that his real name is Jayson Crawford Castleman, since you seem to be close friends. You met while attending Dartmouth, no?"

"We did." He eyed me warily. "And how do you know him so well?"

"Jay is an old acquaintance of my family." I squared my shoulders and sat straighter in the saddle. "And, if you'll remember, I mentioned that I was once engaged to be married."

"Yes, I remember."

I tamped down the distressing thoughts of how Dexter might react once he knew everything. Surely, he would be angry. Would he send me home? Never speak to me again?

"It was Jay I was engaged to…a long time ago. It was a secret; hardly anyone knew of it, save for one of my brothers and my sister."

"Did you know he was at Everston? Is that why you took the job with—"

"Not at all. Yes, I knew he worked here before Mrs. Granton brought me, but I had no say in the plans. In fact, I dreaded the thought of seeing him again."

"You're certain you have no lingering feelings for him?"

At his question, my grip on the saddle horn tightened involuntarily.

Dexter must have noticed, for he persisted, "You're not just saying that because he's going to marry Miss Cole?"

"No attraction remains," I rushed to assure him, "though I'll admit to feeling cast-off, witnessing a former fiancé betrothed to another. But Jay Crawford is most decidedly not the man for me. As awkward as it is to find myself in his company again, I am happy for him and for Greenlee. She adores him in a way I never could have. Jay needs that."

"And what is it, exactly, you think you need?"

No reflection was necessary for me to answer. "Someone who sees my worth without judging me by the family I come from or how much money I have…or don't have."

"Crawford was a fool to let you go," he muttered as he caressed Knightley's mane.

My chest swelled at his words, but I was wise enough not to take them to heart. Not until he repeated them after learning the complete truth of the matter.

"But I'm glad he did," I admitted. "At least, I am now. Five months ago, my feelings were quite the opposite."

"Five months?" Dexter frowned. "I thought you said this occurred a long time ago."

"I—I held on to unreasonable hope for some years. I was young and foolish, and I wouldn't give up the idea of him. But in June, something happened, and I finally realized that I never really loved him. I was just clinging to a vision of my preferred future."

"How ever did you meet him?"

"Jay used to come to Bar Harbor quite often."

Partial truths—were those all I'd ever have the courage to share with him? I wanted to tell him everything. I needed to. I just hoped I'd see the same light in his eyes I saw now when he looked at me as Estella Everstone instead of as Elle Stoneburner.

"I know now what I want...what I need."

He made no response, so I continued off subject, "I hope Greenlee will be happy as a missionary. I hope she loves him."

Dexter shook his head, as if to dispel a thought from his mind. "I believe she does," he answered, keeping his eyes on the trail ahead. "And that alone is proof enough to me that even the most difficult things we go through in life are part of a bigger plan. If she hadn't been held captive by Ezra for those months, she never would have met Jay."

I thought of Dexter's father and brother, and the tragedy that had befallen their family. It wasn't altogether unlike what had happened to my family earlier that summer. And I knew that if either of those tragedies had not occurred, Dexter and I likely never would have met—under any circumstances.

My gaze returned to Jay. He'd known I wasn't what he needed. I just wished he'd told me when he'd figured that out. Maybe he had loved me once, but I suspected it was more that I'd been a small, shiny thread connecting him to the life he'd been born into and hadn't been certain he wanted to give up as he accepted the call of a missionary.

I glanced at Dexter, gently leading Knightley. He looked up at me, his brownish-green gaze serene and steady.

That was another thing that drew me to him—the peace I felt whenever we were together. Even with the raging emotions his closeness caused within me, he managed to impart a sense of calm that I'd never felt with anyone else.

"What are you thinking about?" he asked next.

I thought for a moment. "How very strange life is."

"You don't have to convince me." He smiled reflectively. "I never thought I'd call Everston my own."

"I'm sorry I responded to the news in such an unladylike manner. How was it that you came to buy Everston, exactly? You never did say."

"I think I told you that after graduating from Dartmouth, I took a job at one of Bram Everstone's hotels along the coast. We lived simply, Mother and I, while Roxy stayed at the sanatorium. We saved everything we could and added it to what Father had left us. My goal, for the longest time, was to get back to Everston." Dexter glanced at me and caught me staring. He paused for a moment. "You see, Father and Cull were—"

"Roxy told me what happened."

"Probably the mild version. It's the only version she knows."

"I'll admit that the details she shared were vague."

He nodded. "Good. She's confided in you more than I ever dreamed she would. I wish she wouldn't hide herself away. She would stay in her room for weeks on end, if we let her. She gets that from Father."

"What was he like?"

"Absent, mostly." Dexter chuckled. "He was a British naval captain, retired about the time we began to holiday at Everston; but for most of my childhood, he was at sea. When Cullen and I were young, Mother brought us to America to live near her sister in Portland, since my father was hardly home." He cleared his throat, his eyes on the trail. "Since Roxy's begun, I'd like to tell you the rest of the story, if you don't mind."

"I'd very much like to hear it." I watched him intently as he walked alongside Knightley. I realized that Wulfric had disappeared—the vast amount of trees and wild animals likely too much a temptation to keep him near.

"I went back to Dartmouth that autumn, while my parents and Cull traveled to California. What Roxy doesn't know is that

Cull fell in love that last summer we were at Everston. He asked the young lady to marry him, and she consented, until her mother relayed that she didn't feel Cull was good enough to marry into their family. It didn't seem to bother the young lady's father—actually, I know for a fact it didn't—but in the end, her mother persuaded her not to accept Cull."

"That all happened at Everston? You must relive those memories every day."

"I revisit the ones I choose…the ones involving my family being together, since that was such a rarity."

"I'm sorry," I said hoarsely.

"It took them over a month to get to California, and from what Mother told me, Cull became more sullen and depressed each day. Months after they reached the West Coast, I received a letter from Mother."

He stopped walking and pulled the reins, bringing Knightley to a halt. I looked ahead and saw Jay helping Greenlee to dismount.

Dexter tied Knightley to a nearby tree and helped me down from the saddle with a firm hold on my waist. I consciously controlled my breathing as my boots touched the rugged terrain.

We hadn't ridden to the top of the mountain but to an overlook offering a view of Everston—it looked small enough to fit into the palm of my hand—and the southern half of the lake, sprawling out for miles before us. The view was magnificent and well worth the ride, which I hadn't minded as much as usual.

Jay put his arm around Greenlee's shoulders, and the two strolled to the edge, taking a seat on a giant stone protruding from the mountain.

I glanced at Dexter, whose gaze was not on the lake at all, but on me. Clasping my hands together, I fidgeted nervously with my fingers. "I suppose they might like some privacy."

"They're not the only ones." Dexter reached out his hand. "Come with me."

I placed my hand in his, and he started toward the trail. "There's another lookout close by, with a bench."

I followed him silently, wondering what I would do if he made another attempt to kiss me. Would I let him? Where would I run this time? Down the rocky mountain trail?

The bench he'd mentioned turned out to be a large log stripped of its bark and wedged in between the trunks of two giant pines.

"Please, take a seat."

When I did, Dexter let go of my hand and began pacing in front of me. "Within months of arriving in California, in an effort to take his own life...."

So rapt had my attention been on Dexter—his eyes, especially—that it took me a moment to absorb the meaning of his words.

"My brother accidentally shot and killed my father."

What could I possibly say to that? I felt sick at the thought of the pain his family had suffered. When I looked up, Dexter held my gaze for a long moment.

"Father had walked in on Cull and endeavored to stop him. They struggled...and the pistol went off." Dexter removed his hat from his head and sat down next to me, his eyes on the lake below.

"Days later, after the funeral, Mother wrote to me again. I received the two letters in a matter of days: the first, about the death of my father; the second, the death of my brother. Cull had finally succeeded in ending his life."

I stared down at Half Moon Lake. "Why...why would your brother want to—"

"He was always extremely sensitive...more than was healthy, I suppose."

I brought my gaze back to Dexter as he pushed a hand across his brow and down his face.

"It was because of the rejection of the girl he loved. Did she ever...?"

"Yes, she found out. I made certain she did."

It sounded uncharacteristically callous of him, but would I not have done the same thing for my own brother? Would I not want the man who had murdered Will to know how he'd left Will's new bride a widow on the very day of her wedding, destroying her heart, her very life?

"When her brother found out, he went and told the sordid tale to anyone who would listen, thereby ruining our family's name in polite society."

Suicide was nothing short of scandalous, it's true. "Yet you're telling me."

"That's because I needed for you to know." His eyes met mine for the briefest of moments. "My mother was never the same after suffering as she did. After losing her husband and her son, she traveled alone from California to Maine. She wasn't always this unstable, this dependent on…ways of forgetting the pain."

"What do you mean?"

"She takes 'Hoffmann's drops'…commonly known as ether. I don't approve, but I've done everything I can think of to get her to—"

"And Roxy hardly knows anything?"

He nodded. "We'd like to keep it that way."

"Of course. I wouldn't dream of telling her."

"I knew I could trust you, Elle." Dexter met my gaze with his brilliant eyes. "It doesn't change anything, does it?"

It was amazing to me how one simple question, made of the most ordinary words, could ask so much.

"It doesn't change a thing," I whispered.

I only prayed he would be as understanding when it was my turn to ask the same question of him.

Hearing Jay and Greenlee coming down the trail, we stood and went to meet them.

Greenlee, who'd spoken hardly a word to me since I'd come to stay at Blakeley House, sidled up beside me and said, "Well, aren't you glad you came?"

I smiled warmly. "Indeed, I am. Thank you for inviting me, Greenlee. It turned out to be just what I needed."

She kept her gaze on the lake as she whispered, "It was nothing, Miss Everstone."

My breath caught in my throat. Jay must have told her. It seemed she was willing to keep it a secret, just as Roxy was.

But with the circle of people who knew the truth expanding, I knew the chances of Dexter's finding out from any one of them were becoming more and more likely—which meant I really needed to find the courage to tell him myself, and soon.

TWENTY

The Fall

"Did my heart love till now?"
—William Shakespeare, *Romeo and Juliet*

On the way back down the mountain, my fear of riding returned. I knew the horses to be capable of negotiating the impossibly steep trail, but somehow that knowledge did not translate into feelings of confidence. I clenched my jaw and gripped the saddle horn for dear life.

Dexter chuckled. "You don't need to be nervous, Elle. Knightley has traveled this trail a hundred times or more."

"It's just...I haven't ridden in a long time, and going up the mountain seemed far less risky."

"We'll go down slowly, then."

"Thank you."

We didn't say much as we made our descent, but I wasn't exactly in a talkative mood. We'd conversed a great deal already, and I needed a chance to absorb some of the things he'd shared with me.

When we'd nearly reached the base of the mountain, Jay and Greenlee were out of sight, having made the trek at a fair faster pace. Suddenly, a barking Wulfric bounded out from the dense trees, chasing a large bird across the path in front of us.

Knightley reared, wrenching the reins from Dexter's grip. "Hold on!" he yelled—quite needlessly. I was still grasping the saddle horn in desperation. But as I tipped backward, I lost my grip and grabbed the next thing within reach—Knightley's thick black mane.

Knightley's hooves crashed upon the ground before he reared again, and I was tossed forward, then back again. I kept clinging to his mane, my legs awkwardly draped over the sidesaddle, the skirt of my dress becoming taut beneath me as my left foot caught in the stirrup. The next time Knightley reared, I fell backward into empty space. Everything went black for a moment.

When I regained consciousness, my entire right side hurt—especially my throbbing skull. I could hardly open my eyes. I couldn't speak or move; I felt as if I weighed a thousand pounds.

And then I felt Dexter's arms around me. But why couldn't I open my eyes? And why did my head hurt so dreadfully?

"Elle? I'll need to carry you back," he said, his tone urgent. "Knightley's run off, and—"

"I like you, Dexter Blakeley. I really do." For some reason, that seemed to be the most important thing for me to say.

He didn't respond right away, which left me to wonder if I'd even spoken the words aloud. But then he whispered close to my ear, "I like you, too, Elle Stoneburner."

⟡

The next thing I knew, I awoke and those words were the only thing I could remember.

Dexter stood before me, just as he had in my dream weeks before, right next to Jay. But, for some reason, my wrists were bound tightly with rope and shackled to some kind of stake in the ground. My skin had been rubbed raw as I struggled to escape.

"Please, let me go," I pleaded. "These ropes burn."

"They're for your own good, Estella," Jay answered. "You don't know what's best—you don't know what you need. There's a reason you've been held back."

"Nobody knows what I need because no one knows me." I faced Dexter. "No one but you."

He stepped forward, between Jay and me. "Do you know what you want—what you need, Elle?"

"Please…can I stay?" I looked into his vibrant hazel eyes.

"You thought you wanted me," Jay said. "And you were wrong."

Dexter's eyes were fixed on me with an intensity that told me he might welcome what I had to say next.

"I want you, Dexter Blakeley. I need you. I belong with you… and I think I love you."

He smiled and stepped closer. He reached out his hand to take mine, and the ropes binding me to the stake in the ground were instantly gone. But what he said next didn't match his smile: "Do you know what you're saying?"

In the next moment, Jay somehow vanished, and I felt the comfort of Dexter's arms disappear from behind me—though I didn't remember how they'd come to be there—and I landed on soft heaven.

"Please don't leave me."

"I need to, sweetie. Hannah will be here in a moment, and it isn't—"

I opened my eyes and found Dexter seated on the edge of my bed—in my bedchamber. At the thought of him leaving, I impulsively clutched at his arm, his wrist. He didn't withdraw from my grasp, so I brought his hand to my cheek and held it there. His touch felt so good, and I just wanted him to stay there while I fell asleep.

He brought his other hand to the back of my head, where his fingers gently touched the tender area from which my blaring headache seemed to originate.

I closed my eyes again. It was easier that way. The room was too bright.

"I'll stay until Hannah or Crawford comes, but I'm certain they won't approve—"

"I don't care." I clutched his wrist, feeling the blood pulse in his veins. With my other hand, I reached for his arm and gripped his tense muscles beneath the material of his shirt.

Turning my face into his hand, I kissed his palm. And then his wrist. I heard him suck in his breath.

I wanted him to be as near me as possible. I didn't care what Jay thought. I just needed Dexter to love me.

He slowly pulled his arm away.

"Dexter, please...."

"Ah, you remembered your promise to use my first name." There was a smile in his voice as he pressed his cool fingers to my forehead.

I burrowed my head into my pillow and wished desperately that I could ask him to use mine—my real name. For a moment, I considered telling him the truth right then—but the words wouldn't come. All I could think of was his hand as it gently caressed my skin. I never wanted him to stop.

"I fell off your horse...right? Is that why my head hurts?"

"Yes, but I think you'll be fine."

I lifted my eyelids just enough to catch a glimpse of him. He *was* smiling.

"I'm not sure where Crawford is at the moment, but I'll make certain he sees to you as soon as—"

"Miss Elle!" Mrs. McGuire rushed into the room. Dexter stood and stepped out of her way. "You fell from Knightley? Is that what happened, Mr. Blakeley? I'm sorry I wasn't here when you brought her in."

"Yes, Hannah. A partridge flew across our path near the base of the mountain. Knightley spooked, and I was unable to reach her in time to break her fall."

"Well, off with you now!" She shooed him away with her hand. "Thank you for bringing her in, but it's time I took over. I see you've put her in good spirits, despite her pain. But do be off; you can return later to bring back more of her smiles, I'm sure of it, after you hurry and go for Dr. Crawford. He left for Everston as soon as he and Miss Cole returned from the ride, so he isn't aware she fell, is he?"

"No."

"Well, thank goodness she doesn't seem too badly hurt. She can't be, if you've got her grinning like a giddy schoolgirl and all."

"She said some rather odd things as I carried her in; I'm not sure she's completely awake. I think she's been dreaming." Dexter's voice sounded distant, as if he were leaving.

I struggled to sit, though my eyes were still heavy. Mrs. McGuire came to the side of the bed and gently tried to make me lie back down.

"But I meant every word, Dexter. Every word." Making this declaration seemed quite important, even imperative—so much so that tears sprang to my eyes at the thought of him doubting me.

As I finally reclined once more, I forced my eyes to stay open enough for me to watch Dexter slowly back out of the room and close the door.

I shut my eyes again as Mrs. McGuire fluffed the pillows behind my throbbing head.

She clicked her tongue. "That man. He doesn't know what to make of you, does he? But you know what I think, Miss Elle? I think you're the best thing to happen to Mr. Blakeley in a long, long time."

"But I…I haven't done anything," I mumbled.

"Oh, don't you worry, dearie; you've already done more good for that man than you could ever know." She moved to the end of the bed and began unlacing my boots. "Never could picture him falling all over some girl...at least, not until you came around. How distracted he's been lately!"

I threw one arm over my eyes and pretended not to have heard her, though what she'd said sent a wave of warmth through my chest.

And then, Dexter's last words registered in my mind—about my being incoherent and saying odd things as he carried me to the house.... When had what I'd been saying in my dream become reality? And just how much had I spoken aloud?

The thought of what I might have said was too mortifying to dwell upon, so I let myself drift off, surrendering to the sweet sleep that had been hounding me since I'd awakened to Dexter sitting before me on my bed.

TWENTY-ONE

Recovering

"Everyone believes very easily whatever he fears or desires."
—Jean de La Fontaine, *Fables*

What seemed like days later, I awoke to a burning pain in my right hip, as well as an awful ache at the back of my head. I rolled to my side in an effort to escape the glaring sunlight streaming in through the windows. By its brightness, I knew it must be past noon—later than I'd stayed abed in years. I closed my eyes tighter and draped an arm over my face.

As I lay there, a memory flashed through my mind—Dexter in my bedchamber.

He'd sat right there at the edge of my bed...and I'd dared kiss his hand. His wrist. Was that all?

What had I said to him before Mrs. McGuire had come into the room? A strange mix of memories assailed me. I wasn't sure what had been real and what I had dreamt.

I opened my eyes wide and stared at the gas chandelier that hung from the ceiling in the center of the room.

The next thing I remembered was telling Dexter that I wanted him. That I thought I loved him. Had I actually said those things to him? Or had I merely imagined doing so?

Flopping over, I burrowed deeper beneath the covers and buried my head under my pillow, suddenly hot with embarrassment and shame.

No, it couldn't be true. I would never say such things, even in a state of delirium—would I? And what had he said in return? I was almost certain he'd asked me if I knew what I was saying.

Obviously, I hadn't known!

But it was the truth, and I did know what I wanted. Whether I would ever have it was yet undetermined. Would Dexter's feelings for me survive my telling him the truth? And what would my father think? He liked Dexter, but in a strictly professional capacity. Could he entertain the thought of having him for a son-in-law?

I removed the pillow from over my head, stuffed it under my arms, and blew out a sigh.

Dexter had felt compelled to tell me of his family's illustrious past, clearly believing complete transparency to be a crucial basis for two people in a budding relationship. And I still hadn't had the decency to reciprocate.

His confessions, while startling, hadn't changed how I felt about him. He was still the same man I'd come to know over the last six weeks—faithful, loving, loyal, and steadfast, always striving to do whatever he could to help others. I didn't think there was anything he could have said to change the way I viewed him.

Did it matter to him that I'd once been engaged? I'd explained that Jay had been the one to end things, the public knowledge of which would have ruined my reputation. But would Dexter want a woman who'd been rejected by another man?

It hadn't seemed to matter to him. It was after learning of my past relationship with Jay that he'd decided to share with me about his family's disgraced reputation. And he'd said he liked me, hadn't he, while he carried me to Blakeley House? I remembered that quite vividly.

Dexter's comment about my broken engagement the first time I'd mentioned it, weeks ago, returned to me: "*What more could he want?*" And then on the mountain, "*Crawford was a fool to let you go.*"

But he'd made those remarks in ignorance of who I was. And when he found out, his stance was sure to change. He wouldn't like me. Not as Estella Everstone.

A knock on my door startled me out of my miserable musings. Roxy opened the door a crack and whispered through the narrow opening, "Elle? Are you awake?"

"Yes. Come on in." I turned over and sat up with some pain.

Roxy pushed my door open wider and entered the room, followed by Mrs. McGuire with a tea tray.

"Oh, lovely." I smiled groggily. "Thank you, Roxy, Mrs. McGuire. This is just what I needed." I was thirsty but not hungry; for some reason, the thought of eating anything at all made me feel nauseous.

The housekeeper set out my tea as Roxy came to sit in the chair by my bed. She seemed agitated or unsure about something.

When Mrs. McGuire left the room, Roxy didn't say anything for a little while. I drank my tea and waited. I still hadn't the slightest idea what time it was, or how many days I'd been asleep, having half awakened only a few times to see either Mrs. McGuire, Roxy, or Greenlee standing over me, sometimes offering me a sip of water.

"What is it?" I finally asked. "What's the matter?"

"Estella, I really think you ought to tell Dexter who you are."

"I know. I've been meaning to tell him, but...."

"You have?"

"I realize it's only a matter of time until the truth comes out, and I'd rather he hear it from me. He told me my father was coming here soon, and I imagine he'll want to take me back home." The thought of departing Blakeley House—leaving Dexter and

Everston—turned my insides into knots. "It would be better for your brother to find out before Father comes."

For so many reasons.

Roxy leaned back in her chair. "He's stayed around Blakeley House a lot more since your accident. He's been concerned...." She trailed off, as if contemplating whether to divulge more. "I've never seen him like this," she continued. "Dexter's never looked at a young lady twice, as far as I know. As I've told you before, he thinks me a fool for dreaming of falling in love someday; to him, romance has always been the most ridiculous thing...."

I remained silent, my eyes searching hers, as I waited for her to go on.

"Until now."

I knew now that Dexter's long-held disdain for romantic love had likely stemmed from what had happened to his brother—the way his love affair with a wealthy socialite had ended in heartbreak, leading to murder and eventual suicide. Cullen Blakeley had been unfortunate enough to fall in love with a woman who was too easily persuaded that marriage was a matter of status more than a matter of the heart.

"I wonder if he hasn't had something against young ladies in general, as if they pose some sort of threat to him." Roxy leaned closer. "But I think you broke through his defenses somehow, Estella."

With a tiny groan, I pulled my knees to my chest and pressed my forehead against my arms.

"Do you see why you need to tell him?" Roxy urged me. "Unless...unless you don't think he's good enough for an Everstone—"

"No, that's not it, Roxy. I just...I'm afraid he'll despise me," I moaned, my words muffled by the sleeves of my nightgown.

"What?"

I finally lifted my head. "I've heard him speak of the young girl Estella Everstone, the friend his little sister loved and never forgot. And I've heard him speak of Estella Everstone, the pampered, privileged young socialite who whiles away her days without a care in the world besides doing and having whatever she wants. I don't think he has anything against young ladies in general...just the wealthy, spoiled ones like me. Or like I used to be."

"But he cares for you a great deal," Roxy insisted. "I can tell. As can Mother."

"Maybe so. But he also has a heart for all women in need. Greenlee, myself, Violet Hawthorne...we all have some sort of friendship with your brother that stemmed from our unfortunate circumstances."

Roxy's eyes widened. "Violet Hawthorne?"

"She works the front desk at Everston. Do you know her?"

"I know *of* her. But never mind; that doesn't matter right now. You owe it to my brother to tell him the truth, because I know for a fact he's in love with you."

"If you're right, he's in love with Elle Stoneburner...and that's not me."

"It *is* you, Estella. It's not a name he's in love with; it's who you are. He'll see that; I'm sure of it. But you need to tell him. As you said, your father is coming soon, and I'm certain Dexter would rather hear the truth from you than from him."

⌒

I soon learned that three days had passed since my fall when Roxy came to speak to me about Dexter. I remained in my room for another two days, not knowing what else to do. I had such an anguishing fear of seeing him again, with what I needed to tell him, and also with the awkwardness of what I'd said and done to him as he'd sat at my bedside after my accident.

I shook my head at the memory of kissing his hand and wrist, of begging him to stay with me. Oh, how freeing, and how dangerous, the lack of inhibition when one was incoherent. In the midst of my delirium, everything in my heart had come forth. There was no use in denying it—being with Dexter Blakeley was what I wanted. I'd fallen in love with him, and now he knew it.

From my scrambled recollections of the moments following the accident, I remembered the feel of his cool hand on my face, and how I couldn't imagine permitting the intimate gesture from anyone else. Although I was almost certain I'd been the one to initiate contact, he hadn't fought me, not even when I kissed his wrist. He'd simply smiled.

He must have thought me amusing, my words and my kisses, after I had spent weeks resisting his advances. But he would soon understand the reason for my reluctance. Hopefully, he would appreciate my wanting to wait until he knew the truth, and believe that it was never my intention to lie to him.

I stood, pulling the coverlet from the bed and wrapping it about my shoulders. The weather had turned colder, and Mr. and Mrs. McGuire had many tasks to handle besides keeping the hearth fires stoked. If only there'd been a dressing gown in the assortment of clothes Roxy had loaned to me.

There was a tap on the door as I took a seat at the vanity table. "Come in."

Roxy peeked her head inside. "Estella! You're feeling better?"

"Shhh, Roxy!"

She came into the room and closed the door. "Please say you'll come down for dinner. Dexter can't join us tonight." She flung herself onto my messy bed and propped herself up on one elbow. "It's too bad you didn't come down last night. Dexter stayed after dinner, and Dr. Crawford taught us how to play a game called euchre. It was so confusing! Dexter was familiar with it, but it didn't signify, for you play with partners, and neither Greenlee nor I had any idea what we were doing!"

"It's been ages since I've played," I replied, ignoring her comment about her brother. She knew I'd been hiding from him. "What is the plan for tonight? I suppose Dr. Crawford will be staying after dinner to entertain Greenlee?"

"Of course, but I don't think he'll want to play his game again. Especially if Dexter isn't around."

"I'll come down for dinner, and for whatever else is planned, Roxy. For your sake."

And since Dexter wouldn't be there.

My heart and my actions were at such odds. What I wanted most was to see him, to be with him. Yet I knew very well that I needed to resist my feelings for him. That it hadn't been wise to indulge them even as little as I had. Until he knew exactly who I was, so that he could make an informed decision on how he felt toward me, I could not allow myself to encourage his affections.

I'd done entirely too much of that already.

After dinner, during which Beatrix never stopped glaring at me, she retired for the night. Jay, Greenlee, Roxy, and I congregated in the front parlor for a reading of poetry Jay had selected with his fiancée in mind.

He seemed to be genuinely in love with her—a strange thing to witness, since, after how he'd treated me, I'd thought him incapable of love.

How long had he planned her rescue? And how had he achieved it? I imagined it wasn't easy, but perhaps he'd had help. I couldn't ask him, no matter how curious I was.

As Jay commenced his poetry reading, I sat in my favorite chair in the corner, drawing in my sketchbook, while Roxy occupied the matching chair beside mine, working on her fancy ribbon embroidery.

There weren't many people besides Roxy Blakeley I could honestly say I enjoyed simply being with. Mrs. Granton had been another, even if I'd spent most of my time with her reading aloud.

And, of course, there was Dexter. I'd never known I could feel so content with a man as I did with him. Jay's company had never produced that effect. I hadn't realized it at the time, but the rare moments we'd stolen away together were so superficial, like a dance that neither one of us knew but were still loath to quit.

When Jay had concluded his reading, he stood from the sofa where he'd been seated with Greenlee and offered to help her up. She took his hand with a smile.

"Well, I had better be off," he said. "It's getting late."

Roxy went to see them to the door, and I followed suit, not wanting to be rude. After Jay had gone, Greenlee went upstairs, while Roxy and I returned to the parlor. I intended only to collect my sketchbook and pencils. Roxy helped me gather the pencils, which were strewn about the side table. I quickly grabbed my sketchbook, lest she peek inside and see how many drawings there were of her brother.

"You don't have to hide in your room, you know." She handed me the pencils she'd gathered. "He won't make you feel uncomfortable. He would never do that."

"It's too awkward. I'm too embarrassed," I whispered. "Too ashamed."

"Of what? Falling off Knightley?"

"I said some things to him that day...I wasn't thinking clearly." I groaned inwardly. I knew I couldn't hide from him forever.

"Well, whatever it was, believe me, it worked for your benefit, given the way he's been anxiously waiting for you to emerge. He can't wait to see you again. I don't know why you doubt me."

"Because when someone is told she can't have what she wants, it's hard to switch to believing she can."

Roxy shook her head. "I look forward to saying I told you so when it all works out the way I've prayed it will."

I wouldn't let myself dare hope that Roxy's prayers would be answered.

Mine never were.

"We'll see."

"Do you *want* to go home with your father?"

"No."

"Home" didn't mean anything to me anymore. Being with Dexter was home, and I was afraid that when he learned the truth, I'd find myself homeless yet again.

"Then you should stay here and marry Dexter."

"Roxy, you really are too idealistic."

"You just have too little faith, Estella…in yourself and in God. Don't assume that because He didn't give you one thing you wanted, He isn't ready to give you something else you might want more. He knows our desires better than we do, after all."

I wasn't in the mood to hear a sermon just then, so I feigned a yawn. "Like Dr. Crawford said, it's getting late. I think I'll retire for the evening. Good night, Roxy." And with that, I left her in the parlor.

She let me go without another word.

TWENTY-TWO

The Hall

"I've always known myself.
But he was the first to recognize me. And to love what he saw."
—Charlotte Brontë, *Jane Eyre*

As I prepared for bed, I reflected on Roxy's words and ultimately resolved to resume the usual routine starting the next morning. I would go downstairs for breakfast, and when I saw Dexter seated at the head of the table, as usual, I would eat my meal as if nothing had happened.

I had just climbed into bed when Mrs. McGuire came in to add wood to the fire in the hearth.

"So glad you're feeling better, Miss Elle. We've missed you at mealtimes."

"I think I'm mostly back to normal now, yes, thank you. I should be down for breakfast in the morning."

"I'm glad to hear it. I know someone down there has been missing you something dreadful."

I recalled then that she had witnessed my shameless proclamation to Dexter before he'd left my room. What must she think of me? I doubted she'd be as keen on the placement of her esteemed employer's affections when she, too, learned what a liar I'd been.

When Mrs. McGuire finished with the fire, I thanked her and snuggled under the covers, Roxy's two cats lending their warmth.

I brought my knees to my chest, closed my eyes, and covered my face with my hands, thinking how I never wanted to leave Blakeley House. And yet, with every passing day that I kept up my charade, the eventuality of my departure became more certain.

Yes, Dexter had come to care for me—I knew he had. It was evidenced in every word he'd ever said to me, in every look. But as a poor girl named Elle.

Was it so bad that I came from a wealthy family? He liked Father, it seemed, and he'd kept in contact with Nathan and Vance. Was that merely for business' sake? So he could eventually acquire Everston?

I had a sudden urge to continue working on my latest drawing of him. Sitting up in bed, I opened the drawer of my nightstand and pulled out my sketchbook and pencils. This particular drawing was of him at the spring, leaning with his hand on the rock wall, as he had been when he'd almost kissed me. When he'd admitted that I terrified him, that he thought me dangerous.

I hadn't been at all prepared for that. Perhaps, if I had been, I might have let him kiss me. And then I would have told him everything. Surely, I would have. And the entire matter would have been resolved.

I studied the likeness of Dexter. I could still envision the look in his eyes from that day. A look that said he knew me. That he saw me, and he liked what he saw.

I grabbed my pencils, desperately wanting to finish the drawing then and there. But my favorite one was missing. I searched the drawer, the bed, the floor; it was nowhere to be found. I figured I had left it downstairs, but did I dare leave my room without getting properly dressed again?

I sat there for a moment, weighing my options. It would be a quick jaunt; I wasn't likely to see anyone, save for maybe Mrs. McGuire, who would hardly be scandalized to see me in my nightgown.

I slid out of bed and wrapped a worn quilt around my shoulders, over my nightgown. Carrying a small lamp lit low, I tiptoed down the back staircase and along the hall to the front parlor. There on the carpet beneath my favorite corner chair was the pencil. I snatched it up and scurried back to the hall.

I was passing the foot of the main staircase when I heard the bolt of the front door unlock. Knowing just who it would be, I blew out my lamp, quickly set it on the hall table, and ducked into the small alcove formed by the curve of the stairs, my back pressed against the wall.

As my eyes adjusted to the darkness, I could barely make out Dexter as he came into the house and closed the door behind him. The wick of my lamp smoldered beside me, and I prayed he wouldn't get a whiff of it as he went to his study across the hall.

He whistled a tune that was unfamiliar, though perhaps that was because of his terrible pitch. I found myself grinning, despite my fear of his finding me. His steps slowed as he neared his study, and he stopped whistling mid-tune when he reached the door a few feet from me—where he stood in silence for almost a minute, his back to me.

I'd been holding my breath ever since he'd entered the house, but my lungs chose that moment to give out. As soon as I exhaled, Dexter twisted around. "Who's there?"

At the shock of hearing his voice, I dropped my pencil and let out a small shriek.

"Elle? Is that you?"

"Yes," I whispered with a sigh.

Dexter's left arm immediately came around my back and pulled me close, while the fingers of his right hand came to my lips. He had me pressed to his chest; my arms were trapped at my sides, bent at the elbows; my hands were between us, clutching the edge of the quilt.

I couldn't think of what to say, beyond his name. "Dexter...."

He cradled the nape of my neck and raked his hand through my hair. "Elle," he whispered. He still hadn't removed the fingers of his other hand from my lips; they now glided over the soft flesh. "I don't want to be your friend."

Such straightforwardness from him didn't surprise me anymore, though it did seem a strange thing to say at such a moment. At least until he leaned in, slowly removed his fingers from my lips and kissed me.

Then it made all the sense in the world.

Taking in a deep breath, I delighted in his nearness—his smooth lips, the coarse growth of whiskers on his chin, the heady smell of his skin. And it was no surprise to him, I was sure, that I kissed him back. When I lifted myself up on my toes, a gentle moan escaped his throat, and his hands pressed against my back brought me even closer.

We soon had to stop to catch our breaths, and then we stood there for a few minutes, cheek to cheek. At some point, my hands had released the quilt and had clutched the front pockets of Dexter's wool coat.

After a while, he drew back; even in the darkness, I could tell he studied me. "I want to be so much more than friends." His normally gruff voice sounded even more thick and uneven, and he was still out of breath.

I smiled. I was a little breathless, myself.

"Elle?" There were so many questions in the utterance of that name.

And I had to be careful how I responded…because it was still the wrong one.

"I don't want to be friends, either. I want…I think I want all of the same things you want, Dexter." Daringly, because I needed him to believe me, I let go of the front of his coat and slid my hands to his strong shoulders. "I thank God for bringing me here every time I think of you…which is quite often. But I need to…." How was I supposed to tell him? I stalled with a question: "You've really never been in love?"

"Never." He choked the word out. "And I never thought I would."

Then he kissed me again. But this time, his manner was more serious, more focused, as his hand traveled from the back of my neck to the front, fiddling with the ribbons that fastened the high collar of my nightgown. He looped them around his fingers and pulled until the pleated fabric was loose enough for his lips to reach my collarbone.

He held me quite close as he explored my throat and shoulder, and something I'd never felt before—a strange clarity—rushed from deep inside, and I shivered. My tense, worry-worn shoulders immediately relaxed, and I exhaled, raking my fingers through his thick, dark hair. I didn't mean to; I simply couldn't help it. I never wanted him to stop.

He made a sound that fell somewhere between a chuckle and a growl, then abruptly stopped the kiss with a low groan as he brought his face back to mine, his nose caressing my cheek while his lips stayed at my jaw.

Then he stopped and swallowed hard. "I shouldn't have done that."

"It's quite all right," I breathed.

He brought his left arm around my shoulders. "Because of what happened to Cullen, I never thought I could allow something like this...but I didn't seem to have a choice in the matter when it came to you." His right hand tightened its grasp at my waist, bringing me closer, even when it seemed there was absolutely nothing between us. "Ever since first meeting you in the stagecoach with Mrs. Granton, each time I saw you, I became further convinced that I never wanted to see you go."

"I was inexplicably drawn to you then, as well; and now...there are so many things I need to tell you, Dexter—"

"What is this?" He tugged at the quilt, which now hung loosely about my shoulders.

"It's a quilt from my room. I had to use it as a wrap over my night—"

"Is that all you're wearing—a nightgown?" He tensed and released me with a sudden jerk. "Forgive me, I didn't realize— I should go." He backed all way to the door of his study, and I heard him bump into it. "You should go back to your room. What were you doing down here, anyway?"

"I had to retrieve...a missing pencil." Feeling incredibly foolish, I bent over and picked it up off the floor. I straightened, not sure what had caused his sudden change of mood. "I didn't expect to see anyone. I didn't have anything better to put over—"

"Forgive me, Elle, I really must go. Please go to your room before anyone hears and comes down and finds us—"

Completely horrified with myself, I asked, "Are you ashamed of me?"

"No, Elle—goodness, no! I'm ashamed of myself. I'm not sorry I kissed you, only that I wasn't thinking clearly enough to—" He let out a deep breath, sounding quite exasperated with himself... and likely also with me, even if he hadn't said so. "I shouldn't have kissed you like that, at night in the dark. It could have—"

I started toward the back stairs, my bare feet padding quietly on the carpet.

"Elle, wait." He came after me, and as I turned around, he took my hand in his. "Please don't think I'm upset with you. Finding you down here simply took me by surprise. You're all I've thought about for days, and it didn't occur to me what you'd be wearing, I just needed to—"

"I should go, like you said." I strove to pull my hand from his, but he wouldn't release me.

"Blast it, Elle, I'm not mad at you." He brought my hand to his lips and kissed my palm, as I had done to him the week before.

"Then why your sudden brusqueness?"

"Because I love you." He almost growled the words. "And this could have ended quite badly."

His admission both shocked and thrilled me. "Oh, Dexter. I love you, too—but I think I've told you already, haven't I?"

Dexter chuckled and let go of my hand. "I'm glad to know that wasn't just incoherent mumbling." He took hold of my shoulders, turned me around, and gave me a little push. "And it's all the more reason for you to get back to your room."

Insufferable man! But I grinned all the way back upstairs.

TWENTY-THREE

The Barn

"Sometimes, only one person is missing,
and the whole world seems depopulated."
—Alphonse de Lamartine

Dexter wasn't at breakfast the next morning, but I wasn't surprised. That would have meant a lot of running back and forth between Everston and Blakeley House in a short amount of time. And perhaps he hadn't expected me to be there, since I hadn't been down for breakfast in over a week.

And what a difference that week had made. I glanced around the table at Beatrix, Roxy, Jay, and Greenlee. Could they tell there was something different about me? I felt different. I felt like I'd finally found my place; and I was both excited and anxious for them to find out about Dexter and me. How would they react? I knew that at least Roxy would be pleased.

For now, none of them seemed to have any clue—though Beatrix did stare at me from down the table a little longer than usual. Was it because of the way I was smiling? I really couldn't help it. I'd been kissed before, by Jay, but Dexter's kisses had a completely unprecedented effect on me. Everything I'd seen in his eyes had come through to me as his lips had found mine in the dark. He'd been so assertive, like he knew just what he wanted—and it was me.

Jay had never kissed me like that. His kisses had always seemed tentative, hesitant—something I never realized before kissing Dexter Blakeley. I'd never had any basis of comparison. And now that I did—what a difference!

Dexter had kissed me as if I was the only thing he wanted, the only thing that mattered. If only it hadn't been dark in the hall, and I could have seen the smile on his face after he kissed me. I remembered feeling the lift of his lips against mine, and that particular recollection had created perpetual flutters within me all morning.

And his eyes—what kind of light would fill them when he next saw me? I couldn't wait to see.

It would have been better, of course, for me to have been more appropriately clad for our kiss; but the quilt had been just as effective as a wrap, if not more so. I suspected that Dexter was embarrassed for having untied the collar of my nightgown, likely thinking it was the frilly collar of a regular dress; but I wouldn't hold it against him. It wasn't as if he'd been seeking to remove my nightgown, only to gain better access to my neck.

I shivered at the memory.

"Elle, are you all right?" Roxy asked. "Are you cold?"

"I'm fine, thank you." I took another bite of a biscuit covered in gravy to conceal my broad smile. In that moment, I noticed the lamp I'd carried from my room the night before, resting on the sideboard behind Greenlee. I stared at it for a moment, wondering who had moved it there. Hopefully, whoever had done so didn't recognize it as having come from my room.

"Do you know if your brother plans to come around today?" I asked Roxy, trying not to sound too curious.

"I think he's leaving for Severville this morning," Roxy said.

"And stopping in Laurelton on his way back to collect Reverend Whitespire for our wedding tomorrow," Jay put in as he stood.

He took Greenlee's hand and helped her from her seat. "If you'll excuse us, we'll be in the next room."

"I'm not certain what's taking him to Severville," Roxy told me as Jay and Greenlee moved to the parlor, "but I'm sure he'll stop by to see us before he leaves. He always does."

"Why does it matter?" It was the first time Beatrix had addressed me in over a week. She spoke with a scowl, her eyes narrowed to slits.

"It doesn't," I replied, staring at my plate. "I only asked."

"You've never cared to ask before."

"Mother, please leave Elle alone. She hasn't done anything wrong."

"Hasn't she?" Beatrix stood from the table and grabbed the lamp from the sideboard. "You left this downstairs last night."

So, she had recognized the lamp.

"Yes, I left one of my pencils in the parlor last night, and I came down to fetch—"

"Why did you leave your extinguished lamp in the hall?" She stared at me, awaiting my answer.

"Mother," Roxy chided.

But she had every right to ask. I just wasn't prepared to answer. And, rather tired of lying, I decided to simply excuse myself, leaving most of my breakfast still on the plate. As I crossed the hall, I glanced at the corner where Dexter and I had met in the night. Had Beatrix overheard our encounter? Or even witnessed it?

I squared my shoulders and took a deep breath. There was nothing I could do about it now.

Before breakfast, I'd had one thing on my mind: how I would reveal my identity to Dexter. I planned to explain everything calmly and thoroughly, all the while holding his hands, or maybe with my arms wrapped around him, as they'd been last night. That was where I belonged, and hopefully he would think so, too, even after learning the truth. He would see that I'd grown to become utterly unlike the average socialite who frequented Everston.

Admittedly, my vision was extremely optimistic—but how could it be otherwise, now that I knew for certain how he felt about me?

Knowing made it all the more imperative I tell him the truth... and made me all the more desperate for him to accept it—and me.

I took my faded blue coat from the hook in the hall, struck afresh by my new attitude about apparel. Dexter never had commented on how much better I looked in Roxy's colorful, fashionable dresses than in the ugly brown ones I'd worn while at Everston. He'd always been focused on the inward things that made me who I was. And it amazed me that he had always considered me beautiful even when I thought I looked abysmally plain, without my elaborate hairstyles and expensive Parisian-made gowns.

I couldn't help but think how backward his view of me was. He thought I was poor, without family and without anything better to wear than clothes borrowed from his sister. Would he still think I was beautiful—inside and out—after he knew the truth? Or would his opinion of wealthy Estella Everstone remain as it had been before meeting me?

I opened the front door just in time to see Dexter dismount from Knightley near the barn. I hadn't heard him ride up, probably because I'd been in the dining room being chastised by his mother.

He looked devastatingly handsome as he walked across the yard with his smiling hazel eyes focused on me, while Wulfric followed at his heels.

I still couldn't believe I'd captured his heart by simply being me. No inheritances, no fancy parties, no giant houses, and no rules dictating why and when and where—just me. It was exactly what I'd always wanted—to be loved even when stripped of all worldly wealth and status.

Surely, a man who could love me as a nobody could also love me as a somebody. Especially since that somebody no longer existed, except in name alone. The Estella Everstone of yesterday was forever gone.

It wasn't as if I wanted to take him back to Boston, to the world I was eager to disown; I wanted to stay right there with him at Everston and be exactly who I'd been for the last two months.

Meeting me at the foot of the porch steps, Dexter took my hand and kissed it.

Instead of greeting him, I blurted out, "I have something I need to tell you."

With a questioning glance to me, he commanded Wulfric to stay on the porch.

We strolled to the barn, and as we reached the wide-open door, he rotated me around to face him, then stooped several inches to bring his eyes level with mine and touched my chin with his thumb and forefinger. "Are you all right?" A glint of doubt flashed across his face. "You don't regret what you said last night…?"

"Of course not!" Though we stood in plain sight for anyone to see, I put my arms around him and nestled my head against his shoulder. I wanted to burrow into him, to somehow reach inside to his heart and secure his love for me—secure it, so I could know he would love me, no matter my name.

Dexter straightened with a glance toward the house. "I must leave soon for Severville."

I closed my eyes as I pressed my cheek against his coarse wool coat. "Yes, Roxy told me."

"I'll be back tomorrow afternoon—before you know it."

I pulled in a deep breath and brought my hands to his chest, then slid them under his scarf until my cold fingers reached his warm neck, his muscular shoulders.

He shivered at my touch, and his hands gripped my waist.

207 The Captive Imposter 207

I lifted my head to find his eyes taking in every part of me. He let out a long breath. "You're so—"

Rising up on my toes, I brought my mouth to his and kissed him passionately, deeply, hoping he would remember it well—and everything else he knew about me—when I told him who I was. If he changed his mind, if he didn't want me as Estella Everstone, I didn't know how I would get over him. He was a better man than any I'd met, and his kisses were beyond describing; I could hardly believe he'd never kissed anyone before. He was so very good at it.

His mouth broke from mine, but after a deep breath, he immediately pressed in for more. After some time, he made a low sound deep in his throat and leaned back, leaving me breathless.

"You know, when you relaxed into my arms on the road to my house from Everston that night, I couldn't bear the thought of your leaving, the thought of not holding you like that—like this— forever. I felt for you before then, but that made it real; and the idea of your having to leave…it hurt." He buried his face in my hair for a moment, then drew back and studied me with furrowed brow, a mystified expression in his gorgeous eyes. "I just can't believe I've fallen in love. How did you get me to do that?"

"I don't know," I whispered. "But I'm in love with you, too. And I hope you'll believe that for a very, very long time—"

"There's no doubt I will…with pleasure."

I knew it was time to bring forth the confession I'd rehearsed. He knew me—the real me—better than anyone else did. All except for my name. And I had to believe he would still love the real me once he knew.…

"Dexter?" Beatrix called from the porch. "Are you not coming in before you leave?"

He pulled away and took my hand in his as he drew his time-piece from his pocket with the other and clicked it open. "Mother's right. I need to be at the train station in Severville by eleven, so I really ought to go." He put his watch back in his pocket and pulled me close one last time. "I meant to be here earlier, Elle, to see you for a longer time before heading off. There's so much to say...and do." The corners of his mouth lifted in a grin.

Beatrix and Roxy waited for us on the porch, Beatrix wearing her customary frown. She clearly knew there was something between us, but she didn't say anything as Dexter and I ascended the porch steps hand in hand. Roxy was smiling; I could tell she was pleased because she believed I'd made my confession.

Jay led Greenlee onto the porch; oddly, his eyes were on me, and he wore a curious expression. Honestly, I didn't care what he thought. He would be gone the next day, as soon as he married Greenlee.

Dexter didn't let go of my hand until he was about to leave.

"Stay close by the house today," he told Jay. "Ezra Hawthorne was at Everston this morning, accompanied by that Frenchman who appears to be of the same sort."

Jay nodded soberly. "Thank you for the warning." They were obviously concerned about Ezra Hawthorne's certain desire to reclaim Greenlee.

I then recalled my brother Vance's fear that his brother-in-law might seek to vindicate his deceased sister, whom Vance had compromised and been forced to marry while in France. Could Jacques Gerard have followed me to Everston? Or would he be more interested in Vance, who, as Jay had mentioned, wasn't too far away, in Bangor?

As I weighed these concerns, Dexter hugged and kissed his mother and sister good-bye, then took my hand again and guided me down the steps and across the yard toward the barn.

It was only four words: *I am Estella Everstone.* But I didn't want to speak them so abruptly. I needed time to explain things properly, to answer his questions. I was quite certain he would have more than a few.

"I'm afraid I must be off. As I said, I meant to have more time with you, but things were a little chaotic at Everston this morning." He slowed his pace as we neared Knightley.

"What happened?"

"Oh, just Ezra Hawthorne bothering his sister. I don't know what he said to Violet, but whatever it was had her awfully upset."

"I hope he isn't around when Greenlee rides through in the stagecoach tomorrow."

"She'll be fine," he assured me. "I'm going to rent a closed carriage in Severville for her and Jay for their departure." He entwined his fingers with mine, and his eyes traveled over me, from my hat to my boots, his love for me evident.

I had put it off long enough. Whatever the outcome, it was time to make my confession. "Dexter, I really need to speak with you. I have something—"

"Elle, I really have to go. Can we talk tomorrow? I'm sorry we didn't have more time." With one final kiss, Dexter wrenched himself from my grasp, quickly mounted Knightley and rode off with Wulfric bounding down the road after them.

TWENTY-FOUR

The Special Guest

"To be yourself in a world that is constantly trying to make you
something else is the greatest accomplishment."
—Ralph Waldo Emerson, *Essays*

It was late the next afternoon when I heard the pounding hoofbeats of a team of horses and the creaky wheels of a carriage
come down the lane. Beatrix stood from her seat across the room
and made her way to the front door.

Greenlee hastened down the stairs to greet Jay, whom Dexter
had planned to collect at Everston on his way back to Blakeley
House. She stood beside Beatrix at the front door, watching for
the carriage.

As Roxy and I stood from our chairs in the corner of the parlor,
she linked arms with me. "Everything will be fine," she whispered.
"You'll tell him, and everything will be fine."

I could only hope she was right.

We joined her mother and Greenlee in the hall and stood
beside Greenlee's small trunk, which I'd helped pack with her
favorite borrowed dresses and a few other household items Roxy
had decided to pass on to the newlyweds.

Even though Greenlee had shared that she gladly would have
eloped to Laurelton, Jay had insisted they have a proper wedding
at Blakeley House. And so, Greenlee, Roxy, and I were dressed in

three of Roxy's brightest, most fashionable gowns. Mine was one I'd admired for some time, a soft aqua-blue with white and beige accents.

We watched as Wulfric came bounding out of the closed carriage, and then Dexter, Jay, and Reverend Whitespire climbed out. Greenlee grabbed her coat and went outside to greet Jay with a hug. After a moment, Roxy and her mother went out, as well, leaving me in the entry alone.

In the mostly empty house, I could hear Mrs. McGuire in the kitchen, preparing the pre-wedding dinner.

Finally, I took my blue coat from the hook, put it on, and walked out to the porch, pausing at the top of the steps. My pulse raced at the sight of Dexter as he spoke with the driver, and I couldn't wait for him to kiss me again.

Once Dexter noticed me on the porch, a smile transformed his face, and he immediately strode toward me, pausing only briefly to greet his mother and sister. He took the steps two at time until he stood before me, then took me in his arms and held me tight. "I know I was gone but one night, yet I missed you dreadfully. How are you feeling…in regard to Crawford's imminent wedding?"

"Honestly, I've hardly thought about it. I've thought only of seeing you."

"You are kind to forgive him." Then he stood back and looked me in the eyes. "I can tell you have, because I know you. It surprised me when you told me he was the one to whom you'd been betrothed, but I'm almost glad. Now I won't have to wonder about some stranger's possible claim on your heart."

"You certainly won't. I am completely over my feelings for Jay, and I'm happy for him and Greenlee."

"You're an extraordinary woman, Elle Stoneburner…so beautiful, inside and out. I'm so glad God brought you to Everston… and to me."

"I wish I could kiss you," I whispered.

Dexter brought his left hand to my chin and gently fingered my lips with his thumb. "I promise to kiss you later, don't worry," he said with a playful smirk. Then he took a step back and took my hands in his. "Right now, I'd like to properly introduce you to Ben Whitespire, and to allow you to reunite with your previous employer, Bram—"

"What?" How had I missed Father exiting the coach? Had he watched from across the lawn as I greeted Dexter with such familiarity?

"That's who I needed to meet in Severville." I could tell Dexter's eyes were on me as I scanned the scene below. "I thought you knew."

"I knew you were stopping to pick up Reverend Whitespire on the way through Laurelton." I still didn't see Father. Had Dexter had left him at Everston?

My pulse raced as Dexter led me by the hand down the steps and toward the carriage. A hundred questions raced through my mind as I stared at his hand over mine. In the day of travels they had spent together, had Father said nothing to Dexter of desiring to pick up his daughter Estella and take her home? Surely, that was his primary goal in coming to Everston. But if Dexter had shared his feelings for Elle Stoneburner, perhaps Father had decided to say nothing on the matter.

As we reached the carriage, Father stepped around from the other side, talking with Jay. I wanted to run back into the house and lock myself in my room, but Dexter kept a firm grip on my hand. "Miss Stoneburner, I realize you've known him as your employer, as I have; but now I'd like you to meet Mr. Bram Everstone as a friend—the man and mentor who has made me who I am today."

I let go of Dexter and schooled my facial expression as I took the hand Father offered me. He appeared content to play along with my charade, for now.

"It's nice to see you again, Mr. Everstone," I said, trying to keep my voice steady, my tone reverent.

"And it's a pleasure to see you, as well, Miss Stoneburner." Father gave me a cryptic smile from beneath his thick beard. "It appears life has treated you fairly since your change in position."

"Yes, very well, sir," I answered.

Dexter draped his left arm possessively around my shoulders, and I leaned into him, reveling in the comfort he offered.

As Father looked on, I saw the glimmer of comprehension in his eyes. Did that mean he approved of our match? It was a rather strange sensation, for I had rarely felt the warmth of my father's approval; more often, he had seemed to think I didn't know at all what was best regarding my life or my future.

But then, he'd been right. I hadn't known, at least when it had come to Jay.

I wanted desperately to speak with him in private, but then Dexter guided me over to where Reverend Whitespire stood.

"And this is my friend Benjamin Whitespire, pastor of the church in Laurelton. Ben, meet Miss Elle Stoneburner."

"A pleasure, Miss Stoneburner."

I smiled politely. "It's nice to finally meet you, Reverend Whitespire. I've heard nothing but glowing reports of your parish."

I stayed by Dexter's side as he introduced his mother and sister to Father and then discussed the day's plans with Reverend Whitespire. Beatrix said hardly a word during the entire exchange, which didn't surprise me, considering how openly she despised my family.

As the group headed toward the house, Dexter and I hung behind, allowing everyone else to go ahead of us. I watched Father's eyes on Jay and Greenlee. He didn't seem troubled, only curious. It was no secret to my family that I'd been fixated for years on Jay Crawford.

"Were you nervous to meet Bram Everstone again?" Dexter asked quietly as he helped me out of my coat.

"It was a surprise, I must say." I left it at that. I didn't need to pile any more lies onto the mountain I'd made since meeting Dexter Blakeley.

TWENTY-FIVE

The Wedding

"I have been bent and broken, but—I hope—into a better shape."
—Charles Dickens, *Great Expectations*

After Reverend Whitespire had offered a word of grace, the wedding feast began, and I made my best attempt to eat. Across the table from me, Greenlee stared at her plate, looking just as bewildered as I felt. She seemed scared out of her wits to find herself in the company of so many people.

Everyone else was immersed in a conversation regarding Jay and Greenlee's plans following their wedding.

"So, where are you and this beautiful young lady headed to next, Dr. Crawford?" Father asked, as if he didn't already know.

"We'll take a post with the Boston Inland Mission Society in Aberdeen, Washington," Jay replied with a quick glance my way. "It's a small town along the coast, and, while newly incorporated, it's quickly made a reputation for itself…not a favorable one, I'm afraid."

"That sounds like some of the lumber towns around here," I put in, not wanting to seem aloof.

"It's far worse, actually, Miss Stoneburner. It's not a place I imagine you would ever want to visit."

Dexter reached under the table and took my hand in a silent show of solidarity. The deeper meaning of Jay's words was not lost on him.

I gave him a tiny smile, thankful I'd at least told him the truth about my past engagement.

I had planned to tell Dexter the whole truth that day. If only the ride back to Blakeley House hadn't ended the way it had. I would have brought it up, and everything would have been settled before our words of love and passionate kisses had made a tangled mess of things.

I had a feeling that our first kiss, that night in the hall—the first Dexter had seen me after my recovery from the fall—had everything to do with the delirious proclamation of love I had made to him.

I'd told him too much of what I shouldn't have, and not nearly enough of what I should.

For the rest of the meal, I remained quiet as I kept stealing glances at Father. What must he think of me, of my obvious affections for Dexter? It had been very cavalier of me to take up a new life for myself at Blakeley House without consulting my family, but it really happened with no premeditation on my part.

After the meal, we congregated in the parlor for the wedding ceremony. Only Beatrix was absent; she had made it abundantly clear she did not want to have anything to do with the joining of any two people in marriage.

As Reverend Whitespire led Jay and Greenlee through the exchange of vows, I had a difficult time keeping my focus on anything besides Dexter. He stood on the other side of Jay, consuming me with his eyes. Everything that gaze communicated took my breath away. He loved me—he who had always been convinced he would never love anyone.

When the short ceremony concluded, we all congratulated the newlyweds. After a final word of blessing from Reverend Whitespire for their journey, the couple headed outside to the waiting carriage, which would take them to Bangor to catch their train west.

As the rest of the group began to file out after them, Roxy caught my eye, then tossed her head toward Father. I would thank her later for instinctively knowing the two of us needed to speak privately.

"Oh, Dexter, was that not the sweetest wedding?" she asked her brother as she linked arms with him. "I've always dreamed of going to one. Wouldn't it be grand to have a wedding at Everston?"

"Yes, someday, dear sister." He sent me a wink. "And maybe sooner than you think."

"What, no scathing response about how pointless and deceptive love is?" Roxy turned to the reverend. "Who is this man, Reverend Whitespire, and what have you done with my brother?" She took his arm with her free one and led both men toward the hall.

The three of them gone, I stood alone with Father. He quickly crossed the room to me. "Are you in love with him?" It was so like Father to get right to the point. "There's no use denying it. I can tell you are—I can see your heart; can see right through you, in fact."

He'd always been able to see through me, but that no longer seemed to be a bad thing. All those years I'd felt misunderstood, unknown…perhaps he'd understood me better than I'd thought.

"Do you…do you approve of him?"

He considered me for a moment. "Dexter Blakeley is one of the finest men of my acquaintance. I approve of him without reservation."

My heart swelled, but he wasn't done.

"I just don't approve of his not knowing the truth."

"I know." I bit my lip. "I've tried to tell him, ever since I had an inkling of what was happening, but…."

"You need to tell him now, before this goes any further." He reached inside his coat, pulled a small envelope from his pocket, and offered it to me. "This is from your sister. She and George are still at Everwood, for the time being."

I took the envelope, broke the wax seal, and peeked inside to see a photograph of Natalia holding the baby she'd waited so long to have. Without looking up, I asked, "Did you come here to take me home?"

"I did, and I was nearly on the verge of telling him so when he confided in me about his 'beautiful, wonderful' Elle Stoneburner. I realized then what had happened, and that it wasn't my place to tell him but yours. Which you need to do, Estella. Today."

"Oh, Father, I've made such a muddle of things. I don't think he would have fallen in love with me if he'd known me as anyone but poor Elle Stoneburner."

"Estella." His voice, stern yet calm, somehow steadied me. "We don't know that. And I'm sure everything will be resolved, but not until you tell him. And if you don't, I'm quite certain Vance will when he gets here. He's coming up from Bangor either today or early tomorrow."

"What about Jacques Gerard?"

"As far as I know, Vance doesn't sense much of a threat from him. And I want the chance to see how he's faring. From my limited interactions with him over the past months, he doesn't seem to have recovered from what happened, though he's put up a convincing front."

"But Dexter said he ran into a Frenchman at Everston yesterday."

"I doubt it was Gerard. There are guests coming down from Quebec all the time. Vance would have told me if he thought Gerard was around, I'm certain. He knows you've been at Everston, after all."

The front door opened, and Father and I turned toward the hall as Dexter strode into the parlor, beaming. "Getting reacquainted?"

I held up the envelope from Natalia. "There was...this...for me...."

Father moved across the room to join Dexter in the doorway. "From our short conversation, Miss Stoneburner seems to enjoy her position here immensely."

"I've gathered that." Dexter looked my way with a grin.

"Are the newlyweds packed and ready to go?" I asked.

"Yes." Dexter turned to Father. "And the carriage is ready to take you back to the hotel."

"It will be nice to stay at Everston again. It's been too long."

As we made our way outside to join Dexter's mother and sister, I wished I'd had a chance to ask Father why he'd agreed to sell Everston to Dexter.

Before I knew it, Father and Reverend Whitespire had joined Jay and Greenlee inside the carriage. We said our good-byes, and then they were off.

As I stood there in the coolness of the early October evening, holding Dexter's hand and watching the carriage roll down the drive, I imagined what it would be like to be left there for good as Dexter Blakeley's wife. The thought nearly took my breath away.

I turned to Dexter. "May I—"

"I need a word with you, Dexter," Beatrix interrupted me, clamping her hand possessively around his upper arm.

He gave me an apologetic smile. "Let me first have a word with Mother. It won't be long." With that, he turned and followed Beatrix toward the barn.

A mixture of relief and dread ran through me. The thought of telling him had always twisted my insides into knots, and now it was time—after this latest delay.

I was about to return to the house when Roxy grabbed my hand and started in the direction of the barn.

"What are you doing?" I whispered.

"Don't you want to know what Mother has to say to Dexter? I sure do."

I didn't really, but it was impossible to wrangle free of Roxy's grip; and it wasn't as if Dexter and his mother were making any effort to be quiet as they conversed just inside the barn doors.

"Elle will be staying on here, no matter how you feel about it, Mother."

"Not that she's ever done anything with Miss Cole or your sister. Isn't that why you brought her here? She's spent all her time with you! Miss Cole is gone now, and Roxy's doing better. We don't need her!"

"Mother, it isn't that simple."

"You want her, don't you?" Beatrix spat. "Just like your brother wanted that vixen who destroyed him! Haven't I taught you better than to fall for flighty girls who are sure to break your heart? Did you learn nothing from what happened to Cullen?"

"Elle's not like that, Mother. She doesn't have anything—"

"That won't stop her from ripping your heart to shreds! Don't you remember what happened to your poor brother?"

"I've decided I'd rather take my chances, Mother. For her." After a long pause, Dexter continued, "It wasn't part of my plan. I never would have imagined I could—"

"Nor I! And you thought you could hide it from me, didn't you? But you couldn't! I've seen everything, heard everything. Every look that's passed between you two, and her attempt to seduce you during your clandestine tryst in the hall the other night—I heard it all!"

Dexter's only answer was silence.

"Do you deny it, Dexter? What else would she have been doing downstairs in the middle of the night but waiting for you, wanting to sink her teeth into your unsuspecting heart?"

"That's not how things transpired, Mother; and I wasn't unsuspecting. I knew what I was doing—even the other night. I've known it for weeks."

"What?" Beatrix screeched. "What have you known?"

"That I love her, and that she's going to remain at Blakeley House—as my wife. It's my plan to propose, and I have little doubt she'll accept."

My heart swelled in my chest. He wanted everything that I wanted! Surely, God had heard my prayers—and would respond favorably to the one that was yet answered....

"How could you forget what happened to Cullen?" Beatrix wailed, sounding much the same as when I first saw her, the night Jay had brought Greenlee to Blakeley House.

"I haven't forgotten, Mother! But Elle has nothing—no money, no family to disapprove. I'll give her everything—"

I pulled my hand free from Roxy's and fled for the house, scared that Dexter or his mother would suddenly exit the barn and find us eavesdropping.

Roxy came quickly behind me. "What did I tell you? Oh, Estella, we'll soon be sisters for real, just like we always wanted when we were little!"

Never in my wildest dreams would I have expected my silly childhood wishes to become a reality. God had listened to my little-girl prayers back then and had orchestrated the events of my life, even the painful ones, to produce a present reality beyond my greatest hopes. How great were His ways compared to ours!

Roxy followed me up the porch steps and into the house. "I still need to speak with him," I told her in the front hall. "I need to tell him—"

"Go wait for him in his study. When he comes in, I'll tell him to meet you, and I'll make sure Mother doesn't—"

"Thank you, Roxy." I have her hand a squeeze. "I hope this works out well."

"It will—I'm sure of it! He'll forgive you. He'll want to know the details, of course; but you've already done the impossible by finding your way into his heart. I can't imagine he'll let you leave. He loves quite fiercely, as you've probably come to realize."

For some reason, her final words left me feeling somewhat unsettled rather than reassured. Even so, I went to the study, stopping first in the parlor to retrieve my sketchbook and pencils. I needed them in order to tell Dexter my real name the way I had planned. I wasn't sure exactly how it would work out, but I did know that having those vestiges of childhood with me would help, if only to lend a measure of comfort.

TWENTY-SIX

The Confession

"Talk not of wasted affection; affection never was wasted."
—Henry Wadsworth Longfellow, *Evangeline: A Tale of Acadie*

I'd been in Dexter's study only once before, on the first night I came to Blakeley House. That day had signaled the true beginning of my friendship with Dexter. As he'd walked me by twilight back to Everston, I'd realized what an extraordinary gentleman he was—a stark contrast to my first impression of him from the stagecoach ride.

Maybe it wasn't that my first impression had been unfavorable, only that it felt strange experiencing a connection with someone—especially a complete stranger—after spending so long thinking I was in love with someone else.

I sat down at the desk and opened my sketchbook to the drawing I'd made of Roxy and him that summer my family had spent at Everston. Then I emptied my case of pencils and fiddled with them, adding color to the background of the old, familiar drawing. Once I heard Dexter enter the house, it wasn't long until he strode into the study, smiling self-assuredly. He closed the door behind him and let out a long breath. "What a day. And I have more to do…I haven't finished my sermon for tomorrow."

"Were you planning to stay here to work on it?"

"I'd better. If I go back to Everston now, I'll likely get caught in a conversation with Bram—and I'd rather be here with you, anyway. Do you want to help me?"

"Work on a sermon? I don't think I'd be any good at that."

"The hardest part is converting my abstract thoughts about what God has taught me through the study of Scripture into relevant examples for others to identify with."

"I can hardly imagine." I flipped to the next page in my sketchbook, simply for something else to do besides staring nervously at Dexter. The drawing happened to be of Natalia and a beau of hers from years ago. "How do you select the Scripture verses to preach on?"

"I pray for God to reveal those He wants me to share, and I listen closely for the guidance of His Holy Spirit, trusting Him to move in each person's heart as He sees fit."

"That Sunday I heard you preach, every time you recited a verse and explained what it meant, I felt as if you were speaking straight to my soul. I think I could have sat there all afternoon and simply listened to you talk."

"Well, you can sit with me now and watch me, if you'd like. I know I'd like that."

"If you don't think I'll be too much of a distraction."

Dexter studied me, his gorgeous eyes silently echoing the things he'd spoken aloud to me over the last few days. "You would be quite the distraction, whether in this room, down the hall, or at Everston. It doesn't matter where you are; you're all I think about. You...and being with you."

I felt my cheeks burn. How many times had he kissed me and told me he loved me? And yet, there I was, embarrassed because of a simple compliment.

"How long will you continue holding services in the woods?" I asked.

"Until the weather turns too cold for sitting outside for an hour. Tomorrow's service will probably be the last of the season. After that, anyone wanting to attend a Sunday service will have to travel into Laurelton, to Reverend Whitespire's church."

I stood, collecting my sketchbook and scattered pencils, then moved to the upholstered chair in the corner so that Dexter could sit at his desk. I knew I could talk all day with him about everything under the sun, but there was only one thing I needed to discuss. And I wasn't leaving the room until I'd done so. "Thank you again for giving me my sketchbook."

Rather than sit, Dexter leaned against the edge of his desk, facing me. "You've taken full ownership of it, then?" he asked with an amused smile.

"It's been mine...." I averted my gaze from his and started sorting my pencils, arranging them according to the colors of a rainbow. My confession wasn't going at all the way I'd planned. It was so easy to get lost in him, to speak with him about anything and everything, or to simply sit and stare at him—all of him.

"But first, it belonged to Estella Everstone—"

"—who is, I'm sure, never going to give it a second thought. She's probably replaced it with a hundred other sketchbooks by now."

"But she hasn't—"

"Elle, I've wanted to speak to you alone all afternoon." Before I knew it, Dexter was kneeling before my chair, his elbows propped on the armrests, playfully blocking my escape.

"But you have, silly. On the porch, when you first arrived...." I was stalling, for I knew that if he kissed me, I'd have a much harder time confessing.

"No...I meant alone, like this." He leaned forward and wrapped his arms around me, his hands at the small of my back. I met him halfway, still gripping my sketchbook in my lap as he kissed me, long and slow.

When he pulled away, I couldn't help it; I pushed forward for more, letting go of the sketchbook and looping my arms about his neck for a longer, deeper kiss. After that, he stayed just as he'd been, holding me at the waist, his cheek pressed to mine.

"Elle, I want to give you more than pencils and paper," he breathed into my ear. "I want to give you all the dresses you could want...everything, everything I have...Blakeley House and Everston...."

I knew exactly what he meant—and I also felt heartsick because I couldn't give him the answer he wanted to hear. The answer I wanted to give him.

Not until I told him.

I leaned back against the cushions. "You've already given me everything, Dexter. Being with you is all I've wanted since meeting you. And that's what I'm trying to explain. You don't need to—"

"I *do* need to. I want to keep you, to spoil you. I can't bear the thought of you anywhere but with me."

"And neither can I, truly, Dexter, but you need to—"

"Will you marry me, then? I never imagined I'd ask such a question of any woman, but you—just knowing you, who you are—you give me no other choice. Our hearts have been fitted together; you feel it, too, don't you?" With his face just inches away, his eyes locked on mine, I saw everything he was willing to give—even his whole heart—written plainly in his pleading expression.

"Yes, I feel it; I do." I shoved the sketchbook and pencil case in between the armrest and cushion. I could no longer imagine using them as I'd planned. The conversation had intensified much too quickly. "But I... You have no idea how complicated this is."

"Why make it complicated?" he whispered. "All you have to do is say yes." He kissed my cheek, then just stayed there, so close.

I took in a long breath. "I want to." The words came out as I slowly exhaled. I reached for his face, my fingers traveling lightly over his cheeks to his jaw. I just hoped it wasn't for the last time.

He met my eyes, his hopeful look having turned to one of confusion. "Then why don't you?"

"Because...because my last name isn't Stoneburner...and Elle is just my nickname. Because you probably won't like what I'm about to tell you." My heart thudded violently in my chest, and I could hardly breathe.

He backed away a few inches but still knelt before me. "Go on...."

I took a deep breath. "My name is Estella." I leaned forward, resting my head on his shoulder, so he couldn't see my face. "Estella Everstone."

He went as rigid as stone and removed his hands from my waist. Then he scooted back, sitting on his haunches in a rather undignified manner, and stared at me.

"I know it's—"

"What are you saying?" There was a tone in his voice I'd never heard before—a tone of betrayal.

I didn't know how to respond to the anger burning in his eyes. I touched his left hand, with which he'd been gripping the armrest.

He pulled it from my grasp, slowly got to his feet, and turned away from me. Then he rubbed his hands down his face, raked them through his hair, and let out a long breath. Without a word, he walked over to the stone fireplace and propped one elbow on the mantel. With his other hand, he covered his eyes.

I moved to stand before him, but he didn't acknowledge me as I waited, terrified of what he might say, already feeling the pain of the heartbreak I was now certain was coming.

Finally, he asked a simple "Why?" that spoke a dozen questions.

"When Will was murdered, Vance thought it best that I go into hiding. And Father—"

"Bram Everstone...your father." He spoke slowly, but his eyes revealed the same burning fury.

"Yes. I knew from the letter you gave me in the lobby that day we had breakfast together that Father would agree I'd be safe here with you, once Mrs. Granton was taken away—"

"He told me in the carriage this morning that Elle…." Dexter licked his lips, as if he couldn't believe what he was about to utter. "He said Elle Stoneburner was an excellent choice for a wife. Why would he say that?" He was addressing me, looking in my direction, but not seeing me there.

I took a step closer but didn't dare touch him. "Because he likes you. Because he approves of you…of you and me, together."

He dismissed my words with a shake of his head. "But he knows why that would never work."

"Why not?" I hated that I sounded like a pouty, petulant child. "We love each other, and Father approves. I'm sorry for being dishonest about my identity, but, as I explained, it was for my own safety. I was to live under an alias until Vance dealt with the man who murdered Will."

"What else did you lie about?" Dexter demanded. "What of your engagement to Crawford?"

"That was the truth. He asked me to marry him, but when he felt God had called him to mission work, he broke off the engagement. He didn't think I would be a suitable—"

"I imagine not."

Those words hurt. "The only truth I kept from you was my name. But you know me—the real me. While here, while with you, I've discovered who I truly am; I've uncovered what I truly want."

"And what is that?" he asked slowly, as if he wasn't entirely sure of my answer.

"I belong with you, Dexter, and I want to be with you more than I've ever wanted anything. You know me better than anyone ever has, whether by the name Elle or Estella. I'm the same person. I didn't present a false persona; I just fibbed about my name. Is

229 The Captive Imposter 229

that so bad?" On the brink of tears, I brought my fingertips to the corners of my eyes.

"Elle—Estella—Miss Everstone." He seemed to struggle with every single name, as if he didn't know what to call me. "It's not that you purposefully lied...about anything." His every word seemed to require great control.

"Then what is it?"

"You wouldn't know, would you? You were just a little girl at the time...Roxy's friend." He spoke absently again, as if to himself. Taking his arm from the mantel, he paced the room several times before his eyes finally returned to me. "She knows who you are, doesn't she? That's why she stole your drawing the first night you came. She would have recognized you better than I, since the two of you were so close."

"Yes, but you're not making any sense, Dexter." I crossed the room and gently touched him on the arm. "Why don't you think we can—"

"Because it was Natalia."

My heart skipped at my sister's name. Had I heard him correctly? "What do you mean, it was Natalia? What does she have to do—"

"Natalia was the one who broke Cull's heart. The one who backed out of the engagement because of your mother's wishes. Your brother Will spread the rumors that destroyed my family's reputation."

He looked down at me, his gorgeous eyes already devoid of any of the light I'd sparked by kissing him that night in the hall. Now they were empty, as if the joy I'd brought to his life now meant nothing. I released his arm and stepped away, convinced he now despised my touch.

Without another word, Dexter left the room. Then I heard the crack of the front door as it slammed shut after him.

It was no wonder Dexter hadn't been as keen to talk about Natalia and Will as he had about Nathan and Vance. Dexter would never want me now, no matter my name. How could he, when it was my sister who had caused such unspeakable heartache for him and his family?

I looked at the sketchbook in my hand. The "Mr. Collins" from my long-ago drawings I'd remembered was Cullen…and the mother who'd been against his match with Natalia had been my own. That must have been why Dexter had become taciturn when we'd flipped through my sketchbook together that afternoon on the hill. It must have brought so many old memories to mind. Was this part of the reason Father had sold him Everston? To somehow make up for the pain Natalia and Will had both caused?

I thought back to my conversation with Father. He'd been so insistent I tell Dexter the truth…but he must have known what the outcome would be. Why hadn't he simply told me about Natalia and Cullen?

Upon reaching my room, I changed into the ugly brown dress from my days as Mrs. Granton's companion, collected the bear my mother had made me, and positioned the sketchbook and pencil case at the bottom of the wardrobe, beneath the tattered quilt I'd worn for my "tryst" with Dexter. I never wanted to see them again.

I'd maintained my composure thus far, but once I sat down on my bed with my back against the headboard, my hands clutched around my knees, I couldn't help but sob into my arms.

Dexter didn't want me, no matter that he'd told me he loved me and had kissed me and had asked me to marry him. He only wanted Elle Stoneburner, who had nothing but him—no money, no status, and no sister who had committed a seemingly unpardonable sin against his family.

If only I'd been able to leave Everston with Mrs. Granton, I never would have fallen so dreadfully far in love with him. How easy it would have been to forget the strange preoccupation I'd had with him those first weeks. Then he would be merely someone I might remember at random in years to come, rather than someone who now unwittingly held too much of my heart for me to go on as if nothing had happened between us.

I sat there, wracked with sobs, as the reality set in: It didn't matter that I had changed, that I was no longer the spoiled young socialite Estella Everstone. What mattered was that Natalia was my sister—a fact I was powerless to change.

TWENTY-SEVEN

Everston

"The broken heart. You think you will die, but you just keep
living, day after day after terrible day."
—Charles Dickens, *Great Expectations*

Dusk settled and turned to dark as I walked the cold,
lonely mile to Everston. Leaving Roxy's warmer blue
coat—it wasn't mine to take—I had worn the ugly lighter-weight
jacket from the travel suite I'd worn to Everston.

I'd left quickly, determined not to see Beatrix, and especially
not Roxy, on my way out. Since Roxy didn't know the details of
her family's tragic past, the news of her brother's reaction wouldn't
make sense to her unless I divulged more than Dexter wanted her
to hear.

I felt a new heaviness as I neared Everston for the first time
since meeting Dexter on the road to Blakeley House. Just four
weeks had passed since then, but it felt much longer. I never could
have envisioned that my time there would end this way, and yet I
saw no way of rectifying the situation. I couldn't imagine anything
besides going home with my father...and my broken heart.

Upon reaching the hotel, I climbed the steps to the veranda,
which appeared virtually deserted now that high season had
passed.

I was grateful to find Father seated alone in one of the many available rocking chairs. He seemed to be waiting for me, or maybe for Vance.

When he saw me approach, he stood and slowly walked to meet me. "This unlocks the room I'd secured for Vance," he said, pressing a key into my palm. "We'll get another room once he arrives."

"Do we have to stay?"

He sighed. "I take it your confession didn't end well."

"He won't have me. He asked me to marry him and then took it back the moment I told him. He doesn't want me."

"Of course, he wants you. He's simply shocked. He'll get over—"

"No, he's changed his mind, and he told me why. He told me about Natalia. Why didn't you say something?"

"Would you have gone through with it if I had?"

He was right; I probably wouldn't have.

"He was in love with Elle Stoneburner," I sulked. "Not me."

"But is there any difference between those two women, aside from the name?"

"None at all," I affirmed.

"That's right, Estella. It wasn't your name but your core attributes—your compassionate spirit, your unwavering love, your quiet resilience—that Dexter fell in love with. He described you to me, just as you are. He knows you, Estella, and he loves you."

"He left the house in a fury that would suggest otherwise," I huffed. "He was quite angry with me, Father...with the whole situation, I imagine."

"Is he aware you walked from his house to Everston at dusk? You shouldn't have—"

"I couldn't stay there. His mother has been against me from the start; she'll hate me all the more once she knows who I am.

And Roxy is oblivious about Cullen and Natalia; I don't want to be the one to explain, and I promised Dexter I wouldn't—"

"I see. And you think hiding yourself away at Everston and then going home to Boston—ignoring the situation altogether—is best."

"You didn't see his face—how disgusted, how perplexed, he seemed as he contemplated what you said to him on the way from Severville. He could barely stand to look at me." Tears threatened to spill down my cheeks for the second time that night. I hated crying, especially in front of Father. I sucked in a sob. "If it's all right with you, I think I'll retire for the night." I held up the key he'd given me. "I don't feel like seeing anyone."

"We'll be here for at least a few days, Estella."

I heard the disappointment in his voice—it was the same tone I was accustomed to hearing from Father whenever we spoke. It seemed I never did what he thought I should, especially in regard to men.

"And there's church tomorrow," he added.

"But Dexter's preaching. He's supposed to be working on his sermon right now." I didn't know how he could. What kind of sermon would he deliver after such a terrible evening? I dreaded hearing it almost as much as I dreaded seeing him again.

"I'd like to go, for Vance's sake. I know he'll go if we both do."

I sighed, knowing he was right. Attending church had never been a priority of Vance's, but he wasn't about to skip out if we didn't.

"I'll go, Father."

But I would also pray that Vance wouldn't make it to Everston in time for church the next morning. I didn't want to face Dexter again. I wasn't sure which would be worse: experiencing the sting of rejection yet again or being ignored altogether.

How could this be happening to me again, and so soon after getting over Jay?

Even the combination of countless attempts I'd made to convince Jay that he was mistaken in breaking off our engagement wouldn't compare with how humbled I would feel if Dexter refused me even just one more time.

～

Sunday, October 25, 1891 · Everston

Vance arrived on Saturday evening, but I didn't make a point to see him. I stayed in my room on the fifth floor, just down the hall from the room where I'd stayed while employed by Mrs. Granton.

It felt odd to walk that hall again, to be assaulted by memories of an inebriated Lester Imbody, a sleepy Mrs. Granton, and a spiteful Ursula Imbody throwing accusations at me.

Father had brought a few trunks of what had long been considered my customary wardrobe, including a few black and gray House of Worth mourning gowns and matching black accessories. He hadn't brought a maid for me, though; apparently he hadn't thought about who would style my hair to match the austerity of those gowns. But I'd become quite skilled at pinning up my own hair, and any wayward or plain coiffures were easily covered with my gray velvet hat covered in ostrich feathers that had been dyed black.

On Sunday morning, I faced the mirror in the corner of the room as I put the final touches on my ensemble before heading down to meet Vance for breakfast. Dressed in a pewter-gray ruched silk gown and an elaborate feathered hat, I didn't feel like myself. It was no longer comfortable wearing them, these clothes I'd wanted so badly two months before.

And then, there was the luxurious mink fur mantle Father had brought for me. The weather had turned much colder overnight, making it appropriate; and I would have to wear it, no matter how I regretted that Dexter would see me in it, since the brown travel coat wouldn't fit over my gown—not that it went with it at all.

I didn't look forward to going downstairs, or to the church service—anywhere except into the stagecoach that would take me quickly away from the memories, the heartache. Dexter was likely at Everston somewhere, either downstairs in his office or upstairs in his living quarters on the sixth floor.

He had to know I was there. Where else would I be?

And Roxy—did she know where I'd gone? I'd left her without saying good-bye, and I would probably never see her again. Dexter, I was certain, wouldn't want me to.

Looking out the window at the familiar view of the surrounding mountains, I lamented that I would likely never see Everston again, either. I couldn't bear to relive the pain it would bring. I actually hadn't thought of it much since taking up residence at Blakeley House, probably because it belonged to Dexter...and so did I, or so I'd hoped.

Now I would lose both.

In two months' time, I'd gone from being lost and overwhelmed to having the courage to recognize and acknowledge exactly what I wanted.

Turning away from the window, I took one last, long look in the mirror. I truly felt overdressed, as if adorned just to make other people look at me. But I knew too well that, just like before, they wouldn't really see me. I had gone back to being invisible. All anyone had ever seen or cared about me was the dress, the hat, the jewelry, the money...and nothing about me at all.

The thought of going back to my lonely existence amid society crowds in Boston depressed me; but as I left my room and made my way down the elevator, I attempted to mentally prepare myself.

But it was impossible. I was a different person now. Dexter had seen in me everything I wanted to be, but it didn't matter now.

Misery flooded me as the elevator doors opened to the lobby. There weren't many people about, but as I stepped into the hall, I felt the knowing stares of the few who were loitering about.

I lifted my chin, just as I'd always done, for I knew what they were thinking: *It's Estella Everstone. What do you think she's been doing here, posing as Elle Stoneburner? Why would her family send her away? What does all this have to do with her brother's murder?*

Soon I heard Dexter's voice from the hotel office behind the front desk. "I know you were supposed to have had the entire weekend off, but this will be the last Sunday I'll need you to work. I'm sorry, Miss Hawthorne."

"It's quite all right, Mr. Blakeley," I heard Violet answer.

From around the wall of the office, I heard the door shut, and then Violet answer the telephone—which created the perfect chance for me to slip by unnoticed. With my shoulders squared and my head held high, I walked past the front desk. Violet stayed busy jotting something down as she held the telephone receiver to her ear.

As I walked by, my eyes drifted to the door separating me from Dexter—not that it was the only thing. I slowed my pace, half wishing for it to open, for Dexter to see me and smile like he had so many other times. For him to forgive me, for having been a snob for most my life, and Natalia, for what she'd done to Cullen.

Then, to my shock, the door swung open. There stood Dexter, framed by the dark wood doorway, dressed in his usual black custom-fitted suit.

And he stared through me. As if he didn't even see me.

I'd already felt as if my heart had been ripped to shreds from everything that had happened between us the day before, but that look of complete indifference hurt me like nothing else could have. I froze, unable to move, paralyzed by the pain in my chest—a physical ache that prevented me from breathing and made me want to retch.

Then Dexter turned and said something more to Violet before heading back into his office slamming the door behind him.

After pausing for the briefest of moments to grasp the emptiness of that look, I hurried on through the lobby to the dining room to meet Vance for breakfast.

Dexter clearly wanted to forget me. It seemed he'd started to already.

TWENTY-EIGHT

Vance Everstone

"We must not always talk in the marketplace
of what happens to us in the forest."
—Nathaniel Hawthorne, *The Scarlet Letter*

Father told me you're in a hurry to leave Everston. Why is that?" Vance asked me at breakfast.

Everything up until that horribly invasive question had been mere chitchat. But Vance had always been blunt, albeit in a much different way than Dexter. Vance meant to cut to the chase, even if it resulted in hurt feelings and bruised egos, while Dexter always remained a gentleman, even if somewhat abrupt at times.

"I just want to go home. It's been so long," I finally answered.

"I don't know why you didn't just stay at Blakeley House."

Vance seemed a bit troubled that I'd broken character, and I hoped that it would incline him to want to leave that much sooner, so I could go with him. Did he still think we were in danger?

"You do know that Father plans to stay on into the week, don't you?" Vance asked me.

"Of course. He needs to meet with Dex—I mean, Mr. Blakeley."

"Hmm. You're on a first-name basis with him already, are you?" Vance studied me, his black eyes narrowed skeptically. Then he glanced out the windows overlooking the lake and Iron Mountain.

"Nothing's changed much around here. It seems like he's been keeping Everston respectable."

"Of course he has."

"And you? Blakeley's been keeping you just as respectably, I assume?"

"He stayed here while I was living at Blakeley House, if that's what you mean."

"Sure, that's what I meant." Vance took a sip of his coffee, keeping his eyes on me. "I wouldn't want you to forget just who you are while pretending to be nobody."

"I never—"

"Probably didn't like finding out he'd been keeping one of the hated Everstones under his roof, did he?"

I glanced about the dining room, thankful that it was mostly empty. "No, he didn't seem to…." I forked through my omelet, hunting out the mushrooms I didn't remember asking for. "I don't understand. Does he hate you, too? And what about Father?"

"Oh, I imagine he despises him just as much; he merely keeps up an appearance of civility as part of the deal. Men can be great pretenders, you know, Stella."

From what Dexter had said about my father, I couldn't believe him capable of hating him.

"Did he tell you about Talia and his brother?"

"Yes." I made an effort to ignore the questions streaming through my mind, but it was impossible. Vance probably knew all about that summer. "Did you know Cullen Blakeley?"

"Well, sure, we all did. The families practically lived together that summer. I guess you were too young to know what was going on."

"Why didn't someone tell me the Blakeley family would hate me—especially after I wrote to Natalia that I'd be living with them?"

"Yes, well, I suppose she forgot to mention it."

"In the one letter I'd received, Natalia had said that Dexter was an old family friend—someone I could trust."

"Hmm. Well, that's the truth. He is a trustworthy fellow, I'll give him that." Vance brought a hand to his chin and seemed to be in great thought before adding, "Perhaps she thought you might like him as much as she liked his brother." A mocking look lit his eyes.

I swallowed hard. As shrewd as Vance was, I needed to take care about what I said of Dexter, or he would guess just how far I'd gone in trusting Cullen Blakeley's brother. "Yes, perhaps."

Vance studied me for a moment, then went back to his breakfast. "All I know is, she was well aware it was Cullen's brother Father sold the hotel to last summer."

I set down my fork with sudden force. "Why was I not told? It was quite a shock when I heard it from Violet Hawthorne."

"I suppose no one thought you would care." Vance took another sip of coffee, suddenly avoiding my gaze. "Do you know this Violet Hawthorne very well?"

"She works the front desk. I'm sure you'll meet her eventually, if you haven't already. She's there right now, in fact." The jumble of memories from my last full day at Everston was strewn about my heart like a puzzle of pieces that no longer fit together. "I was merely under the impression Dexter Blakeley was the manager of Everston when we were first introduced—not the owner."

"Were you?" Vance leaned back and assessed me with his perceptive dark eyes.

Vance and I had never been close, yet it seemed he could read me rather well.

"It was weeks later when Violet inadvertently told me the truth of the matter. I suppose I should have told him who I was back then, once I knew…." I clasped my hands in my lap, wondering just how much I should tell Vance. "But then, I suppose he wouldn't have offered me the position at Blakeley House. He probably would have sent me home, glad if he never saw me again."

"Surely, the Blakeleys don't hate *you* that much. Especially your old friend Roxy. You two were just children at the time. You didn't have anything to do with what happened."

"And you did?"

"Nathan and I might have said a few things to encourage Cullen's interest. We thought they were a good match. I never dreamed Mother wouldn't approve. She never seemed to have a problem with Talia spending time with Cullen before she found out just how serious they were."

"Why didn't Mother approve?"

"I was under the impression she'd met someone else that summer with whom she wanted Talia to form an attachment. You know, someone better suited for inheriting Father's empire."

"You can't mean George Livingston."

"Of course not."

"But she married him just over a year later, right after Mother passed away."

"As far as I know, Talia simply encouraged the first man who showed any interest in her after Mother's funeral. If you'll recall, she married him before her mourning period was anywhere close to being completed. It's not as if it was something that needed to be shared with an eight-year-old. And, I have to admit, we didn't pay much attention to you back then, did we?"

"Most people don't pay much attention to me, unless they're men in search of a hefty inheritance to marry," I murmured.

"Come on, Stella—it's not like there's nothing to you beyond your wealth and family name. You have plenty of desirable assets." He smirked rakishly; it seemed he couldn't help behaving in such a manner, no matter whom he was addressing. "Besides, you are awfully pretty. But that's no surprise, considering your striking resemblance to me."

"Thank you, Vance." I could tell he was trying to cheer me up. "Why do you think Natalia was so easily persuaded to refuse Cullen? Did it seem she truly loved him?"

"I have no doubt she loved him. I remember when Dexter came around to tell her about...what had happened. She was sick with grief. She didn't speak for over a month."

"I can imagine." I'd been thinking through the whole sad situation and the multitude of ways it had affected so many people: Dexter, Beatrix, Roxy, Father, Will, me.... "I wish Natalia had told me in her letter, or that somebody would have alerted me before.... I wouldn't have...."

"You wouldn't have what?"

Taken the position at Blakeley House. Rekindled my friendship with Roxy. Fallen in love with Dexter...so many things.

"I would have telephoned Father when Mrs. Granton left Everston." I took one last sip of the hotel's trademark blueberry tea.

"Did you not like staying at Blakeley House?"

"No, it's just...I wouldn't have become so dreadfully attached to everything here." I set my teacup on its saucer. "And now I *have* to leave."

Our breakfast complete, Vance and I stood from our table and walked arm in arm toward the lobby. "Come on now, Stella. If you wanted to, you could live at Everston indefinitely. Just pair up with some old lady like Mrs. Granton and rent a room. It's that easy."

"I couldn't."

"Why not?"

"Dexter Blakeley despises me."

"What does that matter? I'm likely not his favorite person, either, but I'm here." Vance guided me to the coatroom.

Once I had the mink mantle draped over my shoulders, we went to the lobby, where we were supposed to meet Father before heading to church.

Dexter was nowhere to be seen. Violet stood alone at the front desk. She looked right at me and smiled brightly as I entered the room on Vance's arm, but as we came nearer, she appeared a bit flustered. She came out from behind the counter to meet us.

"Elle! I'd heard from Mr. Mulduney that you no longer work for Mr. Blakeley? That you've taken a room here, and that—"

"Yes, it's a long story," I interjected before she could say anything else. I was actually surprised she didn't know the whole truth already. "I'll be going back home to Boston to live with my family."

"Your family?" I watched her as she took in the fineness of the fur cape.

"Is this Violet?" Vance asked dryly. "The girl seems harmless enough. Just tell her the truth."

Violet looked almost transfixed as her gaze traveled over Vance. His arresting good looks and intriguing aura often had that effect on women.

"Vance, meet my friend Miss Violet Hawthorne."

He extended a hand to Violet, and when she took it, he shook slowly, which surprised me. Whenever he interacted with a young lady—no matter who she was or where she came from—he usually poured on the charm, planting a kiss on her bare knuckles or even—scandalously—her palm.

But he didn't do any of that with Violet. Instead, there was a peculiar look on his face as he studied her, as if he recognized her.

"Violet, meet Mr. Vance Everstone…my brother."

"Your brother? Is he your half brother, then?"

"No. Everstone is my name, as well. Estella Everstone."

"Not Elle Stoneburner, lady's companion?" For some reason, she didn't sound surprised. She kept her eyes on Vance, who had yet to release her hand.

"I'm afraid not."

"I had wondered about that," she said absently, looking past me to Vance.

"You did? But how—"

"Not about your name, per se; I simply noticed that you seemed utterly unlike any other lady's companion I'd met—and I've met a lot. As I said before, you're a rare mix of culture and humility. And I guess I was exactly right, if your father used to own Everston. You must be unbelievably wealthy."

"You might say that," Vance supplied.

"Won't you stay a while longer?" Violet asked, finally looking at me. "I would hate to see you leave so soon. And I can't imagine Mr. Blakeley wants to see you go."

"Oh, I'm certain he's come to terms with the situation by now," I replied, trying not to pique Vance's curiosity. If he knew the details of the "situation," he was likely to take it upon himself to repair the breach between Dexter and me, and that would only make matters worse.

"Well, Stella, I think we should go," Vance said, finally letting go of Violet's hand. "The surreys are already lined up outside, and we don't want to miss our ride to church." He grasped me by the elbow. "It was a pleasure meeting you, Miss Hawthorne," he added with a dip of his chin.

As we waited outside for Father, Vance turned to me sharply. "What happened between you and Dexter Blakeley, exactly? Don't lie to me and say 'Nothing,' because I can tell there was definitely *something.*"

"It's a long story," I admitted hesitantly.

"Well, you're not alone in having one of those. And it can't be that long of a story; you've been here only seven or eight weeks." He paused expectantly.

"It doesn't matter now."

"You told me he stayed at Everston while you were at Blakeley House, but how often did he come around? What exactly has he done to make you—"

"He is a gentleman, Vance. He hasn't done anything untoward; he's been very good to me."

"All right, then; since something *has* happened—and you can't tell me it hasn't—why did you wait until yesterday to let him know who you were?"

"I tried and tried, but then…well, he proposed, and then I was forced to tell him. I was already terrified of what he might think of me, but I didn't know how bad the situation was until he told me about Natalia and Cullen, and I left Blakeley House."

Vance looked as if he might deliver a punch to the nearest porch pillar. "I didn't know he booted you out of his house! How dare he—"

"He didn't boot me out. I left of my own accord."

"Have you seen him since?"

I nodded. "In the lobby this morning, before I met you for breakfast."

"So, he's here."

"Of course, he's here. He almost always is."

"Did he say anything to you?"

"He didn't see me."

"That's not likely."

"He looked right through me."

"Well, I'll be sure to talk to him before—"

"Oh, please don't! There's nothing more to say. He doesn't want me now, Vance. He only wanted Elle Stoneburner."

"But he proposed? And you love him? Whatever happened between the two of you should be—"

"It cannot be fixed. The situation is irreparable. If you try to intervene, I won't talk to you ever again."

"But I'm certain I can change his mind—"

"I don't want you to. I want him to love me, to want me in his life, because he needs me to be there. Not because my brother convinced him to."

"If he wanted to marry you yesterday, before you told him who you are, I have no doubt he can be persuaded to want to marry you again today. Stella, you're one of the most sought-after—"

"He won't be, I'm certain. You would believe me if you'd seen his face when—"

"I will see his face. When I speak with him."

"Please, Vance, don't interfere. What do you know about love, anyway?"

Vance gave me a scathing look, and I immediately regretted my thoughtless remark.

"Please don't say a word," I pleaded. But I knew I'd already sealed my fate.

"I'll show *you* what I know about love. And it's more than you think."

His spiteful words still hung in the air when Father walked out to join us.

"There's no changing my mind," Vance continued, bringing Father into the conversation. "Now I just need to figure out where to corner him. It's a shame dueling isn't done anymore."

"Corner whom?" Father asked, just as I knew Vance had hoped he would.

"Blakeley. He can't tell Stella he's in love with her one day, and the next, act as if she's—"

"Father, please, make him stop!" I cried. "Dexter made it all too clear he doesn't want me because of my family, and what we've done to his. Nothing Vance may say or do can change that."

Father gave Vance a bemused smile I found quite infuriating. "You'll have a chance to see Mr. Blakeley this very morning, at Leightner Hollow. Estella says he's giving the sermon."

"Is that right?" Vance leered wickedly at me. "How perfect."

Vance took the steps down to the last surrey in the line headed to Leightner Hollow.

My stomach twisted into knots at the thought of Vance speaking with Dexter. Where would I hide myself as he did so? I clenched my fists under the cover of my mantle. "Why does Vance insist on interfering?" I lamented to my father, "I purposefully tried to keep the details of what happened with Dexter from him, but he somehow wheedled them out of me."

"I wouldn't worry yourself excessively, Estella. I believe everything will be fine. I don't know many men who would fall out of love as easily as—"

"I didn't say I don't think he still loves me. From his actions and his words ever since I met him, I have to believe he does; but that doesn't mean he wants to."

"Unlike Jayson Crawford Castleman, who wanted to love you but, in the end, couldn't bring himself to, truly. Am I right?"

My father's perceptiveness left me speechless.

"You have to understand, Estella, that Dexter isn't Jayson. I've known them both for a very long time, and I'll be the first to tell you Dexter Blakeley is the better man. By a long shot. He would never toy with your affections."

"I'm the one who toyed with him, by not telling him who I was for so long."

"But you didn't know...we didn't know it would matter. The thought never occurred to us that you and Dexter would fall in love."

"I wish we hadn't." I could already feel the hardness of disillusionment overtaking my heart. I was only one-and-twenty, and already I'd failed at love twice.

I never wanted to fall in love again.

But then, I hadn't aimed to fall in love with Dexter.

In fact, I'd tried my very best not to.

TWENTY-NINE

The Hollow

"Clarity of mind means clarity of passion, too; this is why a great and clear mind loves ardently and sees distinctly what it loves."
—Blaise Pascal

I took my seat in the surrey with Father and Vance just before the line of vehicles started down the drive through the green pines and brown- and orange-leafed birches. When we got to Leightner Hollow, we were the last of the hotel guests to reach the benches, which meant most of the seats—there weren't many to begin with—were taken, obliging us to sit in the front row.

Where I kept my attention focused in my lap.

I hoped to keep Vance from speaking to Dexter—not that I knew how. Why did Vance not care how humiliated I would be for him to speak to him on my behalf? Dexter didn't have any intentions concerning me anymore. Not even Vance's most persuasive argument would change that. There was nothing he could do or say to fix it, for the chasm between Dexter and me had been created by hard facts, old scars, and relational circumstances between our families that he clearly could neither forgive nor forget.

After a few minutes of staring at my lap, I couldn't stand it any longer; I lifted my gaze to Dexter.

And then, no matter how I wanted to—knew I needed to—look away, my eyes wouldn't move from his form as he paced behind the pulpit. He looked dashingly handsome, as always. He held his Bible to his chest, clutching it with both hands, and appeared to be praying silently. Soon he would open his eyes and see me with Father and Vance, and then what would he do? What would he think? Would he even see me, or would he see past me once again? I almost hoped so, for I didn't want to be a distraction as he delivered his sermon.

I closed my own eyes to pray. *God, help Dexter to concentrate, that he might convey his message as he's been called to do. He needs Your peace right now. He needs You more than he needs me. And I need You more than I could ever need him. Why do I keep forgetting that?*

When I opened my eyes, I somehow restrained myself from raising them to the stage, to Dexter. It was a good thing I'd left my sketchbook and pencils purposefully at Blakeley House. Having the drawings of Dexter on hand would have been too strong of a temptation. I wouldn't have been able to resist studying them, and that would only have kept reopening the wound on my heart.

Led by one of the young ladies from the congregation, we sang "Joyful, Joyful, We Adore Thee," our voices making a heavenly sound as they reverberated off the ceiling of the hollow. Of course, I didn't feel joyful; I wondered if I ever would again.

Beside me, Vance surprised me with the sound of his rich deep voice. He didn't usually sing in church, on the rare occasion he attended.

When the hymn was finished, and we were seated again, Dexter prayed, "Let us come to the Lord, humbly...." He remained silent for quite a while before continuing. "Savior, You're the only One who can save us. Help us to remember that. Help me to remember that." He paused again. "You are the Alpha and the Omega. You see everything from beginning to end, from start to finish, and You make all things good, even when it doesn't look that way to us. You have revealed to us what is good, and Your

Word reminds us what is required of us: to do justly, to love mercy, and to walk humbly beside You in Christlikeness." He took a deep breath before concluding: "Lord, help us, for our hearts are weak. In the name of Jesus Christ we pray, amen."

As Dexter began to preach, I endeavored to keep my attention on his words rather than on how good he looked and how confident he sounded. I knew I couldn't afford to dwell on him—the second man I'd loved and had nearly been able to call mine.

Father had been right in perceiving that Jay's wishy-washy affections—his coming in and out of my life multiple times, always making me think he'd changed his mind, only to change it back again—had done some long-lasting damage to my heart.

I'd thought my confidence in Dexter's love had been strong enough, but every time I recalled his reaction to learning the truth about my identity, I sank further and further into disbelief that he could ever want me again. The doubt was something I didn't know how to overcome.

As I refocused my attention on Dexter's sermon, I heard him quote a verse he'd alluded to in his opening prayer: "'*He hath shewed thee, O man, what is good; and what doth the* LORD *require of thee, but to do justly, and to love mercy, and to walk humbly with thy God?*'"

Beside me, I was surprised to see Vance reading along from a pocket-sized Bible.

"Do you know the reference to that verse?" I asked him quietly.

Vance tilted the page for me to see. "Micah six, verse eight," he whispered.

"We love to complicate things," Dexter continued. "We make a ritual out of our efforts to please God; we wrap it up in nice paper and seal it with a bow, thinking we're going above and beyond, making ourselves more valuable to Him. But we're to *just* do what is right and know what is right by reading the Word. We're to *just* show mercy as God has shown mercy. We're to recognize that God is the only One worthy of praise; nothing we can do will ever make us worthy of adulation."

After a long pause from Dexter, during which I continued to study the luxuriously soft fur of the mantle draped over me, Vance leaned over and whispered, "He hasn't stopped staring at you."

I didn't answer him. And I didn't glance up to see whether he was telling the truth.

"It's almost as if he were in love with you, or something. And why wouldn't he be? Just because you're Estella Everstone and not some nobody named Elle Stoneburner?"

His comments stoked a small ember of hope in my heart, but it petered out then I remembered how very scheming Vance could be.

"You can't fix everything, Vance," I muttered.

"Sure, I can. Just you wait."

"*For now we see through a glass, darkly....*'"

Hearing those words from Dexter, I couldn't help it; my gaze shot to him, and he was, indeed, watching me, his eyes dark and intense. Butterflies replaced the knots in my stomach.

"*...But then face to face: now I know in part; but then shall I know even as also I am known.*'" After completing the verse, Dexter continued, "God says, simply, to do what is right: to show mercy as you humble yourself before God and others. He's speaking to you...and to me."

As his deep voice boomed over the congregation, I wished I'd been less preoccupied with my own heartache during his sermon. I recalled the first time I'd heard him preach—how mesmerized I'd been as he'd spoken. His words and his heartfelt passion had begun to weaken my resistance to everything else I found attractive about him, and it hadn't been long thereafter that I'd realized what a truly exceptional man he was.

He was still watching me, as if I were the only person in attendance. I couldn't tell why he studied me, though. Was he examining me, trying to figure out if the "new me"—the one dressed so extravagantly and seated between Bram and Vance Everstone—was really the same woman as Elle Stoneburner? I prayed he would realize that I was exactly who I'd always been, albeit now dressed in more expensive attire—attire I no longer felt I needed or even wanted.

"Miss Franklin, would you mind leading us again in song?" Dexter asked the young lady who had led us in the opening hymn. "Let's stand and sing 'Savior, like a Shepherd Lead Us.'"

"Savior, like a shepherd lead us, much we need Thy tender care...." As the hymn floated to the roof of the cavern, the compelling lyrics and sweet melody caused a swell of emotion in my chest. I wasn't ready for the service to be finished. I didn't know what to think about Dexter's message, about his staring. What did it mean?

We had just finished the hymn when Vance grabbed my hand, pulled me from my seat, and stalked toward the forest path to Half Moon Lake. I didn't fight his urgent grip, for something about his demeanor during the service led me to hope there was a transformation going on in that stubborn heart of his. I hoped that Dexter's message might have whittled away somewhat at the wall Vance had long hid behind.

After a short hike through the woods, we made it to the edge of Half Moon Lake, near the spring.

"What was that about?" I asked Vance when he finally released my hand.

He stood upon the rocks along the shore and stared at the great expanse of water for what seemed an hour before answering. "Dexter was getting to me."

"He does have a way of doing that."

"What he said about some people finding it difficult to see, or understand, what's wrong and right...." Vance combed his fingers through his unruly hair.

I must have missed that part of the sermon, so I said nothing but surveyed the space around us. I hadn't been back to the spring since the time I'd come upon Dexter praying...the time when he was so openly interested in kissing me. He'd broken through the wall of my reticence that day and encouraged my suppressed longings for him to grow to the point of being too difficult to ignore.

Standing near the basin of the spring, I lifted my eyes from the mesmerizing blue water lapping at the shore to the mountain range across from the lake as I recalled everything Dexter had said when he'd followed me back to the house. I'd tried to tell him the truth that day, but then he'd held me in his arms and insisted I didn't have to be alone anymore, insinuating what he would later articulate more fully—that he, too, believed we belonged together.

Closing off my mind to the agonizing memories, I asked Vance, "Do you remember this place?"

"Of course, I do. I used to come here all the time." He took a seat on the ledge and gestured for me to sit beside him.

"I don't remember your being all that interested in hiking and exploring back then."

"That's because I wasn't—" He stopped abruptly. "Stella, were you listening to Dexter back there?"

"I was a bit distracted," I admitted, "but I tried to pay attention. It was rather bewildering that he would stare—"

"It's because he's in love with you."

"Or because he was stunned to see me there, dressed as I am." I glanced down at the ruffled silk hem of my gray gown.

"Well, I was listening, and I've never experienced the feeling his words provoked within me." He took a deep breath. "Soon after Will was murdered, I began to experience a sense of heaviness, of responsibility. And, more recently, I've been sensing the enormity of almost every thought and desire I've ever had. Is that what it's like to...to be convicted?"

"Well, yes, I suppose." I'd never thought I would be privy to such transparency from the brother who was known for being hard-hearted and selfish.

"Everything I've done since Will's death—purposefully keeping away from the rest of the family, hiding you with Mrs. Granton—it's strange...." Vance held my hand like a loving brother—as Nathan might have done; like Dexter had done while we sat together on Iron Mountain. But this from Vance, whom I hardly knew, was strange indeed. "I've never been good, but I want to be good now."

"Never been good? That can't be true, Vance. Surely, you're only—"

"It is. I've always hated everyone else for being good...even you, Stella. And I'm sorry for that now. I've been a monster...to so many people."

I squeezed Vance's hand, thankful for the transformation that seemed to have started, and that Dexter's preaching had helped it along.

Before I could tell him so, I caught a whiff of something burning. I turned away from the lake and saw, in the sky behind us, just above the tree line, billows of black smoke. I let go of Vance's hand and jumped to my feet.

When Vance saw the smoke, he grabbed my hand again and pulled me toward the path leading back to the hollow.

"But, Vance, it's Blakeley House! We need to—"

"No, we don't. We need to get you to safety. If the house *is* on fire, it's likely too close to the trees; the whole blasted mountain could be ablaze in no time."

He kept moving toward the trail, but I managed to escape his grasp and ran up the path toward the house. I could hear him following after me, calling my name, but I refused to turn back.

I realized then that I hadn't seen Roxy or Beatrix at the service. Were they inside the house? And what about Mr. and Mrs.

McGuire? I knew they usually went to Laurelton for church. Panic mounted within me.

I hadn't realized how close the hollow was to Dexter's house—just around the ridge that extended to the banks of the lake, with the spring situated almost exactly halfway in between.

When we emerged from the woods, my heart broke for Dexter at the sight of black smoke pouring out from the first-floor windows of his Blakeley House.

Then I saw a man standing in the yard, holding his horse by its bridle.

It was Ezra Hawthorne.

THIRTY

Blakeley House

"When you pray, rather let your heart be without words
than your words without heart."
—John Bunyan

Greenlee Cole! Come on out! I know you're in there!"

Ezra stood there, watching the burning house, as
if he expected Greenlee to run outside and into his arms, and then
he'd ride off with her.

I was all the more thankful that Jay had married Greenlee and
taken her miles and miles away the day before.

As Vance and I hovered at the edge of the woods, hidden,
Roxy rushed onto the porch, dark smoke wafting out of the doorway behind her, and tossed her two kittens over the rail.

"Roxy!" I gasped. "Vance, we've got to do something!" I started
to run, but Vance grabbed me.

"He's got a gun, Stella," he said, nodding to Ezra. "We won't
be much help if he shoots us. We'll help, but when it's safe. Who
is he, anyway?"

"Ezra Hawthorne." I spat his name. "He's after Greenlee, Jay's
new wife, whom he held captive for some time."

"Hey! You, there!" Ezra shouted at Roxy. "Where's Greenlee?"

"No longer here!" Roxy wailed.

"You're lying! Violet told me she was here! Send her out!"

I could hardly believe it when Roxy disappeared inside the house again. What was she doing? Was her mother injured and in need of help escaping?

Apparently having realized Roxy wasn't lying, or figuring—correctly—that Greenlee would rather perish in a fire than find herself in his clutches again, Ezra mounted his horse.

"Vance! What do we do?" I nearly shrieked as Ezra disappeared down the drive. "We've got to save Roxy and Beatrix!"

"I'll get them out, Stella. Don't worry." Vance grabbed me by the arm and steered me toward the back of the barn. He unlatched the door and urged me inside. "Hide in here until you hear Blakeley, or until I come back for you, in case Hawthorne returns."

"Do be careful, Vance!" I cried, disarmed by his display of selflessness.

The barn door closed behind him, enveloping me in darkness. I heard horses whinnying nervously—they probably smelled the acrid odor of smoke and heard the haunting sounds of creaking wood and crackling flames.

Trying to block out the sounds of the fire, I sank to my knees, covering my ears and closing my eyes. "Oh God, help Vance—keep him safe! And please save Roxy and Beatrix. Dexter loves them so. And—"

The sound of footsteps halted my prayer, and I opened my eyes as the barn door swung open, admitting a shaft of bright sunlight. It couldn't have been Vance already; and if it was Dexter, I would rather stay hidden. And if it wasn't Dexter or Vance, then who? I'd watched Ezra Hawthorne ride away in defeat.

Still crouched in the shadows, I held my breath and waited.

"Well, well, well...what have we here?" said a man with a thick French accent.

My stomach contracted as I recalled Dexter's comment about a Frenchman in the company of Ezra Hawthorne just days before.

The gate of the stall where I'd been hiding swung open, and a man stepped into view. I was surprised at the sight of Jacques Gerard, for I'd been under the impression that the family Vance had been forced to marry into while in France had been a well-to-do, powerful sort. But that wasn't how this man seemed at all. He was short of stature with well-trimmed black hair and a sparse mustache and beard, and he wore a fraying jacket and shabby trousers...with the handle of a revolver plainly protruding from the front pocket.

"So, it is the *nonpareil* Estella Everstone I find...hiding in a barn? How *splendide*." He studied me with his fawn-brown eyes. "And *votre frère* is not far away, I presume?"

"No, he's not far; so you'd better take care, Monsieur Gerard."

"We will see. You forget...the fire. Is that not where he is now? Saving your friends?"

"He'll be back."

"Of course, he will. And we will be waiting." He grinned menacingly. "And *votre père*...where is he?"

"He's coming. He'll want to speak to Mr. Blakeley, whose house you burned down. Whose family you endangered."

"Ah, *oui*. We all must make our sacrifices." He fingered the handle of his revolver.

"But he didn't do anything to you."

"What does it matter? And it wasn't my idea; I just did the deed. It was Monsieur Hawthorne who wanted the fire." He took a step forward. "I just wanted you."

I backed into the corner of the stall. There was nowhere for me to go but over the five-foot wall into Knightley's stall, which was virtually impossible.

"Don't fret; I don't mean as you fear. But they will come looking for you soon, *non*?"

"Vance never did anything to you, or to your sister—"

"Ah, but she had his *bébé* and was forced into the *mariage*, only to die on the way to America. Do you not think it rather convenient?"

"Vance said it was appendicitis."

"Vance is a scoundrel. You believe everything he tells you?"

"I don't believe he would have purposefully hurt your sister, no matter the circumstances."

"Well, I hope he does not think the same of me." Jacques hurried at me and grabbed my arms, knocking the fur mantle from my shoulders as he twisted me around. In the struggle, he also knocked off my feathered hat, loosening the well-placed pins from my hair.

I managed to wrangle one hand free, and as he reached for his revolver, I seized the muzzle and pointed it toward the ceiling. He pulled me back against his chest, both of us still struggling for control of the gun. Clutching my waist with one arm, he pressed his knee to the backs of my legs, crippling me for a moment; but as I went down, I grabbed the gun from his grasp and flung it high in the air. A single shot exploded, and I could still feel the earsplitting reverberation as I watched the revolver land in the hayloft.

In the next stall, Knightley reared on his hind legs and let out a high-pitched squeal; then he bucked forward, his kick crashing through the wall and raining sharp wood splinters on Jacques. I looked at him only long enough to see he'd been knocked out, with blood trickling down the side of his face and seeping into his scraggly beard.

I scrambled out of the stall, fled from the barn, and sprinted into the yard, directly into Dexter's arms. We both toppled to the ground.

"Estella—thank God! You aren't hurt, are you?" He pulled me into his lap and cradled me against his chest. How good it felt to be held by him again.

"Your mother and sister, are they—"

"They're fine. They made it out in time, thanks to Vance."

I followed his gaze past the smoldering stone house to where Roxy and her mother rested alongside the gravel drive. They were covered in soot, but at least they were out of the fire, and I could see one of the kittens curled contentedly in Roxy's arms.

Where would they all live now? At Everston?

"Dexter, your beautiful house...."

"You're safe, though. Everyone is safe. That's all that matters." He ran his fingers through my hair, which, free of any pins, now hung over my shoulders and down my back. "Vance had just told me you were in the barn when I heard the shot—"

"Vance!" I broke free from Dexter's hold and scrambled to my feet. Vance needed to know Jacques was in the barn. He could awake at any second, and I hadn't thought to confiscate his revolver. "Where is he? He needs to—"

"I'm right here, you silly goose," came his voice from behind me.

I whirled around. "Vance, Jacques Gerard is in the barn! He's unconscious, and I wrestled his gun away, but it's still—"

Vance was already running toward the barn.

Dexter vaulted up from the ground, his brow furrowed. "Where's the gun now?"

"In the hayloft."

Dexter turned and hastened after Vance.

Just then, Father hurried from around the corner of the barn carrying Roxy's other kitten. "Was that a gunshot I heard?" He scanned the yard. "Where's Vance? Dexter?"

"They're in the barn collecting a rather debilitated Jacque Gerard." I greedily took the kitten from him and held her against my chest, welcoming her warmth. I'd left my fur mantle and hat on the barn floor. "He cornered me, and we struggled, but I managed to wrest his revolver from him. It went off by accident."

"Thank goodness you're alright." Father reached over and gently rubbed one of the kitten's soft, velvety ears between his thumb and forefinger. "Dexter and I arrived just as Vance was helping Mrs. Blakeley and her daughter from the house. They need to rest and recover from having inhaled so much smoke. And Miss Blakeley was quite distraught over not being able to find this little fur ball."

"I should take her to Roxy. Her kittens are all she has."

"I'll take care of reuniting Miss Blakeley with her pet." He looked me in the eye as he lifted the kitten from my arms. "You need to have a talk with Dexter. You owe it to him, especially after what he's lost today."

Before I could answer, Vance emerged from the barn, carrying a still-unconscious Jacques over his shoulder. Was this scrawny man really the threat that had put me on the journey that had brought me to Everston? Then again, when conscious with revolver in hand, he was a threat to be reckoned with.

Dexter came out next, carrying my soiled mink fur stole and the silly ostrich-plumed hat. I looked away from him, ashamed of the gaudy accessories—that they should remain, relatively unscathed, while Blakeley House and all its contents were reduced to charred ruins!

I took my belongings from him without a word, pulling the fur mantle over my shoulders again to ward off the autumn chill.

Vance dropped Jacques' motionless form to the ground, then gave him a light kick with the toe of his shoe, provoking a sleepy groan from the Frenchman.

"Now we can add 'arson' and 'attempted kidnapping' to his list of crimes," Vance sneered cockily down at him. "Father, Estella, I'd like you to meet my brother-in-law, Jacques Gerard."

Father put an arm around my shoulders. "Vance, do be serious. Did you know he would follow you here?"

Vance sighed. "I needed to draw him out, and I figured our presence at Everston would be temptation enough."

Dexter stepped toward Vance. "You would so carelessly put Estella in danger?" The intensity of his hazel eyes startled me almost as much as hearing him speak my real name.

Father held me closer to his side. "Vance, when are you going to learn to think of others before yourself?"

"I thought Stella would still be here, safe, with Blakeley." He motioned to the charred stone walls, all that were left of Dexter's beautiful house. "Still going as Elle Stoneburner and working for him."

I couldn't look at Dexter—it hurt too much. Instead, I stared down at the hat in my hands, anxiously fingering the ostrich feathers.

"You'll need to take him to the sheriff in Laurelton," Dexter said, starting for the barn. "I'll go saddle Pip."

Vance watched him go with a peculiar gleam in his eyes. A jolt of understanding shot through me when I saw that Vance was prepared to begin his discussion with Dexter *right now*.

Before I could escape, Dexter was beside me again. Reaching out, he grabbed my free hand. "Actually, if you don't mind, I think I'd like Estella's help with the horse."

Father released me with a smile.

"I guess she's yours, though I'm not sure how good she is with horses." Vance bent to pick up Jacques again, hefting him over his broad shoulder. "Or if you really want the little minx."

"Oh, I think I do."

My heart soared as Dexter took me by the hand and led me toward the barn. Did I dare hope he meant it—that he wanted me, in spite of everything? That he wanted me, Estella Everstone?

THIRTY-ONE

Dexter Blakeley

"'Stay' is a charming word...."
—Amos Bronson Alcott, *Concord Days*

I wanted to talk to you again last night," Dexter said as he guided
me past the horse stalls. "And this morning, but I didn't see
you—or, I should say, I didn't realize I'd seen you this morning
until I noticed you with your father and brother at church."

"Really?" He hadn't looked right through me in the lobby on
purpose?

"You do look quite different in these clothes." He released me
slowly, then walked to the nearest saddle stand, his back to me,
and stood with his fingers spread upon the smooth leather seat.

"Aren't you going to groom Pip?" I asked.

He seemed thoughtful for a moment. "I think saddling a horse
for your brother can wait. There's a lot to say, but I'm not exactly
sure where to start."

I waited for him to go on, but he remained silent.

Just then, an idea sprang to my mind. "How about we start
anew, with fresh introductions, since we were both presented
rather inaccurately to each other before?"

Dexter pivoted to face me, and I closed the space between us,
extending my right hand to him.

After a slow, steady handshake, I looked him in the eyes. "My name is Miss Estella Louisa Everstone. The daughter of the famed Bram Everstone, I have a massive inheritance, as you may have heard."

Dexter gave a wry smile. "Middle names, too?" he asked, as if the mention of my inheritance meant nothing. "In that case, it's nice to finally meet you, Miss Estella Louisa Everstone. It's been an immense pleasure already, albeit under the misguided impression that you were *quite* destitute." He tightened his grip on my hand and tugged me closer than anyone meeting for the first time would have dared. "I'm Mr. Dexter Kent Blakeley, the esteemed manager and owner of Everston, a grand hotel and resort in the Appalachian Mountains of central Maine. Have you ever been?"

"Perhaps once," I said, echoing my answer to the same question he'd asked the first time we met.

"Estella." He breathed my name, but his eyes said even more, and it suddenly seemed as if the train wreck from the day before hadn't happened.

"Past the use of formal names already?" I teased.

But Dexter was all seriousness as he put his arm around my waist, spreading his palm over the ruched gray silk of my gown, and guided me to a wooden bench nearby. He sat down, then situated me on his lap, tightening his hold on me. "I know we've just met, Miss Everstone, but I'm afraid I must make a rather shocking admission."

He paused, and I prayed he wouldn't hear my racing heart.

"I think I'm in love with you."

"You think?" My breath stopped in my lungs.

"No, you're right; I know I am." He gently framed my face with his hands. "Is it too forward of me, a man you've just met, to propose?"

I was so shocked, I lost my balance and nearly fell from his lap. "Oh! Well then, go ahead!"

"Would you like me to?" He smiled temptingly.

I threw my arms about his neck. "Yes, very much. Please."

He moved his hands to cradle my back, as he surely feared I would fall from his lap from my trembling.

"I'm afraid I don't have a house to offer you, Estella."

"You have Everston. We can live there."

"I might have suspected that was all you were ever after, except for the fact that you didn't know it was mine for half of our acquaintance. And the day you fell from Knightley, you confessed to me everything I longed to hear."

"Oh! That day!" I buried my face in the rough wool collar of his coat.

He and leveled his fiery gaze to mine. "It's no wonder you fought your feelings for me, after I made it clear how I felt about spoiled young socialites." He grinned.

"I was certain you wouldn't like me once you knew...and I tried to do everything in my power to dissuade you. But you wouldn't let me."

"No. And I still won't." Dexter closed his eyes and rested his forehead against mine. "Do you remember the prayer I offered at the start of this morning's service?"

I thought back, but all I could recall was that it was beautiful.

I also wondered how talking about his prayer would lead into the one question I couldn't wait to answer.

"God knew what He was doing, bringing you to me as He did." Dexter pulled back a bit and opened his eyes again. "If you'd come to Everston as yourself, or if you'd revealed yourself to me at any time while you were working for Mrs. Granton, I wouldn't have uttered two words to you again." His breath mingled with mine as he drew me closer, the warmth of this wool coat mixing with the heat between us.

"I'm sorry, so sorry, Dexter, that my sis—"

"What's past is past, Estella. The broken hearts and lives, the tragic losses our families have suffered...it all somehow led to our meeting in the stagecoach that night." He shrugged out of his coat—it *did* suddenly feel quite warm in the barn—and wrapped his arms around me again, this time even closer without the thickness of his coat between us. "And God, in His magnificent ways, worked in my heart to make the impossible possible. I'd long harbored a hardness of heart toward the very ladies I'd been ministering to at both Bailey Hill and Everston. And the way God broke me of it was to introduce you to me, first as Elle Stoneburner and then as Estella Everstone, proving to me that my judgments were wrong."

Dexter brought his hands up my back to my shoulders with a long sigh. Then he kissed my cheek and whispered, "I love you, Estella, and not because of your family connections or your wealth, but in spite of them. And because of who you are when you're locked out of a house in the middle of the night, and who you are when you sit with me on a mountainside, and who you become when I kiss you...."

I kissed him then, pressing forward until he matched my fervor—which didn't take long.

When he broke away, he uttered breathlessly, "Thank God for startled partridges."

"What on earth do you mean?"

"If that partridge hadn't flown across our trail and spooked Knightley, you wouldn't have fallen and injured yourself enough to cling to me and tell me you loved me."

With that, he stood, lifting me to my feet, and grabbed his coat. Then he took my hand, intertwining our fingers once again, and led me outside—still without having officially asked me, as Estella Everstone, to marry him.

"Yes, and if it weren't for that bird, I would have told you the more urgent truth that day."

"I'm glad that ended as it did. Before that ride, I'd told myself I was dreaming...that no matter how attracted I was to you, I could never make it work. You dodged me at every turn, and I didn't know how to get you to fall in love with me."

"But you didn't have to do anything, Dexter. I think I fell in love with you before I exited the stagecoach the night we met. Your soul fits perfectly to mine, and somehow I knew it at once."

"Then you knew it before I did. For me, it was gradual, the way my thoughts of you seeped in, until I couldn't imagine my life without you...no matter your name."

So many words! I loved every one of them, but why did he not ask me what I knew he wanted to?

Dexter leaned forward and quickly pressed his mouth to mine, taking the thought of *any* words right out of my head. After a while, he pulled back, bracing my arms with his hands—as they'd somehow come to be around his neck.

"Don't you want to go share the happy news?" he asked. "I'm not sure about Mother, but I'm quite positive Roxy will be ecstatic; and I'm certain your brother and father will want to know everything's been settled—"

"Settled? Were they expecting this?"

"I asked your father for permission to marry you last night, when you were locked away in your room and wouldn't come out for anything."

"Then Vance knew, too, didn't he—all morning?"

"I suppose he might have." Dexter smiled. "Do you suppose I should ask you, as well?"

"I've been waiting."

His grin widened. "Honor me, Estella Louisa Everstone, in becoming my wife. Say you'll stay and live out all your days with me at Everston. *Your* Everston. Our Everston."

"I want nothing more than to live at Everston, Dexter...." I paused quite purposefully, "...so as long as I am able to...as your wife."

THIRTY-TWO

Mr. and Mrs. Blakeley

"'I'll tell you,' said she, in the same hurried passionate whisper, 'what real love is. It is blind devotion, unquestioning self-humiliation, utter submission, trust and belief against yourself and against the whole world, giving up your whole heart and soul....'"
—Charles Dickens, *Great Expectations*

Friday, November 27, 1891 · Everston

I can hardly conceive that you are Vance's sister! Well, besides the fact that you look alike," Violet Hawthorne remarked as she put the last few strands of my chestnut hair into place. I was grateful for the skills she'd learned from the lady's maids and servants she lived with in the hotel dormitory.

I sat before the mirror of the vanity in my room on the fifth floor, adorned in a Worth wedding gown of silk accentuated with crystals and pearls—a detail that would make the papers, thanks only to Father's wife-to-be, Madame Boutilier. The press had most certainly not been invited to the wedding.

"You really don't seem anything alike." Violet caught my gaze in the mirror and pointed to her chest. "At least, in here."

"Vance and Estella aren't anything alike when it comes to character," Meredyth Hampton supplied as she returned to the room after seeing to something regarding her adopted daughter, Wynn. "But I do believe he's attempting to change for the better."

Upon arriving at Everston the week before, just in time to celebrate Thanksgiving, Meredyth and Amaryllis had accepted Violet, as well as Roxy, into their ranks as friends after I'd explained to them her situation. She really was a very well-mannered young woman who had been raised by her parents to be a lady. It wasn't her fault that her brother had inherited their small hotel and immediately transformed it into a house of ill-repute.

Ezra Hawthorne had come very close to permanently damaging Violet's reputation, if not for Dexter offering her the position as the first pretty face the daytime guests of Everston would encounter upon arriving on the stagecoach.

"I suppose I'll take that as a compliment." My eyes met Violet's in the mirror. "But if you'd known me over the years, you would have witnessed the unfortunate streak of defiance coursing through me, despite my mild-mannered demeanor."

"Estella, you're too hard on yourself," my sister-in-law Amaryllis said from her chair across the room. I'd thought she was asleep; she did spend a great deal of time resting, exhausted from being seven months pregnant. "If not for that streak, I daresay, you wouldn't be marrying Dexter Blakeley today."

"Maybe so," I mused. "It wasn't pretty, but at one time, Violet, I was just as scheming regarding a certain young man from my past as Vance is now concerning most young ladies."

Violet looped a final section of hair around her fingers and pinned it in place. "Scheming? I'm not sure I'd say that."

Meredyth snorted, quickly covering the unladylike sound with a genuine laugh. "I'm glad you think so. It has been the subject of much prayer over the months."

"What I meant is that your brother is a flirt, to be sure."

"That he is, I'm afraid."

I wasn't aware just how much of his flirtations Violet had experienced. For the last month, in Vance's comings and goings between Everston and Bangor, I'd hardly seen them exchange more than two words.

Then again, I hadn't been paying much attention to them, my engagement to Dexter having been somewhat of a preoccupation. I had planned the wedding with the help of the hotel events coordinator, as well as Madame Boutilier, who had sent from Boston everything we could have wanted and more to make for a lavish event, though it would be just a small gathering of family and close friends in the middle of nowhere.

"What has Vance said?" I ventured to ask.

"Absolutely nothing!" Violet assured me. "Not with any words, at least."

"Forgive my brother, Violet, for I fear he knows not what he does to half the young ladies he comes into contact with."

Violet frowned. "Oh. So, he isn't just a flirt… he's a scheming flirt?"

I glanced at Meredyth, wondering what she might say. She'd been on the verge of marrying Vance the previous summer, and probably knew him better than anyone else in the room.

No one responded, however, so I let the subject drop.

Just as Violet lowered the white lace veil over my elaborately coiffured hair, Roxy rushed into the room. "It's almost time!"

My heart nearly burst at the thought of being wedded to Dexter in a matter of minutes.

"We need to be down there before you, Estella," Roxy added, "so we'll have time to get down the aisle and watch as you descend the stairs. I can't imagine anything more romantic than the look that passes between a bride and groom when they see each other for the first time on their wedding day!"

"Every aspect of a wedding is romantic," Amaryllis wheezed, holding a hand to her rounded stomach. "as long as the bride and groom understand exactly what they are doing and why."

"Isn't it because they've found that they're perfect for each other?"

"Some people see it that way, but there's a lot more to it." I looked to Amaryllis and Meredyth, certain they would agree. "Dexter and I have chosen to marry—to become one in Christ— because we want to be together, though we know that there will be times when we aren't perfect for each other. After all, no one is perfect. But that's part of the commitment you make when you marry—to always love your spouse, flaws and all."

Although Dexter and I had both felt a sense that we were "made" for each other, those sentiments had quickly come crashing down around us. If anything, we realized we were the last two people on earth who were supposed to be together, given our divergent backgrounds and the animosity between our families.

But we'd made the choice, regardless of those factors, that we *would* belong together—because we wanted to.

As I stepped off the elevator on the second floor and walked alone to the top of the stairs, I felt for the first time in my life that I had Everston completely to myself. For years, that had been my dream; but as much as I loved the hotel for its charm and the happy memories it held, it was the hotel's owner—the owner of my heart—I most prized now.

The string quartet that Madame Boutilier had convinced to make the long, snowy journey from Boston shifted from the soft strands of Vivaldi's *Four Seasons* to a grander-sounding piece. I really hated the to-do my family had insisted on making of the wedding, but I hadn't complained, knowing it would end with Dexter by my side, forever.

I made my way carefully down the stairs to Father, waiting at the base. He beamed as he took my arm, and together we started a slow procession down the wide, spacious lobby, which had been transformed into a veritable wedding chapel.

My knees went weak when I saw Dexter standing at the altar before Reverend Whitespire, waiting for me.

Had it been just a little over two months since I'd watched him at Jay and Greenlee's wedding, praying, wishing, and hoping with all my heart for what was now taking place?

As Father escorted me down the aisle, I thanked God for the years I'd believed He had put my heart on hold. I'd thought I was waiting for Jay to love me, but that hadn't been the case at all. I was waiting for this.

⌒

"Well, tell me what you think. Be honest." Dexter, my husband of two hours, stood before me, captivating me with the gleam in his eyes and the smile on his lips, as he held open the door that connected the windowed receiving area on the sixth floor to his private rooms.

Now our private rooms. He'd had them remodeled as a residence for us, and he'd moved in just days before, having spent the previous two months living with his mother and sister in a nearby cottage he'd purchased for them.

I stepped off the elevator into the good-sized entrance hall, which boasted dark walls of wainscoting that reached my shoulders and, above that, wallpaper in a gray-blue pattern.

"It's absolutely lovely, Dexter."

"Come and see the main rooms." He closed the door behind me, shutting us inside what would be our own little world. Not that we hadn't already been shut alone in the elevator, kissing our way up the six floors of Everston.

With a wink and another heart-thudding smile, he took my hand and brought me into the parlor. It was decorated much like the one at Blakeley House had been, with a large hollow-back chair in the corner—just like the one I'd favored there.

I hadn't been in the private rooms of the sixth floor of Everstone since I was a child, and I hardly remembered what they used to look like, beyond how I'd rendered them in several drawings in my old sketchbook. I knew Dexter considered the newly remodeled space as his gift to me, and I'd been happy to leave the design to him. All that mattered to me was that we'd be living together within those walls.

The fact that I'd left my sketchbook at Blakeley House, and that it'd been lost in the fire, still caused me pain. I hadn't replaced it yet, but there hadn't been much time for drawing in the last month, anyway.

After showing me the dining room, the study, and the kitchen, in case I ever wanted to make use of it, Dexter led me to two empty bedchambers. I turned to him, for the first time feeling quite bashful in his presence.

He squeezed my hand. "Once we outgrow the apartment, we'll rebuild on the site of Blakeley House, if you'd like."

"These rooms are wonderful, for now. But, yes, rebuilding Blakeley House does sound like a grand plan for the future."

I returned his radiant smile, my excitement mounting to see the room he would introduce to me next. He walked me to the end of the hall and opened a set of double doors to a corner bedchamber with windows along two walls, a beautiful fireplace with hearth aglow, and a high bed of carved wood bed at the center.

Atop the gold coverlet with red embroidery sat a sketchbook. I let go of Dexter's hand and dashed across the room. It couldn't be!

I picked up the book with shaking hands and flipped it open to the middle, to the newer drawings I'd sketched in October. And then I paged back to the ones from thirteen years before. Perching myself on the edge of the bed, I marked my favorite drawing with my finger, then closed the book and looked at Dexter. He was leaning against the door frame, grinning like a mischievous little boy.

"How…? I was certain it had been burned!"

Dexter's smile broadened. "After our last discussion at Blakeley House, I went to the spring to think things through. After what I'd said to you in my shock, I knew you likely thought I despised you…." Dexter crossed the room and sat next to me, positioning his left arm behind me. "When I realized you were gone, I went to your room and found that you'd left with the few things you'd brought with you—only I found this in the wardrobe with the quilt." He placed his forefinger next to mine and opened the sketchbook to the page I'd marked.

It was the drawing of him and Roxy—the only drawing I'd done of him the summer we first met. I hardly remembered him from back then, so I surely didn't remember drawing the fine lines of his face, shoulders, and exquisitely built frame. He'd simply been another subject to put down on paper.

"You like that one?" he asked with a wry grin.

"It reminds me of how good God is, Dexter, that He would give me chance after chance with you, after allowing life to get in the way so many times."

"Don't tell me you were infatuated with me as a little girl, Estella. I won't believe you!" Then he laughed as he embraced me.

I fingered the lapel of his black tuxedo. "Nothing of the sort, Mr. Blakeley! In fact, I was hardly aware of your existence back then." With a sly smile, I leaned forward and rested my cheek on his shoulder.

Dexter turned his head and brought his lips close to mine. "And what about now?" he whispered.

Leaning into him, I executed the kiss that had long been tantalizing us. Then I closed the sketchbook and gently slid it off the bed and onto the floor at our feet, suddenly gaining a vast preference for the flesh-and-blood husband in front of me over the timeworn drawing of his likeness.

About the Author

A graduate of Taylor University with a degree in Christian education, and a former bookseller at Barnes & Noble, Dawn Crandall didn't begin writing until 2010, when her husband found out about her long-buried dream of writing a book. Without a doubt that she would someday be published, he encouraged her to quit her job in 2010 in order to focus on writing *The Hesitant Heiress* (book one in The Everstone Chronicles). It didn't take her long to realize that writing books was what she was made to do.

Apart from writing books, Dawn is also a first-time mom to a precious little boy (born March 2014) and serves with her husband in a premarital mentorship program at their local church in Fort Wayne, Indiana.

Dawn is a member of the American Christian Fiction Writers, the secretary for the Indiana ACFW Chapter (Hoosier Ink), and an associate member of the Great Lakes ACFW Chapter. She is represented by Joyce Hart of Hartline Literary Agency.

The Everstone Chronicles is Dawn Crandall's first series. All three books composing the series were semifinalists in ACFW's prestigious Genesis Writing Contest for pre-published authors, the third book going on to become a finalist in 2013.